EVERYTHING ABOUT YOU

A SECOND CHANCE GAY ROMANCE

JEANNE ST. JAMES

Editor: Proofreading by the Page
Cover Model: Golden Czermak
Photographer/Cover Art: Golden Czermak @ FuriousFotog
Beta Readers: Author BJ Alpha, Alex Swab, Sharon Abrams

www.jeannestjames.com

Sign up for my newsletter for insider information, author news, and new releases:
www.jeannestjames.com/newslettersignup

Warning: This book contains adult scenes and language and may be considered offensive to some readers. This book is for sale to adults ONLY, as defined by the laws of the country in which you made your purchase. Please store your files wisely, where they cannot be accessed by under-aged readers.

~

Dirty Angels MC, Blue Avengers MC & Blood Fury MC are registered trademarks of Jeanne St James, Double-J Romance, Inc.

~

Keep an eye on her website at http://www.jeannestjames.com/ or sign up for her newsletter to learn about her upcoming releases: http://www.jeannestjames.com/newslettersignup

Author Links: Jeanne's Blog * Instagram * Facebook * Goodreads Author Page * Newsletter * Jeanne's Review & Book Crew * Twitter * BookBub

CONTENT WARNING

Child loss (past - discussion only)
Cheating (past - not present day)

AUTHOR'S NOTE

Dear Readers,

While I love the Steel City, I haven't been back in over a decade. So, if I've made any mistakes, please forgive me. I miss Pittsburgh and hope to get back there one day.

Go Steelers!

~Jeanne

PROLOGUE

WHERE IT ENDED

It was your smile.
Your laugh.
The color of your eyes.
The way you looked at me when no one else was looking.
The way you held me.
The way you kissed me.
It was everything about you I loved.

The flattening of that smile.
The silence of your laughter.
The loss of your lips.
The way you left.
The way you destroyed it all.
The way you destroyed me.
Destroyed us.
It was everything about you I hated.

Everything about you.
I wanted.

Needed.
Hoped for.
And that day you not only broke my heart.
You fucking crushed it.

CHAPTER 1

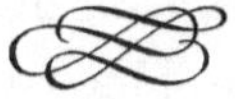

Ronan (Now)

I STABBED the up arrow button on the lobby elevator in my building. My breath quickly returning back to normal and the sweat starting to dry on my body. I looked forward to washing that sweat and grime from my skin once I got upstairs.

Maybe even doing more than that under the warm spray of the shower.

The numbers lit up one after the other as the elevator car traveled down from the sixth floor.

Ding. Five.

Ding. Four.

Ding. Three.

The buzz and click of the outer lobby door unlocking behind me had me glancing over my shoulder to see if I needed to hold the elevator for whoever just entered.

I pulled the sweaty T-shirt from over my shoulder where I had tossed it, and used it to wipe my face, because clearly I was seeing things. Sweat must have gotten into my eyes. Or maybe I was lighteaded because I hadn't eaten anything since much earlier today.

Or...

Or... I was really seeing who I thought I was.

But that couldn't be. I had to be imagining it. Imagining him.

Maybe I was having a stroke or some medical issue and needed to sit down. It was true that I hadn't been running outside as much as I should be and it could be my blood sugar reacting to the intense cardio session.

Or I was simply delusional.

The man who had walked through the front entrance paused in the vestibule lined with the residents' mailboxes. He appeared as if he had just rolled out of bed, even though he wore a suit. It was wrinkled like he'd slept on a park bench.

He couldn't be homeless since he had the code to the front entrance and that was changed once a month. That meant he had to be a current resident, even though I had never spotted him in the building before.

However, not only did he look out of sorts, he was talking to himself. Just like the homeless man who often slept on a bench in Point State Park. The one who occasionally bathed in the fountain and also fished out the change thrown in by tourists and locals alike.

Funny, I never once had my wish come true after throwing a penny into a fountain, but maybe it worked for other people.

I couldn't hear what the man was saying because of the second set of doors separating the vestibule from the lobby, but even with his head tipped down, I could clearly see his lips moving. He could be wearing earbuds and talking to someone on his cell phone.

Or he could be having a full-blown conversation with himself as he dug deep into his pants pocket. Most likely for his mailbox key.

Even after drying the sweat from around my eyes, he still looked so familiar.

Too familiar.

The elevator dinged as it arrived on the main floor and the doors whooshed open. Mr. and Mrs. Callahan from the fourth floor stepped out with their little yappy, ankle-biter Pomeranian, Mr. Pibbles.

I side-stepped to give the older couple room to pass and also so that little fucker didn't take a chunk out of my ankle.

Mrs. Callahan's gaze swept over me and I knew exactly why.

I was wearing nothing but black silky shorts that, when sweaty, clung to my assets, along with running sneakers, ankle-high sports socks and a Penn State U baseball cap.

It also didn't help that my skin wasn't a perfect shade of pale and I sported a wide assortment of tattoos covering my torso and arms.

However, it wasn't the first time they'd seen me after a run and, unfortunately for them, it wouldn't be the last.

Mr. Callahan held the elevator door for me even though it looked like he was sucking on a lemon while doing so.

They were lovely people.

By lovely, I meant judgmental assholes.

Even so, we needed to coexist since we all lived in the same building. Instead of flipping him the bird, I gave him a nod and said, "I'm not going up yet, but thanks," then took a quick glance over my shoulder again toward the vestibule.

The newest resident must've found his key since the metal door to one of the mailboxes now hung wide open while he rifled through a fistful of mail.

Shaking his head, he continued to talk to himself. The only time he glanced up was when the Callahans walked past him with Mr. Pibbles yapping in warning. Mr. Pibbles didn't like strangers.

Hell, Mr. Pibbles didn't like anyone except for the Callahans. And even that was questionable.

As soon as the couple and their orange yap rat stepped out onto the sidewalk, the man shut the mailbox and turned...

And the revolving Earth came to a complete and abrupt stop, as if someone had jerked up the emergency brake.

My heart seized. My lungs emptied. My soul decided to flee the lobby without me.

But my mind… My mind began to spin like a Tilt-A-Whirl with a drunk carny at the controls.

"Oh shit." When my heart kick-started, I yanked my baseball cap lower to hide my face and quickly tugged my damp T-shirt over my head and torso as I hurried into the nearby stairwell.

I made sure the steel door didn't slam behind me and for a second pressed my back to the wall next to it.

I wasn't sure what the hell to do. I certainly wasn't ready to face him.

This couldn't be reality. He couldn't live in the same building as I did.

It couldn't be him. No fucking way!

He left Pittsburgh twelve years ago after he graduated, why the hell was he back now?

My only guess was that it wasn't Tate. That it was someone who looked like him. A doppelgänger.

I was freaking out for nothing.

I was being a foolish idiot.

But to be sure, I slid my back from the wall to the door, flipped my baseball cap backwards, then turned, bent my knees and popped my head up enough to peek out of the little fireproof window.

I watched as he headed over to the elevator and jabbed the button ten times in quick succession. While he waited impatiently for the doors to open, he shuffled from one foot to the other.

Twelve years.

It had been twelve fucking years since I last saw him.

But it was like yesterday.

We both looked different but also the same.

Definitely older. Debatably wiser.

But he looked worn out. Beat down.

As if the easy life he was supposed to be living turned out to be not so easy.

I watched him until he stepped into the open elevator car and the doors shut behind him, whisking him away.

I continued to stare at the empty spot where he previously stood because I had a hard time pulling myself away.

I could only chalk it up to shock.

Once I finally forced my feet to move, I sat on the third step and dropped my head into my hands to try to wrap my head around who I just saw. Unsure why he was here. In Pittsburgh. In the same damn building where I lived. Unsure why any of this was happening.

For a moment in the silence, I was transported back.

To when I had hope.

Dreams.

Expectations.

And, of course, to when those were all crushed.

Ronan (Then)

I SPREAD myself out in the seat with an arm casually hanging over the back of the empty one to my right. I might be a freshman but I came to Duquesne with the intent to not act like one. To not be seen as a boy fresh out of high school.

Instead, I wanted to feel like a man ready to seize the world.

It might not be true, but the saying "fake it until you make it" existed for a reason.

Because of that, I did my best to look confident and like I belonged, when really, deep down inside I was anything but.

I did really well in high school, which helped me earn scholarships and grants. But attending Duquesne University was a whole other world compared to high school.

It would be fan-freaking-tastic if the students here weren't so close-minded like they were at my high school in a small town right outside of Hershey, PA. My roomie in the dorm seemed to be cool so far, but I'd only known him for less than a week and I also hadn't told him I was gay.

Yet.

My hope was that if he got to know me first, by the time he figured it out, he'd discover I wasn't defined solely by my sexual preference. Being gay was just a small part of who I was as a person.

This morning I arrived earlier than usual for this first class—I hadn't been sure where the lecture hall was located—and settled myself in an empty row of seats.

I didn't want to be quite up front, but didn't want to hide in the back, either. There'd be no point since this was Multi-Genre Creative Writing. A class I wasn't forced to take but was interested in because I hadn't quite pinned down my major yet. I had no reason to hide in this class, unlike with my algebra course.

At this point I had no idea what I wanted to do with my life. I was leaning toward a business degree, so I had signed up for a core credit course along with a mix of electives to see if anything caught my fancy.

Since writing was a big part of most careers, I figured it couldn't hurt. While I was a pro at sending texts and casual emails, when it came to professional correspondence, I could use some work. Plus, how hard could creative writing be? Unlike algebra.

Here I was, sitting in the third row, waiting for the professor and watching the seats fill up around me. I had my old Asus laptop set up on the flip-up desktop, hoping my electronic dinosaur held a charge long enough to get me through my classes today. The battery on my three-year old cell phone with the cracked screen was slowly dying, too. I just couldn't afford to replace either *soon-to-be* paperweights.

That reminded me... I needed to find a job in which the hours would be flexible around my classes, studying and, of course, some partying. Since I was putting myself through school, the first and second were the most important. Partying, dating or hooking up with someone would be more of a reward for all my hard work.

I glanced at my flickering screen to skim over the syllabus one last time as everyone finished wandering in. When the chatter came to a halt, I looked up to see the professor wander in, drop off his briefcase on the table, write *Dr. Mario Louden* on the whiteboard and then turn to stand at the lectern.

Dr. Louden cleared his throat. "In case you're lost, this is—"

The door was thrown open with a bang and a student rushed in. He paused, made eye contact with Dr. Louden and grimaced.

"Mr. Harris, *this* is one reason why you are repeating this course. You've known what time this class starts since you got your schedule at least two weeks ago. There is no excuse for you being tardy."

"Sorry. Sorry," he muttered, adjusting the gaping-open backpack half hanging off his shoulder.

"I expect this won't happen again. Right, Mr. Harris? Otherwise, my suggestion is for you to drop out and find another class and instructor to insult with your tardiness, instead."

"I need—" The student shook his head. "I swear I won't be late again."

That sounded like a lie to my own ears, but I didn't give a shit about what was coming out of his mouth. I was more fixated on his actual lips and not the words being muttered from them.

He. Was. Absolutely. Beautiful.

A chunk of thick dark hair fell across his forehead and a flush had crept up his neck and into his cheeks.

I couldn't keep my eyes from my future boyfriend—maybe I'd go so far as future husband even—as he jogged up the steps with his head down. Unfortunately, he disappeared somewhere behind me.

Hopefully, he didn't notice me gawking.

And if he did... Oh well.

He would probably just think I'm staring at him because I thought he was rude to arrive late to class.

I heard the thump of his very heavy backpack hitting the floor a few rows behind me, a loud rustle and a slew of grumbles.

I wasn't the only one who noticed. So did Dr. Louden who stared past me to the future Mr. Ronan Pak.

I liked that. Another man taking my name. If he really pushed it, I'd let him hyphenate. Harris-Pak.

"Are you sure you're ready for me to start class, Mr. Harris?" Dr. Louden called out with one dark bushy eyebrow stuck high up his forehead.

A few sniggers and muffled laughs could be heard and I noticed everyone was turned around in their seats to check Mr. Harris out.

Correction. Mr. Harris-Pak.

A smile spread across my face and I pulled myself out of my fantasy to concentrate on today's lesson as our professor began to teach. I certainly didn't want him calling me out in front of the whole class for daydreaming.

Over an hour later, I was stuffing my shit back into my backpack, including my ancient computer—luckily, it hadn't let me down during class—and thinking about the next time I'd see Mr. Harris, since I didn't know his first name yet.

Yet. But I would.

I would make sure to get to class early on Friday and grab a seat toward the back so I could stare at my newest obsession without anyone knowing. Study him. Learn every detail to memory. For my fantasies.

When I stood, I heard a rush of feet coming down the steps behind me, so I waited and fiddled with my backpack, trying not to be too obvious.

I just wanted to get another look. Of the back this time, since I already liked what I'd seen of the front.

I was not disappointed as Harris jogged down the steps toward the front of the lecture hall. However, his backpack still gaped wide open and all the contents were at risk of falling out.

"Hey!" I called out in warning and quickly followed him down the steps.

He either didn't hear me or was ignoring me as he rushed out of the lecture hall and into the corridor.

I elbowed my way through a group of students standing around and talking, but more importantly, blocking me from my future husband. I got around them and headed out, hoping I didn't lose Harris.

I didn't.

Not because he was waiting, but because what I feared had happened. His backpack was now dumped on the ground and all the items inside had been strewn across the hallway like the contents of a smashed piñata at a birthday party.

What made me almost tear up a little was what looked like a new laptop on the floor.

An utter tragedy. What I would do for a new laptop like that…

Hopefully it wasn't broken and if it was, that it was insured.

Not my problem. My concern was with the broad-shouldered, narrow-hipped man, with a perfectly juicy peach for an ass, now squatting on the floor, collecting his belongings while everyone else walked around him and didn't bother to help.

This was my chance to introduce myself and be his knight in shining armor.

Squatting down while facing him, I began to gather pens, a rainbow of highlighters and various colored sticky notes.

My takeaway was the man carried way too much shit in his backpack. Who hauled around this much stuff? No wonder he couldn't zip it shut.

After my hands were full, I grabbed his backpack and tossed everything into it. If he wanted it organized, he could do that himself and once he was out of hallway traffic.

I stood and moved closer to my future lover, gripping the bag tightly. My brain was trying to trick me into thinking that holding his backpack was the same as holding him.

It wasn't. Unfortunately.

I waited as he stacked some textbooks, and what might be some fiction, into his arms and rose to his feet, his face flushed from either embarrassment or the exertion.

I held the backpack out to him. "Here."

After glancing around to see if he missed anything, his face lifted. And when he reached for his bag, I couldn't release my hold. Once he got a more solid grip on it, our fingers touched and a shock zipped up my arm and a tornado of heat swirled around my gut.

Our surprised gazes locked, and...

I forgot how to breathe.

His blue eyes...

Seeing them up close and personal caused lightning to zap me right in the middle of my chest.

His awkward, crooked smile caused a heaviness in my balls and I hoped like hell I didn't pop a boner right there in the corridor.

"Thanks," got caught in his throat. He cleared it and repeated it more clearly.

"No problem."

"The zipper's broken," he explained.

"Probably because you're hauling around half of your college career in that thing."

"I don't live on campus, so I..." He seemed to lose his train of thought but never once did he lose hold of my eyes. His were locked solid with mine. "I... uh..."

"Don't want to forget anything," I finished for him.

He nodded and that chunk of dark hair fell lower on his forehead. I curled the fingers of the hand not holding the backpack into my palm to avoid reaching out and pushing it off his eyebrow and back into place.

"You can't leave stuff in your car?" It wasn't like I really cared what he carried around like a pack mule, I only wanted to keep him there as long as possible.

"No car." His voice was much deeper than one would think by looking at him since he was on the slender side.

"How do you get to campus, then?"

"My bike or I walk. I sometimes catch a ride with one of my roommates, depending on our schedules."

A little tug had me finally releasing his backpack, even though I didn't want to. I wanted to hold him there, like a hostage. Take him for myself and keep him until he fell desperately in love with me.

Of course, I knew that wasn't realistic. But there was one thing I *could* get from him, if nothing else…

"Cool. By the way, I'm Ronan, but you can call me Roe."

His dark eyebrows pinned together. "Ronan?"

"Yeah, it's Irish. I look Irish, don't I?" I cocked my head and kept my expression serious even though I purposely put him on the spot.

I watched him panic about answering my question and possibly offending me. "Uh…"

I kept my lips from twitching and giving myself away. "I'm actually only half Irish. The front half. The back half isn't." I waited to see if he would ask me about the rest of my ethnicity since I certainly didn't even look half Irish. But he played it safe and didn't, so I asked, "How about you?" I wasn't ready for this conversation to end.

"I'm… I'm not quite sure…"

He scraped his fingers through his hair, messing it up even worse. To me, it made him appear even sexier. I'd love to see his hair like that when I rolled over in the morning and found his head on the pillow next to mine.

"I'm a mutt, I guess. A mix of European. Like German and—"

"I meant your name," I clarified.

"Oh." The redness in his cheeks intensified. "Tate. Harris. You can call me Tate."

When I grinned, I watched something cross Tate's face I was *not* expecting.

Interest. Cautious interest.

Hmm. Could he be gay? Or at least bi?

Could I be so lucky that my future husband actually liked men, too?

Nah, I was never that lucky.

I jutted out my hand. He stared at it for a second like I had just thrown him a curve ball. Then he adjusted his backpack over his shoulder more securely and placed his warm hand with its long fingers in mine.

And, *holy shit...*

I couldn't wait to get my next class over with since I needed to head to the computer lab and start printing our wedding invitations.

I hoped Tate wouldn't mind.

~

Ronan (Now)

IN THE QUIET STAIRWELL, I dropped my hands and lifted my head, taking a deep, cleansing breath to push out the memories.

Out of all of them I couldn't shake, that had been a good one and I needed to stop before they turned to the painful, soul-crushing ones.

Rising to my feet, I pressed my lips together and set my jaw. I began the long hike up the stairs to the penthouse. And as I did so, I realized one thing...

There was no way in hell I was ready to go face to face with Tate Harris.

Not today and maybe not ever.

In the time between the last day I saw him and today, I'd been with plenty of men. But not one had ever been like him and I'd never loved any of them.

Because of that, I never had a loss as great as losing Tate.

After all these years, I thought I was over him.

Clearly, I was not.

CHAPTER 2

Ronan (Now)

I PACED BACK and forth in front of the expanse of windows. The broad and impressive views were the whole reason I bought this building and turned the whole top floor into a penthouse. Like most buildings I purchased, this one had needed a lot of rehab, but now I called it home.

With most of the lights out, the whole city seemed to be within reach of my fingertips. As if I could stretch out my hand and touch everything good about Pittsburgh.

From my penthouse, my views included the city's high-rises, the sparkling lights, and some of the numerous bridges. In the distance I could make out the Duquesne Incline, as well as PNC Park and Heinz Field, the two stadiums where the much beloved Pittsburgh Pirates and Steelers played.

On the nights they did the huge firework display for the baseball fans at PNC Park, I either headed up to the roof or turned off every light in my penthouse, settled myself on my couch in the dark and watched the night sky light up with explosions of color over downtown.

I loved this city. I loved the people. I loved the vibe.

I loved it from the moment I arrived and moved into my dorm room at Duquesne U when I was nineteen.

I loved it so much, I stayed after graduation.

It had everything I ever needed.

Including Tate in the beginning.

Then it continued to include everything I needed except for him.

Tate didn't stay like he said he would. Instead, he left me and the city we both loved so much. The city I thought we'd both call home. Together.

I was wrong.

Even worse was how it happened.

I paused in front of the center floor-to-ceiling window and glanced down at the street. The movement of red and white lights a blurry trail as vehicles wound through the streets filled with people heading to where they needed to be. Tiny people also moved about on foot to head out to dinner or a show, or simply on their way home after a long day.

My attention was pulled from the calming, familiar view when my cell phone finally buzzed in my hand. It wasn't a call but a text with the answer to my inquiry. Alicia was one of my senior property managers. She headed the residential division of Pak Property Management, Inc.

Unit 602. A copy of the sublease is on file if you want to see it. I can email it to you tomorrow when I'm back in the office.

Unit 602.

Before I could respond, another text popped up. *Is there a problem with the occupant that I need to deal with?*

Before I could text back, my phone rang. I swiped the green Accept button and put Alicia on speakerphone.

"Is there an issue, Roe?"

Not one I wanted to admit to. "No. No issue. I saw someone new in the lobby with the access code and just wanted to make sure he lived here. That's all."

Alicia's attention to detail was why she had quickly moved up the ladder in my corporation. I paid her well to keep her and she earned every damn penny. So did the heads of both the commercial and home owners association divisions of my property management company, one of a few businesses I now owned.

I had lucked out in that the original employees I had hired for Pak Property Management when I was just a fledgling investor were still with me. But then, I compensated them well between their salaries and benefits. Along with a generous amount of time off so they didn't burn out.

It also helped that their annual bonuses were more than what a worker paid minimum wage earned all year.

I learned early on to respect and appreciate my most hardworking employees. They, like real estate, businesses and stocks, were also an investment.

The right person was worth their weight in gold.

On that note, so was the right lover.

"Roe?"

I shook my head to shake myself back to the conversation. "Sorry."

"Is something wrong?"

"I just wanted to make sure he was a valid tenant, that's all."

"No. With you." Alicia was also very astute.

"I'm fine," I lied. "Thank you for checking. I'll bring one of those lattes you like from that coffee shop on the corner next time I'm in the office."

A soft snort came from the phone. "You rarely come into the office anymore."

"That's because you, Mike and Abe are so good at what you do that I don't need to."

"That's why you pay us the big bucks."

The corners of my lips tipped up. Even though she was teasing, it was also the truth. "That's exactly why."

"Okay, let me know if you need anything else."

"I need you to enjoy the rest of your evening with your family. I'm sorry for interrupting your family time."

"I'd enjoy it more if you came and took my three wild heathens off my hands for the night."

I laughed softly. "You would need to work for me for a whole year without pay for me to ever consider that."

"So, you're saying a locked cage in the basement would be cheaper," she joked.

"I'm sure we have a vendor that could install one for you at a reasonable price."

"Oops. I think the kids heard me," she said on a laugh.

"They'll get over it as soon as you break out the ice cream."

"They don't need to be hopped up on sugar before bedtime."

I ignored that and insisted, "With sprinkles."

"Fine." She sighed. "Ice cream with sprinkles."

My living room filled with the sound of her three kids cheering and shouting in the background about how they loved their Uncle Roe. That helped drive away some of the dread weighing on my chest.

With a smile, I ended the call, but the second I did, that smile slid off my face as I returned to staring out over the city.

∼

Ronan (Then)

I SLIPPED into the empty seat next to Tate, barely getting there before the lecture started. Dr. Louden had no problem calling out tardy students and I did not want to be his latest target.

I was a lot of things, but usually tardy wasn't one of them.

However, I wasn't in a rush to get to class today since I wanted to make sure my future husband had arrived first. This way I could sit next to him and maybe start some dialogue.

Over the past two weeks, I found it was easier to arrive after him than to get there first and hope he'd sit next to me.

We didn't get to talk as much as I'd like because, even though we were in college and not Catholic school, I wouldn't put it past our professor to get out a ruler and whack our palms for talking.

I needed my palms to be whack-free so I could use them for whacking off to my fantasy man whenever my roommate, Dominic, had a late night elsewhere. I stalked the calendar Dom had hung over his desk so I could schedule some "me time." More like "me and Tate time."

Only Tate wasn't aware he was a participant.

My fantasy man hadn't been late since the first day. Though, his backpack was still overstuffed with all kinds of things. Including snacks. And last Tuesday a condom had fallen out when he was digging for a pen.

A *condom*.

At least someone was getting some action. It certainly wasn't me. Since I didn't have "gay" tattooed onto my forehead, I was relying solely on my gaydar to scope out possible prospects.

My gaydar definitely needed some fine-tuning because it was failing me. If I wasn't underaged, I'd hang out at some gay bar where I could be open and outright ask. I heard about one down in the Strip District called Real Luck Cafe.

Even if I could get my mitts on a fake ID, I had no way to get there to scope out the scene since I didn't have wheels or even a friend with wheels. And forget money for a taxi.

I was working on the second and the third options. The problem with the second one was that I'd have to find a friend willing to go to a gay bar with me. The third option meant I needed to get hired at one of the many places where I put in an application. I was getting desperate since I didn't have anything lined up yet.

It wasn't like I was picky. I just needed flexible hours and some cash in my pocket.

"Hey," I greeted Tate under my breath, hoping Dr. Louden couldn't hear me. I added my signature smile.

"Hey," he greeted back, that unruly thick lock of dark hair falling across his forehead as he reached into his overstuffed backpack on the floor at his feet to get out what he needed for class.

While you're down there...

I bit back that suggestion and instead asked, "Did you get the assigned reading done?" when he sat back in his chair. Because, of course, I was lame like that.

He held out a pack of gum to me. I shook my head. He shrugged, slid out a piece, unwrapped it and popped it in his mouth.

Yes, I admit it, I watched every damn move.

As he began to chew, I also watched his lips, wondering how they would feel moving against mine.

Holy shit, I might as well have "stalker" tattooed onto my forehead, too.

"Only half of it," Tate whispered, keeping one cautious eye on Dr. Louden as he droned on at the lectern. "You?"

"Half?" I asked too loudly, causing the professor to clear his throat at my outburst. I waited until Louden once again got caught up in his lecture before asking in a whisper, "Besides being late, is that also the reason you're retaking this class?"

Tate jerked up one shoulder in a sloppy shrug. Those broad shoulders were covered in an old Foo Fighters T-shirt. I said a silent thank you with how snug it fit him.

He also wore a pair of worn jeans with a tear above his right knee. I was tempted to slide my finger into that hole to touch the skin beneath it, as well as pet the short dark hairs that were in view.

I refrained since I didn't want to be arrested for assault. Not only would that screw up my much-needed scholarship, but I'd have an arrest record and, not to mention, I couldn't afford bail.

So, those were reasons why, besides the biggest one of consent, I kept my fingers to myself.

Shame, really.

"I'll take that as a yes," I said when he didn't answer right away. I needed to distract myself from that damn gaping hole calling out to me like an open invitation.

"I need the credits."

"Why don't you just take something else instead?"

"It's a required course for me. Otherwise, I won't graduate."

His leg shifted and, *damn it,* once again I was drawn to that tempting peek of flesh just out of my reach. I forced my eyes back up to his face, only pausing for a second on his pebbled nipples that were pressed through the soft cotton of his shirt. "Here's a valuable hint then… besides getting your ass to class on time, you might want to do the assigned work."

"I'm trying to do better."

"What's your major?"

"Journalism. Yours?"

Journalism? That sounded dope.

"Undecided." No, I wasn't proud of that answer, but I'd figure it out soon. Hopefully. I had the next four years to figure out my future. It didn't need to be cemented in the first semester.

"How much does one make a year in that career?"

Holy shit. I pinned my lips together to contain my laugh. The hot hunk had a sense of humor. Could this man get any more perfect? "Decidedly not much."

"I haven't seen you around on campus before."

I raised both eyebrows. Was I that forgettable? "I've been sitting near you for the last two classes and I helped you pick up your stuff in the hallway the other day, remember?"

Tate grimaced. "Hard to forget that and I appreciate your help. But I meant before that unfortunately unforgettable moment. Are you a freshman?"

"Well… I *am* a man and, just a warning, I do tend to get fresh."

A laugh burst from Tate before he could wrangle it into an awkward cough. I bugged my eyes out at him in warning.

"Everything okay up there, gentlemen? Is something funny, Mr. Harris?"

Shit. Busted.

"No, sir. I'm sorry. Something got caught in my throat." Tate faked coughed again and slapped a hand to his chest.

I wished it was me caught in his throat.

"Are you sure there isn't a problem, gentlemen? If I'm boring you and since this is the second time you're taking this class, Mr. Harris, you should be able to come down and teach it as well as I can."

"Fuck," Tate muttered under his breath.

"Do it," I encouraged him with an elbow to his ribs.

He jerked away from me, a blush rising into his cheeks.

Damn. I could stare at him all day.

"I wouldn't do the subject matter justice like you do, Dr. Louden."

Kiss ass. I tipped my head down to hide my face and made a soft kissing sound.

That got me a shot in the ribs with an elbow.

I hid my grin when Dr. Louden stared up at us all the way in the back row for far too long. A clock ticked in my head as we waited to see if he'd kick us out for causing a ruckus.

Maybe Tate could afford to repeat classes, but I couldn't. And, again, I couldn't risk my scholarship because I was shamelessly flirting instead of paying attention.

"Since I know I'm irresistible, I'll stop distracting you so you can focus," I leaned in, pressed my shoulder against his and whispered near his ear once Dr. Louden stopped glaring at us from afar.

A little snort came from my left where Tate sat. But that wasn't the only thing coming from my left. He reached out his hand and squeezed my knee.

He squeezed my knee.

If I was a cartoon character, big heart-filled eyes would be bugging out of me right now.

But it was there and gone so quickly, I might have imagined it.

Did I imagine it? I snuck a glance at him.

He was staring down at Dr. Louden, listening to whatever words were coming from the professor's mouth.

I was hoping he'd give me a little smile or a wink… Something to indicate he was attracted to me as much as I was him. Or, even better, that he was gay.

Or at least bi.

Or even bi-curious.

I just needed the tiniest crumb. A speck.

I got nothing from him for the rest of the class. But I had placed my hand on my own knee in the same spot like the desperate fool that I was so it felt like his hand was still there.

When class was finally over and I'd realized I missed half of what Dr. Louden had said, I sighed over my craziness and began to gather my belongings.

I noticed Tate had scribbled a shitload of notes in an actual notebook instead of on his laptop. Did I really miss that much material?

Maybe he'd be willing to share his notes. It could be the perfect excuse to spend more time with him so I could flush out who Tate Harris was and give him a chance to get to know me better, too.

"Hey… uh… do you want to go grab a coffee or something? I would love to copy your notes."

Tate paused and I held my breath while waiting for his answer. I might have even crossed my fingers as I waited. But when he shook his dark head, I slowly released the air I was holding, though my disappointment didn't go along with it.

However, I did notice that he kind of looked disappointed himself.

Huh.

"Can't. I have to be somewhere." He continued stuffing everything back into his backpack. I was surprised it wasn't splitting at the seams. When he lifted his head again, he said, "But I can email them to you after I type them up."

He handed me his notebook and a pen. While I jotted down my

email address, I asked, "Why didn't you just type them directly into your computer? It would be more efficient."

"It's one way that I 'study.' I handwrite the notes first, then type them up later. It forces me to go over the material twice."

"Smart."

"I'm not sure if it's smart but it works for me."

But did it really since he was repeating this class? And how many other classes had he repeated?

"I guess whatever works," I mumbled and followed him down the steps once everyone else filed out.

Dr. Louden's dark eyes followed us as we walked past the lectern.

"Great lesson today, sir," I called out with a half wave and a smile.

Now who was kissing ass?

"You mean you actually paid attention?" the professor asked, knowing full well that I didn't. I'd been too busy mooning over Tate.

"Absolutely. It was mesmerizing. I wish you taught all of my classes." I didn't wait for his response. Instead, we both rushed out of the door and into the busy corridor, trying to contain our laughter.

We stopped right outside the door.

"Well, I'm headed this way," I said, tipping my head to the right.

"And I'm going that way. See you on Tuesday?"

Tuesday was four days away!

"Sure. Yeah." I tried desperately to keep the disappointment out of my voice. I failed miserably.

Clearing my throat, I adjusted my backpack over my shoulder and began to walk away. Well, walk wasn't quite right, more like dragged my feet since I wasn't ready for us to go our separate ways.

"Hey…" Tate grabbed my arm and stopped my forward motion.

Was he about to profess his undying love for me? Right there in the hallway? Good. Because I wanted the whole world to hear it if he was.

I glanced over my shoulder at him and when he looked like he was struggling to get out whatever he was about to say next, I turned to face him and gave him the time he needed.

He dropped his gaze to his sneakers for a moment and when he glanced back up, those blue eyes of his hit mine and shot sparks through me.

Unlike Dr. Louden's lecture, Tate's eyes *were* mesmerizing and they held me in place.

What are you going to say, Tate? Get it out. You're killing me here.

"There's a frat having a party tomorrow night."

What? That wasn't what I had hoped to hear. "You're part of a frat?" I didn't know whether to be impressed or disappointed in that revelation. I leaned toward disappointed. I hoped he wasn't one of those typical frat boys.

Tate shook his head. "No, but a couple of my friends are. But this one's at Pitt, not here. I was invited and now... so are you."

I blinked. That was kind of a weird invite. But... "Why?"

Tate frowned. "Why what?"

"Why would you invite me?"

His frowned deepened, causing creases around his mouth. "Why wouldn't I?"

Oh, how about... you don't know me, I'm gay, I'm deeply in lust with you and you're probably and unfortunately straight... for starters.

"I mean, I'm... uh..."

He tilted his head and stared at me. "You're..."

"A freshman. And not from Pitt. They won't care?"

His frown was now gone and an amused smile replaced it. I definitely liked the smiling Tate over the frowny-faced version.

My attention got caught on the upward curl of his lips for a second.

Or two.

"No, they won't give a shit. And Pitt has the best parties."

"Do they charge anything to get in?" Because that could be a problem.

He shook his head. "They charge for a cup if you want to drink."

"Like how much?" *For shit's sake,* I was so damn lame! And broke.

A look crossed Tate's face. Like he suddenly understood the

reasoning behind my hesitation. "Don't worry about it. I got you covered."

"You don't—"

Tate leaned closer, stared me right in the eyes and said, "I got you covered."

Well, damn. I could read all kinds of naughty things into that. But I doubted Tate meant any of them. "I'll pay you back."

"It's nothing."

It wasn't.

Tate straightened and tossed one strap of his backpack over his shoulder. "So, see you tomorrow?"

"Maybe."

"I'll email you the details when I send you the notes."

"Okay."

Tate jerked up his chin. "Think about it, at least."

"I will."

He turned and headed in the opposite direction.

I remained standing right there in the hallway, watching him. Until he finally got lost in the crowd.

Think about it.

There was nothing to think about. I had already decided I was going.

CHAPTER 3

Tate (Now)

I TIGHTENED my hold on Mazie's hand since my four-year-old had a tendency to run off when I wasn't paying attention. And since we were in the city, I couldn't risk her darting out between parked cars and into traffic.

If I thought my life was messed up now, having something happen to my daughter, especially due to me not being vigilant, would completely annihilate it.

Alec, with his dark head tipped down and wearing a deep scowl, was staying about ten feet in front of me because he wasn't happy and he wanted to make it known to not only me, but the whole world. With every step he took down the sidewalk toward the entrance of my building, when he wasn't kicking the toes of his sneakers into the sidewalk, he was dragging them along the concrete instead.

He was doing his best to get on my nerves and I was doing my best to not let him.

After asking him to stop a half dozen times, I'd given up. But I also warned him that he'd have to live with those scuffed sneakers until he outgrew them no matter what they looked like since we weren't getting him another pair.

My eight-year-old son was clearly telling me with his actions that he didn't want to spend the weekend with me even though he insisted over the phone the other day that he missed me.

The inconsistency that came from my kids was just another joy in a whole list of them when it came to parenting.

Smiles and kisses were what parents expected.

Mood swings and temper tantrums were what they got.

While I loved my kids more than life itself, sometimes I did not love the way they acted.

But I needed to remind myself to have patience, their lives had recently been tossed upside down when Dahlia and I divorced and then again when I moved back to Pittsburgh. A city I never thought I'd return to, even though I had originally planned on never leaving it in the first place.

But here I was, back in the Burgh.

Twelve years, one divorce and two kids later.

My whole young adult life I figured I'd end up married, in a good career and with the two-point-five kids. A "typical" American family. That was expected, right?

Then I met Ronan and everything I thought I was working toward unexpectedly changed. My hopes. My dreams. My future.

Even though I was confused and unsure, I had been excited about that new direction.

Until I wasn't.

Because reality could be a nasty bitch.

And, worse, because I screwed everything up when my life smashed head-first into a brick wall. From there, it never recovered.

After that, I was resigned to the fact I would be stuck living that "typical" American life, that "typical" worn-out American dream, and raising that "typical" American family.

But deep down...

Deep down it had all felt wrong.

Not once had it felt right.

My only real joy in the last twelve years came from the birth of my children.

And still did. Even though they were kind of hating me right now.

Nevertheless, I couldn't be true to them if I wasn't true to myself first. It took me a long time to figure that out and now that I had…

I sighed.

That was how I ended up back in Pittsburgh. In the city I had always loved so much. Missed so much, too.

I returned to the scene of that head-on collision. Went back to where my life took a wrong turn.

Because of my kids, I never thought I'd come back here at all. But when the opportunity came along to return to Pittsburgh, I couldn't say no. Because, truthfully, I couldn't find a better place for a fresh start. Something I desperately needed.

I also needed to return to the place where I originally discovered myself. Who I was. Who I was meant to be.

Despite pushing all of that aside.

At the time I thought I had the right reason to do that. It turned out I was mistaken. All I did was delay the inevitable. My decisions made Dahlia and I suffer through years of pain and anguish when I hadn't meant it to be like that.

When I thought I was doing the right thing.

That I was being a good man. A good father. Even a good husband.

That was what I desperately wanted. To be *good*. And, at the time, I did it the only way I knew how…

I punched in the code at the entrance and as soon as the door clicked, indicating it had unlocked, I held it open and called out to Alec, who had wandered a few feet past the doors. "This way, kiddo."

My heart hurt for my son. My heart hurt for Mazie, too.

My pain was nothing compared to theirs.

Alec turned, his face grim when he walked ahead of me and into the building. My new home. At least temporarily.

I had managed to snag a sublease on a fully furnished apartment. While it was costing me a little more money I really didn't have to spare, it saved me from spending the spare cash I had on furnishings and all the little, but needed, stuff. Like pots and pans, utensils and even appliances.

Once I got my feet solidly underneath me again, I'd find somewhere else. Maybe a house with a yard for the kids. Possibly a place big enough for a dog. Then I'd furnish it the way I wanted. But for now, this had to work. I had no other choice.

"I don't like it here."

"Alec, this is just the outer vestibule. You haven't even seen my... *our* place yet."

"I already know I won't like it," he grumbled.

I bit back a sigh.

"And it's not *our* place, Dad. We live with Mom," he *so* helpfully reminded me.

"You'll be spending time here, too. With me. So yes, it'll be your place, too."

Alec rolled his eyes and yanked open one of the inner doors, stomping his way into the lobby.

"Daddy?"

I glanced down at Mazie as I followed Alec and continued to hold her hand to guide her toward the elevator. "Yes, honey?"

"I don't wanna live here. I don't like the city."

"You don't know this city, Maze. Once you do, I hope you'll love it as much as I do."

"Cities are stinky and dirty and noisy and crowded," my daughter went on, expressing her very strong opinions.

My baby girl would someday grow up to be a very strong, opinionated woman and I would support her every step of the way. I wanted both my kids to be true to themselves from day one. Even when they were being temperamental.

I squeezed her hand. "They're also full of beautiful lights and fun activities, like the zoo. Plus, there are plenty of great restaurants and friendly people. We'll make it fun, I promise."

"Your marriage to Mom was a promise, too," came from my, once again, super helpful son now standing in front of the elevator.

"Push the button, Alec."

Instead of pushing it, he crossed his arms over his chest and huffed.

I didn't muffle my sigh this time. We had a lot of work to do.

I had a lot of work to do.

"I wanna go back to Mommy's," Mazie said with her face turned up to me and her bottom lip pushed out.

"You will. After the weekend. Don't you want to spend time with me?" Truthfully, I was afraid to hear that answer.

Right now, everything was still so raw. I knew it would settle eventually, but until then...

"Alec, push the button, please."

When he didn't, I pushed past him and did it myself.

I turned toward Alec and noticed he was staring past me toward the front doors.

With curiosity, I shot a glance over my shoulder before turning back toward him.

Unexpectedly, the hairs on the back of my neck stood.

As if there was a threat.

Did someone follow us into the building that shouldn't without me knowing? Was I about to be mugged? Or my children kidnapped?

My hand tightened around Mazie's and my heart pounded in my throat.

If I had to, I'd shove my kids into the elevator to keep them safe so I could turn around to confront the threat.

"Hurry up," I mumbled to the elevator, watching the floor numbers count down as it traveled toward the ground level. I quickly glanced back over my shoulder again at the man coming through the doors from the vestibule into the main lobby area.

That was when I lost my breath and my brain glitched.

It couldn't be. I had to be seeing things.

How did he find me here?

How would he know I was here? In Pittsburgh? In this building?

Why would he be here?

Why would he be looking for me?

What the hell was happening?

Maybe I was wrong and it was someone who only looked like Ronan Pak. While this man looked similar to the one I once knew, he also looked different.

Very different.

But then twelve years had passed since I last saw him. A lot could change in that time.

Two of my major changes were named Mazie and Alec.

The man, who looked eerily familiar, froze one step into the lobby, his dark brown eyes taking me in. Then he took in my kids...

That was when I knew...

My instinct was right.

Holy shit.

We stared at each other across the lobby. Me frozen in front of the elevators, him a concrete statue in front of the doors.

Only about twenty feet or so now separated us instead of twelve years.

The elevator dinged and the doors slid open.

Get in the elevator, Tate. Get in. You're imagining this and even if you aren't...

Even if you aren't...

"Wait." I grabbed Alec's shoulder before he could step into the car. "Hold up, Alec."

When my son jerked his shoulder from my grip, Ronan noticed but kept his expression blank.

I didn't know what to do. Had he seen us on the street and followed us inside to talk to me?

And, if so, did I want him approaching me to possibly hash out the past in front of my kids?

No.

No, I didn't want my kids to know who that man was to me... No... who he *had been* to me in my past.

I didn't want them to know how much he had meant to me.

How their father had betrayed him.

Not on purpose but because I thought I had no other choice.

We couldn't stay where we currently were, in this crazy stand-off. I either had to take my kids upstairs to my place and forget I ever saw Ronan, or I needed to find out why he was here. In the lobby of my building.

The first choice would be the smartest. Nothing good would come from us reopening old wounds.

Of course, that wasn't what I did. Mostly because I was a pro at doing the wrong thing and then regretting it later.

"Hold your brother's hand and don't move from this spot. Do you understand?"

Mazie nodded and took a reluctant Alec's hand. My son accepted it but not without glaring at me first.

"Who is that, Daddy?"

I ignored Alec's behavior as if it didn't exist and answered my daughter's question. "Just an... old friend."

Something flashed across Ronan's face. There and gone in an instant.

But what I said wasn't wrong. We had been friends first before...

The rest.

"Stay right here while I go say hello. Don't get in the elevator or go up the steps, okay?"

Alec didn't respond, but Mazie, with her bottom lip now tucked between her teeth, nodded her head.

I stepped away from my present and into my past as I approached the man who hadn't moved even an inch.

When I got closer, I paused and waited for him to say something. Anything. I also kept a close eye on his hands to make sure he didn't pull out a gun to shoot me dead.

When he didn't, I edged my way around him since he was blocking the door and I stepped into the vestibule. I turned to face the lobby so I could keep an eye on my offspring while I talked to Ronan.

However, it took a few more moments for him to finally unstick himself from where he stood and follow me.

Now instead of twenty, we stood only five feet apart.

He was just outside my reach. Even if I stretched out my arm and fingers.

Did I want to touch him? Oh yes.

Did I recognize the fact that the day I walked away from him was the biggest mistake of my life? Also yes.

Was there any way to go back and do it all over again and do it right? I wish there was, but, unfortunately, there was no way to go back to the past and have a redo, even after knowing everything I know now.

The past was unerasable.

I had broken us.

I had stolen his smile.

I had rejected his love.

I had made so many mistakes.

Ronan was not one of them but what I did to him was.

I regretted it every day since.

My heart never healed and the crack widened a bit as I stared at the man I used to love when that same heart had been whole.

I wasn't sure what to say, so I just asked what came to mind first. "You're the last person I expected to run into... What are you doing here?"

I waited for him to echo my question and when he didn't, I realized he already knew I lived in this building. Was he looking for me on purpose or did he find me only out of coincidence?

His answer floored me. It was not the one I expected. "I live here."

"I figured you stayed in Pittsburgh—"

"In this building," he clarified, cutting me off.

He lived *here*? In the same building as I did? What kind of karma was this?

Before I could find words to respond, he continued, his tone more than a little accusatory, "You told me you were moving away from Pittsburgh after you graduated. Or was that a lie, too?"

It was kind of crazy. His voice seemed to be deeper than mine now that we were in our thirties. It was deep and rich and had more of a rasp to it than what I remembered.

What hadn't changed was that it did things to me that I had forgotten.

Okay, I didn't forget. I had purposely pushed them out of my mind. Because back then I figured I would never experience those same things again with anyone else.

Unfortunately, I was right.

I ignored the shot about lying to him. "I did."

"You moved back."

He knew the answer already. I shouldn't have to confirm it, but… "Yes, I moved back." *And somehow ended up living in the same building as you, Roe. How the hell did that happen?*

"Why?" The single word was cold as ice and just as sharp. Like I had betrayed him all over again by coming back to the city we had shared together.

I wanted to snap back, "Why not?" It wasn't like he owned the city. I also didn't owe him an explanation.

The only thing I ever owed him was an apology and I had given that to him twelve years ago.

Just because he didn't accept it at the time, didn't mean it wasn't valid.

I was sorry then. I was sorry now. But I wasn't going to drag myself over slivers of glass for him to feel better.

Not now.

Not all these years later.

Especially when, a couple of years after I graduated, I had too much to drink and in a bad judgment call reached out to him. Of course, he never responded because twelve years ago he decided to never forgive me.

As much as I wished his decision had been different, he had every right to embrace the way he felt.

Back then. And even now.

However, I did not owe him answers. Just like he didn't owe me any, either.

I looked past him to my children, who, surprisingly, still stood where I told them to wait. Both sets of eyes watching us.

Those two were the most important human beings in my life. Even more than the person who previously held that spot.

Because they were watching, and maybe even listening, I didn't want this conversation to turn ugly. I really needed to cut it short now that I knew he wasn't stalking me for whatever reason. Now that I knew that us both living in the same building was simply a strange coincidence.

"Look," I started, driving fingers through my hair, "I don't want this to be uncomfortable for us. I can break the lease and find another place to live."

I really couldn't afford to find another place. Deposits and rent weren't cheap. Moving wasn't cheap. Even without a bunch of stuff.

The thought of having to move again turned my stomach. It would put me in the hole even deeper than I already was. But I would do it.

For him.

Maybe even for my own mental health.

"You'd do that?" he asked with a tilt of his head.

He didn't believe me. I could see it all over his face.

A face that was much more mature than when I'd last seen it. Shallow lines spidered out from the corners of his dark brown eyes. A goatee now circled the mouth I had tasted in the past more times than I could count. It was also hard to miss the tattoos covering his arms below the short-sleeves of his snug T-shirt.

He wasn't so skinny any more, either. His shoulders were broader than what I remembered and he had filled out all over. His thighs, his chest… Even his face.

He wasn't fat, but solid. Very muscular. It was clear he spent a lot of time working on his physique.

He looked good.

Better than good.

But I reminded myself none of that mattered.

I nodded. "I would, Roe. I didn't know you lived here or I wouldn't have signed the lease. I don't want to make this awkward for either of us."

He glanced back over his shoulder at my kids. They were both starting to get antsy, obvious by their shuffling feet and the impatience on their faces.

Both were about to break. I needed to get back to them before they went into full meltdown mode right there in the lobby. I didn't need Ronan to know that I was a failure as a parent as much as I had been as a boyfriend. And husband.

When I turned my attention back to my former lover, I realized he'd been watching me. Closely.

"No, you don't need to move. We're adults now. We can act like it, right? We'll probably hardly run into each other, anyway."

Sure. "We'll probably be like two passing ships in the night," I half-teased on a stilted laugh.

"Right. Two passing ships in the night," Ronan repeated dryly. "With one being a battleship so it could blow the schooner out of the water when they least expect it."

Damn it. "Roe…"

His broad chest rose as he took a slow, deep inhale and then pushed the air out just as slowly. "It's fine. Stay. I don't want you to uproot your kids because of me."

I was tempted to tell him that my kids had no roots here. Not yet. That meant now would be the perfect time for me to find somewhere else to live.

But, honestly, I was relieved about not having to move again. At least right now. Even if I kept running into him. Then, if things got weird or unbearable between us… I'd reconsider it. By then I might have a few paychecks under my belt at my new job and hopefully be more financially stable.

I didn't want to tell Ronan any of that because I was embarrassed by how far I had fallen.

It was my business. We were no longer friends or lovers, nor did we share a future.

We were nothing to each other anymore.

Not a damn thing.

That thought caused sharp shards of pain to explode through my chest.

I pressed my hand to my heart and Ronan's dark eyes followed the motion. "You okay?"

No. "Yes, fine. I need to get back to my kids."

He nodded.

It hit me then that he'd be heading up to his apartment, too. We would have to ride the elevator together and I'd have to introduce my "friend" to my children.

The past meeting my future.

I didn't know if I could do it. Not yet.

Not today.

"Can you do me a favor?" I asked in a whisper, hating to have to ask this of him.

I waited to get a bunch of flak for my request, but surprisingly, I didn't.

"What?"

"Can you wait to use the elevator until I get my kids upstairs? I'm sorry to have to ask that of you, but…" How messed up would it be if we lived on the same damn floor?

His firm but soft, "Go," had me nodding in relief and I went.

CHAPTER 4

Ronan (Then)

I BARELY DUCKED in time to avoid an elbow coming from my left, then a few seconds later, a half-inflated beach ball being batted around overhead. The music was cranked so loud I doubted I'd be able to hear my professors for the next week. But it needed to be at a deafening level to even be heard over the cheers, hoots, whistles, stomping and beer chugging chants.

Noise. That was what it was. An out-of-control commotion made up of questionable music and drunk college students trying to talk over each other.

No, not talk. Shout. They were well past the decibel level where talking could be heard.

Guaranteed, everyone would have a hangover tomorrow or, at minimum, a headache.

Some of the party-goers still wore clothes, some were half-naked and others… not a stitch of clothes could be found. Some bare bodies even had paint on them like at a NFL or college football game. Only the drawings and words would have to be pixelated for national TV.

It seemed like an endless sea of thoroughly pickled cocky guys and ditzy girls. Maybe that wasn't one hundred percent true but close enough. The cocky and ditzy part, not the pickled part. That was definitely true. It also wasn't so much a party as a hookup haven, even though I was being both looked over or looked through.

It was not quite my scene but I was also disgusted and amazed, as well as fascinated and amused all at the same time. However, the amusement waned a bit when the guy standing next to me rushed to the corner to puke. Not in a plant or vase or a trash can.

Hell no.

In some chick's lap.

Mmm. Hot yeasty beer and spicy beef tacos.

With a grimace, I slapped a hand over my nose and elbowed my way through the wall of bodies in an attempt to find some fresh air before the saliva flooding my mouth turned into something more.

I really didn't want to experience tonight's dinner from the cafeteria again. It wasn't great the first time around, it would be even worse the second.

As I made my way through the frat house, I couldn't imagine it smelled much better even when there wasn't a party. Put a shitload of college guys without their mommies in one house and *yikes*... Especially if they played sports.

Sweaty jockstraps, damp socks and crusty, stinky cleats and sneakers.

It was fetish for some, but not for me.

As I made my way through the crowd, looking for the nearest exit to take a non-toxic breath, I half expected the cops to show up at any moment to break up the party and arrest some of my fellow undergrads for underage drinking and drug usage.

Not to mention, indecent exposure.

However, that last one, I was kind of enjoying. A vast array of bitable juicy peaches wandered through the packed frat house. Most a bit pale and some with fuzz, but still edible.

Though, I really doubted any of the owners of those delectable behinds would appreciate me sinking my teeth into a firm cheek. Or two.

With a grin, I took another sip of my now flat, warm beer. I'd been nursing it for the last hour in a red Solo cup that cost Tate twenty bucks.

Twenty fucking bucks.

It was highway robbery since I doubted I would drink twenty dollars' worth of beer. And the atmosphere certainly didn't make up for the difference.

Even though he said he didn't want to be paid back, I planned on doing so, anyway. No matter how long it took me. If I was brave and had my tetanus shot, I'd dig in the frat's couches and probably find enough change to make up that twenty. Only, I was afraid of what else I'd find. I didn't even want to *sit* on one of those couches, forget digging under or in between the cushions.

I should get his money's worth by getting a fresh refill—

My plastic cup was yanked from my fingers when an arm snaked out from between two people, causing me to spill the warm beer over my hand. "Hey!"

After I shook it off, Tate emerged attached to that arm. "Hey."

"Sorry, I thought you were some asshole."

"I *am* some asshole," he said with a lopsided grin and a noticeable slur. Somebody must have already drank his money's worth. And maybe mine, too. "You having fun?"

"Loads," I answered, plastering on a smile of my own. I came to the party to spend time with Tate, not to be hung upside down by my ankles while I shot-gunned carbonated yeast and hops.

He peered into my cup and wrinkled his nose. "You need a fresh beer."

"I need fresh air."

"I'll get you another beer and if you head to the backyard," he tipped his head toward the rear of the frat house, "I'll bring you your beer."

Well, how about that? The man of my dreams was going to *serve* me.

We separated and I somehow managed to worm my way through the sea of students and out the propped-open back door to the just as crowded backyard.

Was the whole damn student body for both Pitt and Duquesne here tonight? It had to be.

I found a tiny bit of real estate to stand on and wait for Tate. In the meantime, I surveyed the scene and saw the same as what I did inside.

At least it didn't smell as bad.

The music changed to *OMG* by Usher and suddenly the whole backyard began to surge up and down in waves, reminding me of a mosh pit. A smile crossed my face and I began to move a bit with the music.

Finally something decent.

Since I got caught up in the song and people watching, I jumped when a red Solo cup appeared in front of my face. I grabbed it and turned to see Tate behind me. Unfortunately, he wasn't alone.

I tightened my fingers around the cup just in time to keep from dropping the beer.

She was beautiful. If you were into that type. That type being female.

I was not.

But I could appreciate her beauty anyway. Just like I could appreciate straight guys.

I looky, I just don't touchy.

I had hoped Tate wasn't straight. Even though I knew that was a stretch, the slightest hope I had clung to was now dashed.

Damn.

"Thanks," I mumbled, then gulped down almost half of it in an attempt to wash away my disappointment.

It didn't work.

"Hey, I want you to meet Dahlia, my girlfriend."

Dahlia leaned into Tate with her breasts pressed into his arm and her arms looped around his neck as she stared up at him with adoration. And what looked like possessiveness.

Shit.

"Hello, Dahlia," I greeted, trying to keep a sour expression from my face.

"Hi..."

"Roe," Tate supplied for her, curling one arm around her waist and keeping her close.

Her little perky nose scrunched up. "Roe?"

"Ronan," I quickly added.

"Ah, okay. Hi, Ronan. Tate says you have Creative Writing together."

Oooh, he talked about me? "We do."

"Dr. Louden's a cranky old fuck, isn't he?" Dahlia asked with a wink. "Tate and I met in his class when we were freshman." She smiled up at Tate. "We've been inseparable ever since."

My takeaway from that was it wasn't only Tate being late to class that made him have to repeat it. He'd probably been distracted by the dark-haired beauty now standing in front of Tate, shimmying and shaking to a Black Eyed Peas song.

Tate had one arm now wrapped around her stomach and Dahlia was pulled against him. Every time her ass swayed back and forth it probably rubbed against his cock. I so, so, *sooooo* wanted to be in her place instead.

But I wasn't and now realized I never would be.

A damn shame, really, but nothing new for me.

I watched the two of them interact with each other for a few moments, then turned back to once again scope out the packed backyard. I figured it would come off as a bit weird if I continued to stare at them, especially since I was having a hard time masking my petty jealousy.

I came to the party to spend time with Tate but as the saying went, three was a crowd and it was me that was the third wheel in this case.

I should leave and head back to campus and my dorm room. I wasn't into drinking myself into oblivion and I also wasn't into chicks, so I was feeling out of place.

It only cemented the fact that I needed to find my own tribe on campus. Maybe even hunt down an LGBTQ organization or think about starting one if there wasn't one already established.

Realistically, I didn't have time to run an organization since I desperately needed a job. And soon.

I circled the rim of my twenty dollar disposable cup with a fingertip and my sigh got lost among the rest of the din.

The job issue was a big one but it also reminded me that once I found one, I might not have time to attend parties, either, so I should enjoy the one I was currently at, even if my heart had been slightly cracked by finding out my former fiancé had a girlfriend.

Hell, that he liked girls.

Tate just friend-zoned me, even though he wasn't aware of it.

I needed to forget that my future husband would no longer be that and just have fun.

Drink. Laugh. Dance. And have conversation without worrying about Dr. Louden kicking us out of class.

When I turned to do just that, Dahlia was just lifting her head from reading something on her phone.

"Lena's heading over to a party in South Side. Want to go?" Dahlia asked Tate over the music, grabbing his hand, holding it up in the air and dancing in a circle underneath it as if he was spinning her around.

Tate's beautiful blue eyes, now a bit on the bloodshot side since he was kind of wasted, sliced from Dahlia to me.

I held my breath waiting for his answer. Was he going to dump me here? That would be the icing on the cake.

"Roe only got here about a half hour ago."

Dahlia stopped dancing, dropped his hand and turned to face Tate. "So?"

Oops, someone sounded a bit bitchy.

"So, I invited him and I don't want to abandon him here."

"There's plenty of other people here to keep him company."

Wow. More than a bit.

"Dahlia…"

"Tate, come on…" she whined, tugging on his shirt.

"What's wrong with this party?"

Dahlia faked a yawn while patting her open mouth with her hand and rolled her eyes.

"Whatever sorority party you want to go to will be the same. All these parties are. We're already here. I spent sixty bucks on the beer and—"

"Do you care if I go, then?"

Tate stared down at her for a few seconds, then asked, "Will I see you later?"

She nodded with her bottom lip caught between her teeth and a smile on her face.

I knew exactly what that meant.

But the turnaround in her attitude was miraculous.

"Okay. Be careful."

She rose up on her toes and pressed her mouth against his. "I'll go find Maggie. She's somewhere inside, I think, and take her along with me. Safety in numbers."

Then she was off with a spring in her step, fighting her way back into the house.

My gaze turned from her disappearing back to Tate. I pressed my lips together so I wouldn't grin since my night started looking better because now I had Tate all to myself.

Well, me and a hundred or more drunks.

But I could work with that.

~

Ronan (Now)

I SMILED DOWN at Jeremy when his hand snaked up my shirt and he tweaked one of my nipples.

I think that was his name.

Jeremy or Justin or Jack. Maybe James.

Something with a J.

And even then, whatever he'd told me might not be his real name since I found him on Grindr. That app was where I found most of my "dates."

Being a twink, he really wasn't my type per se, but tonight my type was anyone able to get my mind off Tate and the fact he now lived in my building. Even if me forgetting my former lover only lasted for a little while.

Because I was tired.

Tired of thinking about Tate. He had invaded my thoughts and dreams all over again.

Sometimes I took my hookups to the William Penn Hotel for the night instead of my penthouse, just in case they were a clinger, or a murdering psycho. I also had a bad experience with a past "date" after waking up one morning and finding some of my things missing.

I was pissed at first that the guy had taken a couple of my smaller art pieces and pinched the cash and black AmEx card out of my wallet. Once I cancelled my card and called the police to file a report and my insurance company to cover the stolen art, I figured if the guy needed the money that badly, he could have it. I guessed it was one way of giving back to the gay community. Just not in a method I had planned.

However, tonight I wasn't in the mood to deal with a hotel. And I'm pretty sure Joe only wanted a quick bang and a goodbye like I did. One reason why I picked him.

So, here it was, Sunday evening and I had met Justin, Jason, or John for dinner at the Primanti Brothers downtown—an occasional unhealthy food splurge for me—and bought him everything he wanted to eat. Afterward, we walked back to my place since the night was perfect and the city quiet for the most part.

Now we were standing in front of the elevator and waiting for the car to finish its descent to the ground floor. I was in no rush to get upstairs since deep down I was hoping to run into Tate in order to prove that I'd moved on and gotten over him.

Truthfully, I thought I had until I'd seen him again. Then everything I had buried bubbled back up to the surface.

It annoyed me that... One, out of all the apartments to rent in Pittsburgh, he chose one in my building. Two, that he still looked so damn good. Three, that he'd had two kids, at least that I knew of, with Dahlia. And lastly, that the heart I thought had scarred over really hadn't.

Just seeing and hearing Tate had driven a wedge into the tiniest of cracks that must have remained in my heart, causing it to split wide open all over again.

I regretted not telling him to find another place like he offered. But then, if I had, it would be proof that his living here bothered me. The exact reason I brought Jeremiah home tonight instead of taking him elsewhere.

Just as the elevator dinged and the doors began to open, so did the lobby doors behind us. I held the doors as I turned my head, hoping it wasn't the Callahans after their evening walk with Mr. Pibbles.

It wasn't.

It was who I'd hoped. I suddenly regretted my plan, just like I regretted eating the kielbasa and cheese sandwich loaded with coleslaw and French fries earlier at Primanti's.

Me being petty wasn't going to hurt Tate.

It would hurt me. Again.

But now I couldn't *not* hold the doors for him. Not without looking like a bitter hag.

Even though I felt like one.

I sighed and hip-bumped Jessie to get him moving into the elevator to wait. I went from holding the door to holding the button on the panel, trying not to stare at Tate as his long, still familiar gait ate up the real estate between us.

I failed.

I was so tempted to close my eyes and get whisked back to our college days, back to when we began to explore each other, not as friends but lovers… Back to when I bottomed for him.

After he left, I never bottomed for anyone again.

I shook that from my thoughts and set my jaw as he stepped into the car, eyeing up Jace in one sweep before his vibrant blue gaze landed on me.

"Sixth floor," his baritone voice rumbled.

I almost answered in a snippy, "I know," but caught myself in time. He had no idea that I knew what floor he lived on.

I didn't bother to hit the button for any floor but his. I wasn't sure I wanted him to know where I lived yet. I could push the button for the penthouse after he exited on his own floor.

When the car jerked into motion, I glanced at Tate and he met my eyes for a second.

Should we greet each other? Or pretend our past together didn't exist?

I opened my mouth, unsure of what to say, but a sharp "Where are your kids?" came out instead.

No *hello*, no *how's your night*, but a demand right off the bat. I was an idiot and he had every right not to answer.

"Back with their mother." His eyes flicked back to Jeremiah, whose head was ping-ponging back and forth between us as he tried to figure out why the tension was so thick in the air.

I pretended there wasn't a problem and went back to thinking about Tate's kids. I had assumed their mother was Dahlia, but I didn't know that for a fact. He could've divorced her years ago and remarried.

I didn't want to ask, either. It was bad enough when he chose

Dahlia over me, but to find out he then chose *another* woman after that…?

I didn't want to think about it.

With an arm wrapped around my Grindr date's waist, I gave it a squeeze like we'd known each other for more than two hours. "Tate, this is Jacob."

"It's Josh."

Shit.

I forced out a laugh and explained to Tate, "It's a game we play. I call him every J name I can think of other than his real one."

"No, we—"

I quickly pressed my mouth to Josh's in a kiss to shut him up. When we were done and I pulled away, Josh was wearing a naughty smile. "Mmm. That was yummy."

Instead of rolling my eyes, I purred, "Yes, it was. There will be more of that once we get upstairs."

Josh tugged on my polo shirt and grinned at Tate, exclaiming, "He's such a tease!"

When Tate didn't smile back or even say a word, not even a greeting, Josh took offense and bugged his green eyes out at me.

It spoke volumes but I ignored that, too.

The elevator car jerked to a stop on the sixth floor and the doors slid open.

"You two have a good night," Tate muttered as he rushed out.

I winced as my date yelled out "Don't worry, we will," much too enthusiastically as the doors slid shut again. "Well, wasn't he pleasant?"

My first instinct was to make an excuse for Tate. I reminded myself that I didn't need to do that.

Josh's eyes narrowed on me and he tilted his head as he asked, "Do you two know each other?"

"Just neighbors," I mumbled, stabbing the button for the top floor, which didn't go unnoticed by the man leaning into me.

Josh gave a little squeak. "That button says PH. The penthouse? You must have a great view of the city."

"That I do."

"I can't wait to see it," he purred, sliding his hand between my skin and shirt again and pinching one of my nipples harder than I expected.

I fought the urge to push him off me. My whole plan of showing Tate how I've moved on had backfired. I no longer wanted to take Josh up to my place. Or fuck him.

Or even have him suck me off.

I *could* fuck him with my eyes closed and pretend it was Tate I was railing. But once I finished and opened my eyes...

Reality would club me over the head.

Before I could suggest cutting the date short and sending Josh on his way, we arrived on the twelfth floor and the elevator opened and we stepped out into the small vestibule right outside my penthouse door.

Josh rushed out, spun in a circle, squealing, "Nobody else lives on this floor?"

"No."

"Wait. *Your* penthouse is the *only* penthouse? It takes up an entire floor? Holy shit, you must be *riiiiiiiiiiiich*." He stopped in front of my door and bounced on his toes with impatience. "Hurry. Open the door. I need to check this out."

My door had a smart lock on it, so as soon as I got closer, it automatically unlocked because of an app on my phone. I also had a couple of fobs with RFID chips I could use in case I lost my phone.

Or if I was careless and it was stolen by a Grindr hookup.

"Whoa, did that door just unlock without a key or a card?"

Josh seemed easily impressed. But then, if he hadn't lied on his profile, he was only twenty. No matter what, he was younger than who I normally "dated."

I nodded and reached past him to open the door and usher him inside. As soon as he stepped over the threshold, he immediately jogged over to the wall of windows that stretched across the south side of my place.

When I had my penthouse designed, I wanted it as open as possible. The less walls to restrict my views, the better.

I wanted plenty of open space and not to feel confined. I got exactly what I wanted and luckily only had to deal with a few support beams instead. The only area of the top floor that was sectioned off was where the bathrooms and bedrooms were. And, of course, at the end of the hallway, where I had built my extensive home office. But even the views from the large windows in those rooms were spectacular.

Everywhere I went in my place, I had a bird's eye view of Pittsburgh and beyond.

However, I wasn't feeling the same excitement with my date as he did when it came to my penthouse. As Josh wandered around taking it all in with his mouth hanging open and a gleam in his eye, I knew he was all wrong for me. Even for a one-night-stand.

Instead of twelve years, it seemed more like two decades separated us. But it wasn't just his age causing the disconnect.

With his slim build, his narrow shoulders and baby face, Josh was so opposite of Tate. That was probably why I had tapped on his photo in the app. Why would I pick someone who reminded me of the man I was trying to forget?

I wouldn't.

But now I was stuck with someone I really didn't want.

Like with my plan to run into Tate, I messed up by bringing home a Grindr date.

I knew it. Josh did not.

Either I had to grit my teeth and go for it, or acknowledge my mistake and cut my losses. But I could at least soften the blow.

Though, I questioned if that was possible when Josh yanked off his shirt and tossed it onto a chair before rushing over to me. "Bedroom?"

"Why don't we have a drink first?" *Before you pull off your shorts next and streak down the hallway naked.* "What would you like?"

"What do you have? Hell, you probably have everything."

The door lock wasn't the only thing "smart." Everything in my penthouse I could set up to be voice-activated, or at least controlled by a remote, I did. Having grown up in a lower class working family, we couldn't even afford a security system, forget modern technology.

"Alfred, open the bar," I called out to my home system.

Josh's eyebrows launched up his forehead. "Alfred? Like Batman's butler?"

"Exactly like that," I murmured, heading over to the now-exposed bar that had slid out of my wall between the chef's kitchen and the dining area.

"Does it make the drinks, too?" he asked on a laugh, following me.

"Now that would be an idea," I answered, plastering on a smile and trying to pull myself out of the funk I was in by seeing Tate.

Josh bumped shoulders with me as we stood side-by-side looking at my vast selection of liquor. "Or you could just pay someone to live here and serve you."

I blinked.

I had a house cleaner who came in once a week. I also had a chef from a very popular restaurant downtown have his staff drop off meals that I could enjoy throughout the week when I wasn't in the mood to cook my own. But have someone actually live in my place with me full-time?

No.

And if I did, it wouldn't be some random Grindr hookup. That was just asking for me to be murdered in my sleep. Or have my whole penthouse cleaned out when I wasn't home.

"What do you want?"

Josh squeezed my ass cheek. "Besides you?"

"To drink," I clarified.

His green eyes again raked over my selection. "Umm. Vodka soda?"

Very original, I thought dryly, then suggested, "Why don't you grab a seat on the couch?" when he became even more handsy.

Guilt was starting to wash over me for wasting his time by keeping him here even this long. But I didn't want to be rude and also didn't want to throw him out like he was spoiled food.

When he wandered back to the stretch of windows, I blew out a quiet breath and grabbed the bottle of Belvedere. After mixing a vodka soda on the rocks, I carried it over to where he stood with both his hands, as well as his forehead, pressed to the glass as he watched the world go by below.

Those marks on the windows would normally bother me but I let it go. Luckily, Mondays were when my housekeeper showed up to clean. It was also the one day a week I made myself scarce and usually headed into my "official" office I kept at Pak Property Management.

"Josh."

He straightened and I handed him the drink. Since my hands were now empty, his brow dropped low. "Aren't you having one?"

I shook my head. "No, but you enjoy."

"But I want to enjoy you. And I see some of your ink peeking out. I'd love to explore them."

I sat on the couch and watched my bad decision prowl around the open area, sipping on his drink, checking out the art that I purchased to support local LGBTQ+ artists, and even thumbing through a couple of the books I had on my marble coffee table.

Eventually, he flopped down beside me and hooked a bare arm around my neck, pressing his naked, hairless chest to my arm. "Hey, are we going to have sex? Or…"

Or…

Or what? "What" was the answer. I just needed to find an easy way to break it to him.

CHAPTER 5

Ronan (Now)

With one hand gripping a lowball glass and the other my bottle of The Macallan scotch almost as old as Josh, I headed up my private winding staircase. After hours, the roof became my personal sanctuary when I wanted to enjoy the night without being disturbed.

The door used by the other residents in the building automatically locked after ten o'clock since that was when the rooftop pool officially closed for the night.

Since none of the apartments had balconies when I purchased the building, and still didn't, I had the roof designed as a little oasis that I allowed my tenants to share.

One long-term resident had even started a raised vegetable garden in the corner farthest from the pool. Several other neighbors now helped tend to it and shared its fresh bounty.

But like my penthouse, I built this space with me in mind and I enjoyed spending time up here as much as I did in my home. Of course, up here the views were unencumbered, unlike in my own place. I had even used plexiglass for the safety railing around the roof's perimeter so it wouldn't block the views.

Pittsburgh might not be New York, Chicago or L.A., but it was home. It was also perfect for me.

I preferred genuine, warm people and the slower pace of this city. The real estate investment opportunities were just as plentiful and more affordable. I doubted my portfolio would have grown as fast and be as large if I'd done the same thing in one of the bigger metropolitan areas.

I stepped out onto the roof from my private access and paused just long enough to fill my lungs with the warm June night air.

When I blew it out, I imagined all the tension I was holding onto going along with it. Floating up to the cloudless night sky decorated with countless stars while the faint and soothing melody of the city sounds reached my ears all the way to where I stood over twelve stories above ground.

It took a while to convince Josh to leave, but eventually he got the picture and left, telling me that if I ever needed a roommate to hit him up on Grindr. Since I would not be doing that, I only gave him a smile, a "thank you" and a genuine "sorry."

Before he stepped into the elevator, he asked, "It's because of him, isn't it?"

I wanted to pretend he wasn't correct, but I couldn't. Instead, I said nothing as the doors shut and Josh disappeared.

It's because of him, isn't it?

Was it that obvious?

Of course it was. The problem was, I didn't know what to do about it.

I thought Tate was out of my system. However, if he truly was, seeing him, knowing he lived in my building, shouldn't affect me the way it was. So clearly, I was wrong.

Maybe if I hadn't loved him so damn much when he broke my heart, things might be different.

But they weren't. I couldn't change the past, but I needed to learn to deal with the future. Because until Tate moved out of River View Heights, I had no choice but to do so.

Distracted with my thoughts, I headed to my favorite pergola on the roof and settled myself on a lounge chair, kicked off my shoes and got comfortable. I opened The Macallan, poured myself about two fingers worth, set the bottle on the ground next to my chair and sat back to stare up into the sky.

While taking the first sip of my favorite scotch, a slight splash caught my attention. When a head broke the surface of the lit pool water, my head jerked back in surprise.

Had I been so caught up in my own head that I hadn't noticed anyone swimming?

From where I sat, it was hard to see who it was. But whoever it was shouldn't be in the pool this late. They had to have come out to the roof before the automatic lock was set. Unless the timer was broken. If so, I'd have to get maintenance to fix it.

Being the owner of numerous rental properties, I had learned to think in terms of "liability." Parties in the pool late at night, especially if they involved alcohol. Someone swimming alone and drowning. Locks not working and a child drowning. Someone jumping off the roof. Lights not working. Security.

Slips. Falls. Fires. Electrical issues.

It was endless and a constant worry. Normally, I let my property management team handle all of that, but I lived here. If I spotted a problem, I dealt with it swiftly. Or at least tried to.

Someone swimming after hours *could* be a problem. One I could deal with easily enough myself, but I'd let whoever it was finish their swim first. They were no longer alone since I was there and if they needed help, I could jump in.

Yes, the building had rules but I wasn't a tyrant.

When the head disappeared under the surface again, I rose in my seat slightly to see the dark figure sliding effortlessly through the illuminated blue water toward the opposite end of the pool. Instead of swimming normal laps on the surface using a butterfly or freestyle stroke, he—I thought it was a he—stayed underwater.

To strengthen their lungs? I had no idea.

The head popped up again at the far side of the pool, then disappeared once more as the person made their way to the end closest to me. Where I sat wasn't close enough to make out who it was until that person was done or I approached the edge myself because the only lights used on the rooftop at this time of night were the string lights. They hung from the six pergolas with the retractable canopies I'd had installed around the pool to give the outdoor area a more resort-like atmosphere. They were also wound around the top rail of the roof's perimeter.

The previous pool had to be completely rehabbed, so I had installed a heater to extend the swimming season. Having both a heater and underwater lights along with the length of the four-foot-deep pool made it a popular feature that attracted renters.

Tenants who usually used it for exercise either swam early mornings or late evenings. Residents who used it for fun or to cool off in the humid summer heat tended to swim during the day.

I took another long sip, the eighteen-year-old scotch sliding smoothly down my throat. But it wasn't The Macallan that warmed my gut.

It was the man emerging from the water and climbing the wide underwater steps at my end of the pool.

He was wet. Slick. As the water sheeted off his skin, it left behind a sheen and a shimmer due to the little white lights overhead.

Tate had been lanky in college, but in shape.

He was no longer lanky. The college boy I fell in love with was now a man. Even though he had filled out, his body fat was pretty non-existent. The ripple of his muscles were visible under a too thin layer of flesh as he strode over to a lounge chair where his towel had been thrown.

Apparently, I had missed that obvious piece of evidence of not being alone, too.

I'd been distracted then. I was certainly distracted now.

His wet bathing trunks clung to his lean, long but muscular thighs and hugged another part of him I had known all too well.

For two years, we worked out together. Running. Lifting weights. We would feed off each other's energy, drive each other to work harder, to push and improve ourselves. Both physically and mentally.

By graduation I'd bulked up, but not like I was now. Over the years, I'd put hard work into my physique as well as my health in general. But my exterior was a never-ending project and I was fully aware more work was needed on my interior.

Right after college, I couldn't afford a therapist. By the time I could, I mistakenly thought I was over Tate.

The subject of my attention wrapped the large towel around his shoulders, using the corner to wipe his eyes and dry off his face. I watched in fascination as he shook his head like a dog to rid his dark hair of excess water.

When he was done, he paused, then turned directly toward me.

I found it interesting that he wasn't surprised to see me. He probably knew the exact second I stepped out onto that roof. Unlike me, who had been lost in my own head and missed the signs of him being there.

But seeing him almost naked just about swallowed me whole.

I fought from being dragged back into the past by gripping my glass even tighter, and digging the fingers of my other hand into the thick seat cushion.

I forced myself to stay put and make him come to me. I refused to go to him, no matter how much I wanted to.

I would not.

If he ignored me and left without a word, I'd be okay with that, too. In fact, it was what I preferred. The fewer words we spoke to each other, the fewer encounters we had, the better. I assumed he'd agree.

Once again, I was proven wrong since Tate came to stand next to me and took his time drying off while keeping his eyes on me the whole time as he did so. Once he wrung out the bottoms of his swim trunks slowly and methodically—most likely on purpose—he sat on the edge of the lounger next to me, facing my direction.

Pretending to ignore him, I took another long sip of my scotch, quenching my sudden thirst in a way that would be less damaging to me, and stared out over the now still pool.

It pissed me off that one, Tate still looked so damn good, despite being too thin for his broad frame, and two, I still wanted him after all these years, even after what he did.

It was a sickness with only one cure. One I couldn't afford.

"What happened to your date? Was it past his bedtime?"

I emptied what was left in my glass in one swallow, grabbed the bottle and refilled it again. This time I poured three fingers worth.

The bottle cost me five hundred dollars and I was drinking the liquid gold like water.

I glanced over at the reason why. "You happened." I probably shouldn't have admitted that, but at that moment I was past the point of giving any fucks.

I had zero left.

Why? Because fate was truly a cruel bitch.

I gulped down another mouthful of overpriced scotch.

"Do you normally drink like that?" His eyes flicked from my glass back to my face.

"Whether I do or don't isn't any of your business, Tate."

He nodded, his lips pressed flat. But of course, he wasn't done. "Josh seemed… nice. If not a bit young."

I sucked on my teeth, biting back any response I was tempted to say.

"Have you two been together long?"

I twisted my head and stared at him. If he wasn't going to get the clue that I didn't want his company, then maybe I should leave instead. "Again, not your business."

My eyes were drawn to his chest and the beads of water he'd missed when drying off. I was so tempted to drink them right from his skin.

I gritted my teeth.

"You didn't even know his name," Tate continued as if I hadn't spoken.

I raised one eyebrow. "Your point?" My eyes dropped to the smooth black circle pendant that hung between his pecs off a long black chain. I didn't remember him ever wearing any kind of jewelry in college.

Tate jerked one bare shoulder up in a half-shrug. I had kissed and tasted that shoulder many, many times. I had leaned my head on it, too. In comfort, in exhaustion, in a sweaty aftermath of tangled limbs and damp sheets.

"You wanted me to think you two were in a relationship."

"I don't do relationships," I cut him off, then winced. I kept showing my damn hand.

Yes, I should put the scotch down and walk away from Tate while I still could. His presence, his proximity, was stirring up things inside me that I wanted to avoid.

"Never?"

"Only once. It didn't turn out so well. After that, I decided the societal expectation of relationships wasn't for me."

The hard truth was, I'd never wanted anyone as much as Tate. Not before. Not since. It was like he had crawled under my skin and once he was embedded there, I couldn't scrape him free.

It had been a curse I'd struggled with ever since the first time we got together. The first time we took the next step and became intimate. When we became a couple, who, in actuality, was not really a couple.

We were only a couple behind closed doors. Only friends outside of them.

"Roe..."

I hated him for the games we had to play back then. The secrets we had to keep.

I hated myself for going along with it, hoping things would change.

They did change, only not in the direction I had hoped.

"No," I said sharply to cut him off from whatever bullshit was about to spew from his mouth. I didn't want to hear it.

I didn't want to hear any more of his excuses. I'd heard enough for a lifetime.

"I—"

"No. Don't you fucking dare, T." I squeezed my eyes shut at the nickname that so easily slipped out, like the last twelve years hadn't happened, and whispered, "Just don't."

When he pried the glass from my fingers, I reluctantly opened my eyes. He put my drink to his lips and waited until I watched. Once I did so, albeit reluctantly, he downed the rest of my scotch before putting the empty glass on the ground near his bare feet.

No words were spoken as our eyes held across the four feet separating us.

Not one damn word was spoken when there was too much to say. Even though none of it should be said. It wouldn't change a damn thing. It would only make the past, the failure and the disappointment hurt more than it already did.

But what he was attempting to do at this moment—by locking gazes with me, by drinking my scotch, by staying when he should walk away—was steal my control. I refused to allow it.

Instead, I had this crazy urge to steal his, to assert my dominance. To show him whose domain he'd entered.

Mine.

His unforgettable blue eyes tracked my every move when I stood and closed the short distance between us, even knowing every step might be my downfall. I did it anyway, convincing myself that I now held the power and he didn't.

That mantra cycled through my head to keep it at the forefront, to remind myself who and what I was now, versus who and what I was back then.

I stood barely inside his spread knees looking down at him with his face tilted up and his eyes intense. With each second that passed, they filled more and more with confusion. Until finally, his gaze dropped from my face to my waist as I slowly, and very deliberately, reached for my belt, then took my time unbuckling it.

The jingling of the metal buckle filled the space between us. Familiar music to our ears as we both relived all those times we frantically tore off each other's clothes, no longer able to keep our hands off one another, no longer able to resist not touching each other.

Once the door was closed, everything flew out the window.

Our control. Our desires. Our worries.

Everything.

Until it was just the two of us. Touching, kissing, sucking and fucking. Our mouths and fingers desperate.

Our whispers, groans, grunts and cries surrounding us in a cocoon.

Back then, I knew him simply by his touch, his scent.

Back then, I knew when he was near me without seeing him.

Back then, I knew he wanted me the second his breath would catch.

Just like I knew what the noise at the back of this throat meant at that very moment.

With excruciating slowness, I lowered the zipper, then reached down and brushed a knuckle across the very short wiry hairs along his tense jawline before dragging the pad of my thumb across his bottom lip. His mouth parted and his warm breath puffed over my fingers.

He couldn't hide the shudder that ripped through him and I doubted he'd tried. That reaction made me continue drawing my fingers up his cheek, along his temple and into his still damp hair.

I rubbed a smooth strand between the pads of my thumb and forefinger, remembering the feel of it. In the two years we were lovers, I had touched his hair a million times.

I had nuzzled my nose in it a million more.

But tonight I drove my fingers through it—once, twice, three times—while my gaze followed the path of my hand instead of meeting his eyes.

I couldn't. Not right now.

Not yet.

Soon.

Because I already knew what I'd see in them.

I knew because if he didn't want this, he could get up and leave. If he didn't want this, his cock wouldn't be so damn hard, causing his wet swim trunks to tent.

If he didn't want this, his body wouldn't be vibrating like it was.

If he didn't want this, his breathing wouldn't be so ragged.

But, the real question was, did *I* want this?

Did I want to give in to my wants and needs and in turn, crack myself open all over again?

I reminded myself to keep my guard up. I couldn't let him break me this time.

Curling my fingers, I fisted his hair and put some pressure on his scalp by pulling slightly. "It's your fault my date was cut short. It's your fault I didn't get what I wanted or needed tonight."

The dilation of his pupils. The quickening of his breath.

The pebbled tips of his nipples.

More proof of how much he wanted me to touch him.

And all of it… Every one of his reactions made my mouth water, my heart beat faster and my own erection flex.

I kept a hold of his hair with one hand and drove my other down my boxer briefs, pulling out my cock and shoving my underwear down enough to tuck them under my balls.

I didn't have to see it to know precum had beaded on the end and was on the verge of dripping and falling.

I knew because Tate now stared at my cock as it pulsed in my hand.

The second he licked his lips and glanced back up at me with a silent question on his face, I knew he wanted to take it into his mouth. To clean the tip off with his tongue. To taste the salty fluid he was only too familiar with.

I imagined his warm, wet mouth encompassing the crown as I began to stroke, not wiping away the precum like I normally would, purposely letting it dangle. Tease. Tempt.

But I would not let him have it. I would not give him that satisfaction.

"On your knees." I tugged on his hair and took a step back, dragging him along with me.

His bare knees hit the ground hard but I didn't care.

Pain would be mixed with this pleasure.

His pain. My pleasure.

Twelve years later and the tables were about to turn.

"Roe," he whispered, staring up at me. His throat working, his eyes dark, his eyelids heavy. A flush blooming up his chest and onto his strained neck.

"No." I yanked again on his hair. "Keep your eyes open and on me. I want you to watch."

I hadn't even begun yet and I already wanted to come. To see Tate on his knees, vulnerable and wanting. Hoping for me to give him what he wanted.

Just that alone was more intoxicating to me than every partner I'd ever had since Tate.

Because none of them compared. Not a damn one.

And I hated him for that.

I hated that he was still my weakness.

I hated that it wouldn't take much for him to turn things around and take over, demanding me to my knees instead. To take over control.

I squeezed the root of my cock hard enough for it to turn purple, making the length bulge and the veins protrude from cutting off the blood flow.

But, *damn it*, I couldn't come yet. Not yet.

I needed to show some restraint. Though, right now it was only held by a very thin thread.

Squeezing and stroking at the same time, I worked on milking more precum to the very tip.

When he lifted his hand, my sharp, "No!" got him to drop it back to his side.

The anger with him that I've carried around for so long, had been sparked again when I first saw him in the lobby. But now it was fueled with each stroke of my fist until it was an out-of-control blaze burning inside me. Searing me.

I flipped the position of my hand and kept a steady rhythm, from the root to tip, making sure not to knock off the long string of precum hanging precariously from the crown.

His hand jerked and this time I dropped my head and narrowed my eyes, giving him a small shake of my head.

He curled his fingers into fists. Most likely to keep from doing it again.

If he didn't like what was happening, Tate could rise to his feet and walk away at any time. He didn't.

He stayed right there on his knees. Watching. His lips slightly parted, his breathing quick. The only time his eyes left mine was when he would drop them to watch me tug on my cock or the pearly string swing like a pendulum.

When he licked his lips again, I almost lost it.

The pressure was building, my muscles became tight. I locked my knees and willed my feet to stay where they currently were.

If I kept my hand on my own cock, I wouldn't touch him.

If I stayed where I was, I wouldn't fuck him.

If I only barked out demands, I wouldn't tell him how he still affected me all these years later.

I hadn't been this hard in a long time and that scared me.

College had been only yesterday. The moment he broke me only minutes ago.

A time warp between then and now.

But it was now and not then.

It was Tate on his knees, not me.

Even so, it was me who was struggling, not him.

And that pissed me off even more.

I jerked my cock even harder, now more for my own punishment than anything.

"Open your mouth and stick out your tongue. I want to paint it with my cum."

Tate shuddered and swayed. When he reached out to catch his balance and his fingers dug painfully into my thighs, I didn't push his hands away, I didn't tell him no this time. Instead, I let him touch me. I let him hang on to prove that he needed me.

Even if it was only to keep him upright.

He opened his mouth, extended his tongue, and set his heated eyes on my cock as he waited, anticipated.

The pressure in my lower gut and the tightness in my balls told me I was close.

So damn close.

Then I was there, my cock pulsing in my fingers as I continued to fist it, squeezing and tugging, yanking and pulling, drawing my seed to the surface.

But instead of coming on his tongue and in his mouth, instead of giving him what he wanted, I shot my load all over his face, making him jerk back in surprise.

Except it was too late.

Thick, white stripes dripped down his chin, crossed his cheeks, his nose, painted his lips, and even a few drops had landed on his furrowed brow.

The sight of it was one I'd never forget. Tate on his knees and his face covered with my cum, covered with *me*.

"Tongue out." My voice was raspy and raw despite holding back on any words or groans or cries. Or even a last grunt when I climaxed. I had kept it all bottled up inside, since I wasn't willing to share any of that with him.

Shock filled me when he obediently stuck his tongue out again and he let me use it like a rag to wipe off the dripping tip.

It was so damn hot and it made me want to rip off his swim trunks, bare his ass, bend him over the back of the lounge chair and drive my cock home until the whole city could hear his cries and the slapping of our skin together.

I wanted to teach him a lesson a lot bigger than the one I just had.

I was no longer his bitch.

I'd never be his bitch again.

I took a step back, tugged my boxer briefs and jeans back into place while keeping our gazes locked as I took my time fastening my jeans and buckling my belt. Straightening my shirt.

When I was done, I waited a few more seconds, daring him to stop me. Daring him to complain or say one damn word. Then I headed back to my private entrance.

Walking away from him at that moment was one of the hardest things I'd ever done. Because when we went our separate ways twelve years ago, it wasn't me who walked away.

Tonight it was.

Tate's voice sounded strained when he called out, "This was punishment."

Yes, it was.

Without a last glance back at the man still on his knees, I let the steel door close and lock behind me.

CHAPTER 6

Tate (Now)

I EXPECTED him to slam the door but it was the exact opposite. Even though the soft click behind me might as well have been a gunshot.

It tore into me, through me and left behind a gaping, bloody hole.

I was bleeding out. Dying a little inside.

I opened my eyes, shakily rose to my feet and located my towel.

Sitting on the edge of the closest lounge chair, I cleaned off my face. I wasn't gentle. I scrubbed as hard as I could.

My tongue swept through my mouth, tasting the salty residue left behind.

Tasting what I've missed, what I've craved for over a decade.

I leaned forward and grabbed the glass from the ground, then stretched out my hand far enough to barely snag the bottle, too.

Reading the label, I recognized the name. It wasn't cheap, but top quality and the average Joe didn't spend that kind of money on a brand like that for their own stash.

And if they did, they certainly didn't leave it behind.

I decided the glass wasn't needed, so I set it back on the ground next to the chair, popped the top on the bottle and took a long swig to chase away the taste of Ronan.

When I put the bottle back to my lips and tipped it a second time, the scotch slid down my throat and pooled in my gut. I breathed through the burn, not used to drinking alcohol straight like this.

After settling back in the lounge chair, I stretched out my legs and stared up at a night sky only marred by the glow of the numerous city lights. Keeping a tight grip on the neck of the bottle, I balanced it in my lap as I went back over what just happened between Ronan and me.

Ultimately, I let it happen.

Admittedly, I *wanted* it to happen.

Now I regretted my moment of weakness.

My vulnerability.

The glaring truth smothered me, making it hard to breathe.

I had fallen in love with Roe when we were only in college.

And, *damn it*, I never fell back out.

～

Ronan (Then)

ANOTHER WEEKEND. Another party.

I wasn't quite sure why Tate kept asking me to go with him, but I knew why I kept accepting his invitation.

I wanted to be near him.

It was stupid because I knew he was straight. I knew he'd had a girlfriend for over a year.

But we had fallen into an easy friendship. In class and out of it.

We laughed, we joked, we teased and pushed each other around. We were constantly sharing funny or stupid stories from our childhood.

Even if that was all I'd ever have with him, I'd take what I could get. I'd remember this time forever because I...

Liked him.

"Liked" wasn't a strong enough description but I wasn't sure what else to call it. But it was more than a simple attraction because of his looks. Which were stellar, by the way.

So… Obsessed? Maybe. But not in a crazy stalker kind of way.

In lust? For sure.

Wishful that he wasn't straight? Absolutely.

Tate was not only hot and handsome, he was smart. At first glance, I had thought he was a bit scattered and disorganized, but it turned out that he was only easily overwhelmed with new situations. Like starting a new semester, which had been the case the first morning I saw him.

But now we were over a month into the school year, he'd buckled down, got organized and was definitely more focused.

I decided to let loose tonight because, for once, I didn't have a shift in the morning at the Power Center, the university's recreation center. While the pay was garbage, the center was located on campus and I could easily walk to and from work. Even better, I could work out before or after my shift.

Admittedly, I started my freshman year as a scrawny guy. Not to mention, awkward as hell. Even though I was still developing and growing physically and mentally, I wanted to help it along faster.

While working at the rec center, I paid attention when the athletes came in and did their workout routines. I began to emulate them and eventually got up the nerve to begin talking to them by asking a question or two, hoping they didn't think I was hitting on them. When I could, I'd give them a hand by spotting for them if they were lifting. I continued to watch their techniques, ask more questions and solicit tips on how to improve my form or what I should be working on.

Most of them loved to share their knowledge because they loved the attention. It was gratifying for them when I openly admired their physique and told them I strived to look just like them.

Except the very muscular, very hot Eurasian gay version. Though, I kept the gay part to myself.

While I was out and open, I didn't flaunt or announce it. Or even wear any clothing that would "label" me as gay. However, if someone asked, I had nothing to hide and would never lie about it.

Luckily, no one asked and they all assumed I was straight. I figured if they knew otherwise, they might not be so willing to help. I could be wrong, and I hoped I was, but I wasn't willing to risk it and lose a valuable source of information.

Only one guy who worked out obsessively was a total dick. My guess was, as huge as he was, he was juicing. While I wanted to bulk up quickly, I didn't want to cheat to do it. I didn't mind hard work and dedication. And I certainly didn't want to end up looking or acting like a meat head the same as that asshole.

As soon as I had landed the job, I mentioned it to Tate one day during the class we shared. When he wasn't busy doing whatever Tate did when we weren't hanging out together, he'd show up either to help my work hours fly by or come work out with me.

Eventually we got into a routine of working out together, spotting each other and pushing each other harder. We turned our goals into challenges. We had mini-competitions between the two of us to keep it interesting and fun.

One day I dared Tate to take a spin class and we both almost died. Afterwards, I couldn't feel my taint for over an hour. I swore I lost three gallons of sweat and walked bow-legged out the door.

Tate wanted to strangle me for even suggesting the spin class but didn't have the energy to do so. For someone who rode his bike to campus most days, I would've thought spin class would've been easier for him. He thought the same.

We were both wrong.

We ended up hobbling out of the building and across the skywalk from the Power Center until we found a grassy patch under a tree where we both collapsed. We did not move for two hours.

Two damn hours.

The whole time we laid on our backs and talked about everything under the sun and also nothing. I'd never forget those two hours.

Because that was all it took for me to fall in love with Tate.

A love I couldn't express to him since I didn't want to freak him out or have him push me away. I ended up doing what was best for our friendship and kept it bottled up.

What we didn't do was ever walk into that spin class again. We began running for our cardio instead. Both outside through the campus and along city streets or, when the weather was shitty and we couldn't run outside, we did it together on the indoor track.

Like our friendship, our running fell into an easy rhythm. Our paces were similar. Our goals similar, too, since we wanted to balance cardio with building muscle.

Sometimes we slowed our pace and talked the whole route. Other times, we plugged in our earbuds and listened to the same song while hauling ass. If the song was particularly catching, Tate would race ahead, turn around to face me and run backwards, playing an air drum solo or singing horribly at the top of his lungs.

I waited for him to crash and burn every time he did it, but miraculously he managed to remain on his feet.

No matter what, he always made me smile or laugh, or almost piss my pants.

Tonight was no exception as we both worked our way around the party being held at a house in Carson on the other side of the Monongahela River. I had no idea who was throwing it or even whose house it was, but I was so damn tipsy, I didn't care.

At least now that I had a job, I could pay for my own plastic cup instead of Tate covering it for me. After the fourth beer, I lost count of how many we'd thrown back. One thing was for sure, we had both drank our money's worth tonight and the night wasn't over yet. We couldn't leave, even if we wanted to, until Tate's roommate was ready to go since he drove. And the last time I saw Jack, he was climbing the stairs with some chick, both of them wearing smiles that made it clear what their intentions were.

Watching them head up to the second floor also made it very clear that I was single and wouldn't be getting what Jack was getting any time soon.

I glanced over at Tate currently in a deep, but slurred, conversation with a guy also working on his journalism and communications degree. According to T, they shared a few classes together.

Not wanting to interrupt their *snewsfest,* what I called Tate talking about anything to do with journalism, I found an empty space along a nearby wall and pressed my back to it, while sipping on my beer and studying my best friend.

His face lit up and he became so animated when he talked about journalism. He said it was in his blood, after listening to him talk about it non-stop, I agreed. He still hadn't decided whether he wanted to be behind the camera or in front of it. I voted for in front.

Tate Allan Harris's stunningly handsome face and equally hot bod should be shared with the entire world. The way his lips moved, those vibrant blue eyes that could spear your heart, his infectious smile, his smooth as honey voice, that defined jawline. Not to mention, his perfectly straight teeth, thanks to braces he hated wearing when he was a teen.

I couldn't forget those broad shoulders…

Yes, I was a bit biased. However, I noticed how girls' heads turned when he entered a room or simply walked past them. What was entertaining was that Tate was clueless they were staring and most likely hoping his clothes would just magically fall off.

Oh wait. That last part might only be me.

But since we worked out together often, I'd seen almost every inch of him in the locker room. I tried not to be too obvious when I snuck a peek, but I couldn't help myself.

However, what I did with those peeks later when I was alone was kind of, sort of, obscene. In a good way.

I really should stop fantasizing about Tate and try to find someone who actually liked men for more than a friendship. I hadn't had sex since the summer before I left for college. Not counting all the sex I had with my five-fingered partner. Truthfully, I couldn't count those since I did it so often I'd lost track.

I got to the point where I could jerk-off under the covers without waking my roommate. Unfortunately, my roommate, Dominic, hadn't perfected that skill yet and I could hear him thwapping his dick at warp speed at the oddest times.

I still hadn't told Dom I was gay yet, but if I did, I'm sure that single-person jerk-fest would quickly end.

I grinned.

Then my heart did a little *rat-a-tat-tat* when Tate's head spun toward me and he gave me a chin lift. As soon as I returned it, he widened his eyes and raised his eyebrows in an unspoken message of, "get me the hell out of here."

I pushed off the wall and headed over to rescue him from having his ear talked off. He'd need both of them if he wanted to appear on camera behind a news desk.

I sidled up next to Tate, planting my hand on the small of his back, and gave the guy sloppily spewing words a nod. With one raised brow, I asked, "Can I grab him for a few?"

And by grab, I really meant that I'd like to slide my hand from Tate's back to his ass and squeeze a handful. I refrained since Tate would probably think I was goosing him in jest instead of appreciating the perfect peach that he hauled around in his jeans.

"Oh sure, sure. I need to hit the head, anyway," the blond guy answered, adjusting his glasses and shooting me a crooked smile. He was trashed.

Tate was close to being totally smashed, too. I only hoped Tate's roommate wasn't drinking as much so he was capable of driving us back. I had ended up crashing on the couch at their apartment a couple of times when we partied too much. But I was hoping to get back to campus tonight since their couch was disgusting and only a scorching hot shower afterward would chase away the willies.

But then, their whole apartment was gross since three college guys lived in it. It was occasionally cleaned when Dahlia came over and could no longer take the filth and would tackle the job out of frustration.

As soon as blond guy stumbled away, disappearing behind a wall of bodies, Tate shot me a very drunk, but also very sexy smile as he rubbed his right ear. "Thanks. My ear was about to fall off."

"I hate to break it to you, but you like to talk, too. It's probably a requirement for a journalism major."

"It isn't, but it's good practice. I need another beer and some fresh air."

I was doubtful he needed more beer but then, since neither of us drove, we didn't have a limit tonight. "Beer or air first?"

"I need to piss."

I rolled my eyes. "You can piss outside in the bushes while you're sucking in fresh air."

"Good idea. You're so smart, Roooow-nan."

"Damn skippy." I tugged his arm and he followed me. "I found a good bush along the side of the neighbor's house. We can both use that."

"Good idea. You're so smart, Roooow-nan."

Why was he dragging out my full name? And repeating himself? "Maybe you don't need another beer. We should find Jack and call it a night."

"No."

"T, there are parties all weekend, every weekend. It's not like this is the last college party you'll ever attend. And we both drank enough to make it worth the money we spent."

"Don't bother Jack. He's prolly getting laid."

That was a given since I witnessed the hike up the stairs, but I doubted Jack needed more than ten minutes. If that.

We somehow worked our way through the thick of drunk college students and outside without crushed toes or bruises. I still had a hold of Tate's forearm so I didn't lose him along the way, and I used it to guide him across the front yard littered with beer bottles, red

Solo cups and who knew what else—I certainly didn't want to look too closely—to the narrow gap separating the two houses. It was a perfect spot to relieve our bladders since it was dark and there were plenty of bushes.

"Roe!" he yelled, even though he was walking right beside me in the tight space.

"Shh!" I hushed him. "We don't want the neighbor to see us watering their bushes." More like killing their bushes with our beer-infused urine.

"Neighbors prolly inside at the party."

They probably were. Otherwise, the cops would've broken up the party hours ago, but I didn't know that for sure.

I stopped at the halfway point between the front and the back yards and used Tate's arm like a rudder to maneuver him around to face the bushes. I pointed. "Point and shoot, dude. Just don't piss all over your shoes."

Tate glanced down. "They're sneakers."

"Don't piss all over your sneakers," I corrected, already working on opening my zipper and digging for my cock. After I pulled it out and aimed, but before I told my bladder to let loose, I glanced over at Tate. He was staring at me in the dark, but not making a move to piss.

"T, do I need to help you or something?" I wasn't opposed to it, but Tate might be.

He shook his head and even in the dark, I could see a thick lock of dark hair fall across his forehead. I fought the temptation to push it off his face and instead concentrated on relieving my bladder.

I snuck a few glances over at Tate to make sure he was doing what he needed to do. He had snapped into action and was finally draining his snake. For a brief moment, I was jealous of his hand.

I shook my dick off and tucked it away, super careful not to get it caught in the zipper. Do it once and you'll never do it again. Guaranteed.

When my equipment was safely stowed away, I turned back to see

Tate rocking back and forth on his feet, still pissing but with his head tilted back.

He was going to lose his damn balance as pickled as he was.

He released a long, low groan, most likely in relief, and then did a few wild shakes of his cock. It made me take a step back in case of splatter.

"You got it?" I asked as he only released his baby python instead of putting it away.

He glanced down like he forgot what he was doing, nodded and finally managed to zip up without injury.

I took a step closer. "You sure you don't want to go? If we can't find Jack, we can call a taxi or something."

I didn't have money for a taxi, but I was sure Tate did. Over the past few weeks I'd learned that, unlike me, who relied on financial aid, scholarships and student loans along with my shitty paying job, Tate's parents were flush enough to put him through school one hundred percent. They simply wrote a check for his tuition. Not even a post-dated one.

They also paid the rent on his apartment every month and gave him an allowance for food or whatever else he needed.

They were hardly strapped for cash. His father was some sort of banker who made the big bucks and when Tate had showed me a picture of their home, I first thought it was a small resort.

It wasn't.

The thing about Tate was, if he hadn't mentioned it in a roundabout way, I never would've guessed he came from an affluent family. He wasn't cocky. He didn't flaunt his status. He didn't even wield it as a weapon as some other rich students tended to do. He didn't wear expensive clothes, watches or anything that would make him stand out. He rode a bike and didn't have a car.

He was the most humble rich guy I knew.

The only reason I pieced it together was from just normal, everyday conversation. In fact, I actually had to cajole him into showing me the picture of his house and his parents.

Tate was the spitting image of his father. His sister took after their mother. But the framed family portrait he showed me hammered home the realization that Tate and I were from two separate worlds. Him, upper crust. Me, a simple plebeian.

Well, maybe not so simple. But I wasn't one of those "sparkly" gays who had flair. I was pretty basic.

"No, not ready to go yet. Need more beer."

Oh, that's right, I was trying to convince him to leave.

When he turned toward me, he tripped over his own feet and began to fall backwards, his arms windmilling wildly as he scrambled to stay upright.

Instinctively, my hand shot out and I snagged his shirt in time to keep him from going down. He ended up overcompensating and fell forward instead, causing our bodies to slam together.

I didn't release him but tightened my grip on his shirt and held him in place while we both gathered our wits and panted from the sudden adrenaline rush.

His from losing his balance and almost falling.

Mine from being pressed against Tate.

We were now close enough for me to pick up the light scent of his soap or aftershave, or whatever he wore. Close enough to be seared by his heat. Close enough so parts of us touched.

Without thinking and while keeping a hold of his shirt with my right hand, I grabbed his face with my left and slammed my lips against his.

He didn't push me away, he didn't step back. He didn't move.

He didn't open his mouth and I kept mine closed, too.

We were sandwiched together from hip to chest and mouth to mouth.

I was as shocked as he was. Kissing him had been instinct for me and I'd wanted to do it for so long. But…

Both of us simply stood there. Connected, but also not.

Not moving. Not actually kissing. Not even breathing.

We were frozen.

For a moment it wasn't a kiss.

It was only two pairs of lips touching.

It was nothing.

Nothing.

Nothing.

Then with a flip of a switch, it became something.

Something I least expected.

The light turned on and became brighter as his lips began to move against mine.

Cautiously and awkwardly.

In truth, I expected that movement to be a demand for me to let him go.

Or a complaint.

Or a curse.

Because again, this couldn't be a kiss.

Like what happened too often, I was wrong.

He *was* kissing me.

Tate was kissing *me*.

Out of instinct or out of want? I wasn't sure.

Fuck, it could be he was drunker than I realized and he thought I was someone else, because...

He couldn't want this.

It was a moment of weakness for me. A moment of confusion for him.

Even so, I knew who I was. I knew who he was. Only too well.

He'd regret this when he was sober. I just knew it.

Because of that, I should end this. That would be best. For him and for our friendship.

Due to my weakness, I let him continue. I let it happen anyway. No matter how wrong I knew it was, I wanted it.

I needed it.

As his lips moved tentatively against mine, the power switched.

I took it and his mouth, as well.

I owned it. It now belonged to me.

Our mouths opened and our tongues clashed.

I don't know who groaned. It could've been me or him. Or even both of us as I deepened the kiss and our tongues continued to tangle, not to push me out, but to play.

I shoved his aside because I wanted to explore his mouth fully. To taste every corner and lock it away to memory, since I knew this would be the one and only time this would ever happen.

After this, it could be the last time we spent together as friends.

Fuck, I hoped not.

I so, so hoped not, even though I was wrong to kiss him. Not only because Tate was straight, but because he had a girlfriend.

It was all wrong, but I still couldn't stop. He didn't make me, either. Every noise coming from deep within his throat, every movement of his lips, encouraged me further.

His cock, hard and thick, being pressed against mine told me this didn't disgust him. That he wasn't turned off by our kiss. Or by our bodies touching as his hands gripped my hips, holding me there, even pulling me closer and not pushing me away.

If he started grinding his cock against mine, it would be game over for me. I've wanted Tate since the second I saw him coming in late to class. I've fantasized about him ever since, too.

And worse, my lust had turned to love along the way.

So, it would only take a few brushes of his erection against mine for me to lose my load in my briefs.

But he was drunk and that meant not making smart decisions. Decisions he'd regret when he was sober.

Since I was the only one out of the two of us not trashed, I needed to be the smart one here.

No matter how much I wanted him.

When I reluctantly ended the kiss and slowly and regrettably pulled away, I expected him to haul off and punch me. Taking a step back to give us some breathing room, I kept my eyes glued to his face so I could read his reaction and prepare for that reality to sink in.

Hell, to hit us both like a bucket of ice water. Him, because he just kissed a man. Me, because it would ruin the hottest and most wanted kiss in my lifetime.

Of course, I was right. Not about him striking out, but being overwhelmed with the realization of what just occurred. His eyes were wide and even in the shadows, I could see them full of shock, mixed with confusion.

But, crazy enough, they weren't filled with disgust.

I was waiting for that to descend over his ghost-white face as he pressed his fingers to his mouth.

He continued to only stand there completely frozen.

I needed more than that from him. I needed *something*. Even if it was rage or revulsion.

My heart pounded in my ears as we remained in the shadows, in a secluded pocket surrounded by the distant noise from the ongoing party.

No one in sight.

Except the two of us.

Shit. I couldn't wait any longer. I had to fix this before it broke us. "I'm sorry. I didn't... I'm sorry. I was wrong. I shouldn't have done that. I got..." *Fuck, fuck, fuck.* "I got caught up in the moment. I lost my head... I—"

"Shut up," he grumbled. "Just... shut... up."

I hesitated for a moment, but I couldn't just let this go. Not until he forgave me. "I don't want what I did to ruin our friendship. Please don't let my stupid mistake do that. You mean too much to me, T. You're my best friend. You're..." *Everything to me.*

But I can't tell you that no matter how much I want to.

"You... like guys?" The last word came out more high-pitched than normal.

Because he'd been drinking heavily, he might forget this whole thing in the morning. Then maybe we could go on like this never happened. "I like a lot of people."

"I mean... like *that*." He flapped his hand in the space between us.

"I thought you knew. I mean, I'm out. I'm open. I've never once hid it from you."

"But you never said anything, either."

What, like a warning? "Of course not. Who introduces themselves in one breath and then announces their sexual preference in the next? Do you?"

Why was I supposed to warn people that I was gay, when straight people didn't have to announce their sexuality? It wasn't like someone could catch it and turn queer against their will. It wasn't a virus.

I had no moral obligation to make people aware that I preferred men over women. That was my business.

At least until now when it came to Tate.

"No. I mean… I guess, that's true." He scratched his ear and his brow furrowed. "Why should a gay man introduce themselves any differently than a straight man?"

I gave him a *no-shit* tilt of my head. He didn't seem to be angry, but still surprised and maybe a little offended I hadn't told him I was gay. But was it because he was a homophobe, or did he think I hadn't trusted him with that info? I doubted it was the first one, thankfully. I never heard him say anything offensive toward the LGBTQ community.

We could explore all of that later when we were both stone sober, not while we were beer-infused and standing in the dark between two houses in Carson.

"Again… I'm sorry. It was the beer talking," I lied. "I know you're straight and have no interest in me that way. Seriously, don't let this… I don't want this to ruin our friendship, T. Can we just forget it ever happened?"

He pressed his fingers lightly to his mouth again. "I'm not sure I can forget it."

"Then, can you forgive me for kissing you without your consent? I should've asked first. I was wrong. I got caught up in the moment…"

Okay, enough excuses. He either accepted them or he didn't. Rattling them off wasn't going to help anything.

Our phones buzzed at the same time, drawing our attention from each other. Tate pulled his from his back pocket while I pulled mine and glanced at the text that had popped up on the screen.

It was from Jack, announcing he was ready to go. *Thank fuck.*

I texted him back quickly to tell him we'd meet him at his car parked on the next block over, since out of the corner of my eye I noticed Tate was struggling to type.

"We'll meet Jack at the car," I announced.

Tate glanced up from his phone and nodded. "Okay."

"You okay to walk that far?"

"It's a block."

"But you almost fell just turning around, T."

"Then I'll hang on to you if I need help."

A sudden sense of relief swept through me that he wasn't screaming at me, that he wasn't cursing me out. That he wasn't telling me to find my own ride back. That he would lean on me if he needed.

"Let's go," I said. "I'm here if you need me."

He stared at me a few more seconds, nodded slightly again and began to head toward the front of the property.

I noticed him wobble a bit, so I rushed to his side.

I almost stumbled myself when he hooked an arm around my neck.

I pressed my lips together to keep from grinning like a fool and we walked that way all the way back to Jack's car.

CHAPTER 7

Tate (Then)

WHEN WE GOT to the car, I texted Jack a couple of times but never got a response back. Ronan and I waited for a while, but my roommate never ended up showing. I figured that meant he had drunk too much.

"Should we head back and look for him?"

Ronan shook his head. "We could split a taxi."

It was probably smart. Maybe Jack curled up in a corner somewhere and was sleeping it off. He also had plenty of other friends at the party to give him a ride home if he needed it.

In the dark, we waited another half hour for the cab to arrive. I had no intentions of splitting the bill with Ronan, though. I would cover it since I invited him. I felt responsible to get him back to campus safely.

Or at least, that was what I told my muddled-brained self.

While we waited, we didn't say much to each other. Mostly because my head was spinning from both the beer and with what happened in the tight space between the two houses. Our shoulders touched as we both leaned back against Jack's car and it was surprisingly comforting, as well as supportive.

I wasn't upset about the kiss but I was definitely confused. This whole thing with Ronan... I didn't understand any of it, honestly.

And I wasn't only thinking about the kiss.

I had only known him for a few weeks. We had class together. We went to parties together. We worked out and even studied together.

We had fallen into an easy friendship because we simply clicked.

When I wasn't with Dahlia—who was busy with her classes, her job, hanging out with her girlfriends or participating in one of the many social clubs she was involved in—I wanted to spend each waking moment with Ronan. I'd never felt this way before with any of my friends. Not even with Todd, my best friend since kindergarten from back home in Virginia.

Even though I liked spending time with my girlfriend of over a year, I was beginning to prefer his company instead. It reminded me of an addiction since this strange pull toward him became stronger every day.

Every day that he plopped into the seat next to me in class.

Every day that he purposely tried to distract me from Dr. Louden's lecture.

Every day that he did his best to get us both busted and kicked out of class.

It had turned into a game with Ronan.

A confusing one. One I didn't quite understand.

I was experiencing feelings I'd never had before and I didn't know what to do with that.

But I knew one thing...

I liked it.

Even if it was wrong. All of it.

It had to be wrong because I wasn't gay. I wasn't even bisexual. So, it couldn't be a sexual attraction. Plus, I had a girlfriend I loved.

But that unexplainable pull was non-stop.

I couldn't wait until our class together.

I couldn't wait to meet up with him to study.

I couldn't wait to grab a coffee with him after class.

Or for us to go on a run together. Or meet up in the gym.

We had fallen into this natural rhythm. What I first thought was only a friendship.

But now…

That kiss…

That kiss.

But now with that kiss, I was worried my obsession with Ronan might get worse.

My strong desire to be with him had already been so sticky, I couldn't free myself.

Not from Ronan.

Not from my thoughts about him.

Not from my unexpected fantasies about him, either.

I hadn't told him about them because I wasn't sure I should even admit I was having them. Part of the reason was, I honestly didn't know he was gay. He hadn't shared that part of himself with me, even though I thought we were close.

The first dream I had about him, about me, about us together, surprised me.

Shocked me.

Outright scared me.

I had shot straight up in bed, drops of sweat beading on my forehead. I panted because I struggled to catch my breath. My heart raced out of both excitement and fear. My response very similar to a nightmare or a panic attack.

But the difference between this dream and a typical nightmare was it hit differently and…

When I woke up I was as hard as a rock. All because in that dream I'd been touching, kissing and fucking Ronan.

That night, I turned Dahlia over, waking her up with those same types of kisses and touches. I told her how much I wanted her. How much I loved her.

All because of the dream I had about *him*.

I had to remind myself over and over, that was all it was. A crazy dream. Nothing more.

I needed to prove that to myself.

That I wasn't attracted to men.

And maybe I wasn't. Not really, not in the way gay men were attracted to others.

Maybe for some strange reason, I only felt that way about Ronan.

How could one guy—someone I met in class that first week of the semester—make me question everything?

My whole being.

My damn sexuality.

My relationship with the girlfriend who'd stuck by me over the last year.

It didn't make sense.

None of it made sense.

So, I assumed it had to be wrong.

All of it.

My brain was broken or something.

I was broken.

I couldn't find another explanation.

No matter what, I needed to fix it. To prove the dream had been just an odd fluke.

In an attempt to do so, I had slipped between Dahlia's soft thighs, so opposite of Ronan's. I kissed her soft lips. So opposite of Ronan's.

I took my time making love to her, slamming the door on the thoughts of Ronan from inside my head.

When I finally spilled inside of Dahlia, I hoped to find relief. Or answers. Or confirmation that I was only attracted to women.

I found nothing. Not one answer. No relief at all.

Even worse, I was more confused than ever. Because this time, I didn't even feel satisfied afterward.

I felt...

Empty.

And that scared the shit out of me.

I needed answers and I had none. I also wasn't sure where to find them. Who to ask.

Maybe I needed a therapist. But my parents would want to know what was wrong, why I needed to see one and I couldn't explain it to them. I couldn't even explain it to myself.

After we climbed into the taxi and the driver asked for the address, I glanced over at Ronan sitting next to me in the dark back seat. "My apartment's closer if you want to crash there tonight."

Tonight. It was more like morning since it was about two a.m.

"Are you okay with that?" he asked, surprised.

He'd already spent a couple of nights on our couch in the apartment. Why should tonight's kiss change that? Or make things uncomfortable?

Plus, if I was being honest with myself…

No, I wasn't ready to be honest with myself. Forget that.

It took less than ten minutes to arrive at my apartment complex since the traffic was pretty nonexistent at that time of morning.

I had sobered up slightly while waiting for Jack and then the cab, but I was still a bit wobbly heading upstairs to our second floor apartment, so Ronan kept a hold of me while we hoofed it up the steps.

Once we got inside, I immediately spotted a problem.

Someone was already crashed on the couch. It had to be one of Thom's buddies. No surprise that they must've partied tonight, too. And Thom must have had the same idea for his friend about crashing on the couch as I did for Ronan.

I was pretty damn sure that was where the similarity ended. I doubted Thom kissed his friend tonight, unlike me.

"Sorry," I whispered as we stared down at the passed-out stranger on the old, worn couch we had found at a local yard sale. "I had no idea."

"I can head back to my dorm."

"No, stay. I can't let you walk back to your dorm at this time of night, Roe. We'll figure it out."

"You want me to sleep on the floor?"

He didn't seem too enthused about that possibility. Jack's bed was empty right now but I had no idea when he'd come home. Not to mention, he probably wouldn't appreciate someone else sleeping in it. Anyway, who knew when his sheets were last washed or changed.

If they were ever washed or changed.

I grimaced.

Having Dahlia come and stay over some nights made me keep up with straightening my room, making sure my dirty clothes made it into the hamper and ensuring my sheets and towels were somewhat clean.

Otherwise, I'd never hear the end of it. Not that I blamed her.

I tipped my head toward the hallway. "My bed's a queen and big enough for the two of us."

With his brow furrowed, Ronan stared at me with his deep brown eyes. "You want me to sleep in your bed. With you? That's not going to bother you after..."

The kiss?

"We're sharing a bed, nothing else," I assured him.

The wrinkles smoothed out on his brow but he continued to stare at me like I had grown a second head.

"I can keep my hands to myself if you can," I added with a crooked smile.

He shot me a teasing grin. "I'm kind of big on consent, T."

The reason he apologized a few times for the earlier kiss, even though I hadn't told him to stop or pulled away. I had given my consent with my response. I would've pushed him away if I hadn't wanted it, too.

Confusion once again swept through me because why had I wanted it? It didn't make sense.

"And we don't have to snuggle," he added, now wearing his

signature smile. The big one that lit up his face and always drew me in.

"What if I want to snuggle?" I asked in a teasing tone as I tipped my head toward the hallway again and headed in that direction.

"I'm a great snuggler."

"Do you have references?" I whispered, trying to keep the noise down as we passed Thom's room.

Even though his door was closed, I could hear a log being sawed behind it. When we first started sharing an apartment, his obnoxious snoring kept me up at night. Now that I was used to it, it was like white noise and I wondered how I'd sleep without it.

"I can give you a free sample if you want to judge for yourself."

I huffed out a quiet laugh and shook my head as I opened my bedroom door. Sweeping out a hand, I invited him in.

I remained in the hallway as he entered my personal domain and I had a sudden flashback to the first night I invited Dahlia into both my room and my bed.

The sex that night had been explosive since it was our first time together and I didn't let her out of my bed that whole weekend, except for small breaks.

A question niggled at the back of my mind. Would it be the same if Ronan and I had sex?

Hold on. Could I have sex with a man?

I did in my dream.

But could I actually go through with it in reality, while I was awake? When it was real?

I couldn't say for sure and tonight was not the time to figure it out. Not when I was pickled and incapable of making good decisions.

I followed him into the room and shut the door behind us, watching as Roe didn't hesitate to sit on the edge of my bed to pull off his shoes and socks. Once he was rid of those, he stood and, without even a glance at me, stripped down to his boxer briefs. He folded his clothes neatly, placing them in a pile on top of my dresser while I did my best to keep my eyes above his waistline. I *really* didn't want to be caught staring at his bulge. I'd already seen it a few times in the locker room at the Power Center before or after our workouts.

But this time would be different. I'd be considering the possibilities. Also wondering if I was really attracted to another man. If *that* was even possible. For me, anyway.

I was worried now that I knew Ronan was gay, it would change the whole dynamic of our relationship.

Not because he was gay, that part didn't bother me at all, but what that discovery would mean to me along with the thoughts I'd had about him that stirred up way too many questions.

"What side do you want?" Ronan wasn't looking at me but at the bed instead.

It took me a few seconds to comprehend his question. But then my brain was still a bit sluggish. "The… uh… right side." That was the side I always took when Dahlia spent the night.

Fuck!

"No, the left. Give me the left side."

He twisted his head toward me, his brow furrowed again. "Okay. I'm going to hit the head and then I'll take the right side."

I had what was considered the primary bedroom in the apartment since my room was the only one with its own bathroom. I paid more rent than my two roommates because of it. Or my parents did, since they were generously covering my expenses while I worked on my bachelor's degree.

Once the bathroom door shut behind him, I unstuck myself from where I stood near the door and hurried to strip myself of my shoes and clothes, quickly sliding under the sheets on the left side.

I grimaced when I realized I should've grabbed us bottles of water since we'd need them. Like Ronan, I also should've emptied my bladder since it had filled quickly after I last pissed in the bushes in Carson. But I didn't want him to see that I had a half-chub from him getting undressed in front of me.

That had never happened before. Not once in the locker rooms. Not once after a run when we showered at the gym.

Not one time.

The only thing that had changed with us, between then and now, was that damn kiss. Was one single kiss going to have a ripple effect that changed everything between us?

As soon as Ronan came out of the bathroom, he slid between the sheets on the right side of the bed and the room went pitch black when he switched off the light on the table next to it.

I stared up at the ceiling, trying desperately not to touch my semi. Trying even harder not to touch Ronan. His heat turned the space between us into an oven and I listened to his slow and steady breathing.

By sticking to the right edge of the bed while I stuck to the left, Ronan made sure no parts of us touched.

I was thankful for that because my resistance was thin tonight and while I completely trusted the man lying next to me, I didn't trust myself.

I knew the exact moment he fell asleep when his breathing changed to a very soft snore. It was almost comforting and I began to count each one like sheep.

Eventually, my eyelids became heavy and I lost track of the number.

Soon after that, I lost track of everything else.

Tate (Then)

MY EYELIDS WERE GLUED TOGETHER. My mouth dry as a desert.

My temples throbbed with the rhythm of my heartbeat. A slow *thump, thump, thump.*

I groaned, keeping my eyes closed since I couldn't remember if I had shut the curtains before collapsing into bed last night—or earlier this morning more like it—after getting back from...

I frowned.

From...

The party Jack wanted us to go to with him.

Us.

Not Dahlia and me.

But Ronan and me.

That "us."

That meant it couldn't be her spooning me. It couldn't be her making me so damn hot. Plus, Dahlia was always cold. Her hands and feet were usually tucked somewhere I didn't want them because of that.

But it wasn't frozen fingers or toes tucked between my ass crack. I slowly became aware that it wasn't Dahlia, either. Unless she had somehow expertly hidden the fact she had a dick.

I cracked my blurry eyes open enough to see the top sheet pushed down to my hips and a muscular arm draped over my waist.

An arm hairier than Dahlia's.

Skin a darker complexion than my girlfriend's.

And definitely without a bit of womanly softness.

What was pressed into my ass crack was thick, hard and very, very hot. The chest pressed against my back was very firm and very flat.

Every muscle in my body turned to stone as I went back over what I remembered of the night.

Most of it was a blur.

Until that one, significant moment...

Then it again turned into a blur...

How the hell did we end up in bed together?

I would remember if something—other than sleep—happened, wouldn't I?

I would feel the effects of... if we... in some way, wouldn't I?

Without moving, I mentally inspected myself from head to toe.

Every orifice, too, for any indication that Ronan and I had done something more than that single, unexpected kiss in the dark.

Reality hit me like an ocean wave in a hurricane.

I kissed a man last night.

I kissed *Ronan.*

Now he was the "big spoon" as his arm clamped me tightly against him, his nose pressed against the back of my neck and his warm exhales swept over my bare shoulder.

I held my breath when the bed shifted slightly and so did Ronan behind me. His movement made his erection slide between my ass cheeks the slightest bit with only our underwear separating us.

Luckily, we both still wore ours.

I needed to get out of this bed and reestablish our boundaries.

We were friends only.

Friends and classmates, that was it.

However, he was a friend I didn't want to lose. I didn't want things to be awkward or uncomfortable between us. It was bad enough when we kissed last night, but now this?

This…

Oh shit… This…

What was he doing? Was he aware that he was now thrusting against me? Like his cock was a hot dog and my ass cheeks were the bun?

I needed to stop this. Get out of bed. Get away from…

The temptation.

What was wrong with me?

Move, Tate. Move!

I began to move but not to leave the bed. Instead, I tentatively rocked against him. Not much, but enough apparently to encourage him further.

Was he doing it in his sleep, or was he awake and aware?

He said last night he was big on consent.

I should wake him up, make him aware of what he was doing. He was probably having a dream about having sex with a man, like I had about him.

"Roe," I whispered, once again overwhelmed. Not with what he was doing, but with how I was feeling about it.

I wanted him to stop.

I also didn't want him to stop.

"Roe," I whispered again.

"Hmm?" came muffled from the back of my neck where his lips now pressed. He planted his hand on my stomach, spreading out his fingers and holding me there as he continued to rock gently against me. "Tell me to stop, T," he groaned.

I opened my mouth to do just that but only a rush of air escaped.

Holy shit. I didn't want him to stop. I wanted him to keep going, to do more, to take it further. To push my boundaries. To let me experience something with him I've never experienced before.

I was safe with him.

He wouldn't judge me.

I also trusted him to stop if I told him to, if things got to be too much. If I wasn't ready for this.

"I can't." Did I say that? Did I really tell him to continue?

I closed my eyes and pressed my back into his chest, pressed my ass against his cock, matching the rhythm of his thrusts as they got bolder, faster.

My cock was so damn hard, it was uncomfortable. I needed him to touch me. I needed relief. But his hand was still glued to my gut.

His low voice filled my ear. "You can't because you don't want me to stop?"

This had to be one of my dreams, right?

I was dreaming this and would wake up at any moment. When I did, I would simply pull one off and then forget all about it. I could take that dream to my grave, too, like the other one. And any future ones.

But if I was only dreaming, what would it hurt if I allowed him to have his way with me? If I enjoyed his attention and touch?

No one had to know.

With my hand over his, I pushed it lower to below my navel and until his fingertips brushed the elastic of my boxer briefs.

My cock flexed with my need for him to wrap his hand around it and pump it the same way he was pumping his against my ass.

This was a dream. Only a dream.

Let it happen and see how it feels. When you wake up you'll realize you're not gay or bi, or whatever, because you're straight. You like women. You love Dahlia.

Dreams were made for you to do all the things you wouldn't do while you were awake.

That was the beauty of them. No expectations, no embarrassment, no self-doubt.

Simply enjoy the fantasy. Something you would never allow to happen in reality.

I shoved his hand further, under the elastic band and until the tips of his fingers brushed over the crown of my cock.

I groaned.

And when his warm, strong fingers curled around my length, my hips shot forward.

"I'll take that as your answer," he murmured against the back of my neck, where his lips were brushing back and forth across my skin, causing goosebumps to break out everywhere.

Even though he was fisting me tightly, I kept a hold of his hand. I was afraid if he began to stroke me, I'd come right away. I gave myself a few seconds to get used to his strong grip, so unlike Dahlia's. The size of his hand, so unlike Dahlia's. The roughness of his palm, so unlike Dahlia's.

So different, but yet... So much better. Or was I just wishing it was, hoping it was, so I wouldn't feel so guilty for liking a man's touch? Or for desperately wanting it.

Cautiously, I removed my hand from his, leaving his behind.

"Do you like me touching you, T?"

I nodded, unable to form words. I had this crazy notion that if I spoke out loud, I'd wake up and this would all disappear.

"Do you want me to do more?"

I nodded again.

His fingers squeezed me harder for a second, then loosened enough to start stroking. Slow and steady. From root to tip. The same as he was doing with his own cock in the crease of my ass. Only not as smoothly since the double-layer of fabric between us was creating friction.

For a second, I wished it wasn't. I wanted to be skin to skin with him.

I wanted us both to be naked. For his lips to be pressed against mine. For his hands to be exploring me all over.

I didn't know why.

I didn't know why I wanted any of this.

This wasn't me.

It wasn't.

I didn't know who I was right now.

I was no longer Tate Harris because that Tate would never want this.

A person I didn't know wanted this. Wanted Ronan.

My heart seized when he used his other hand to grab my hair and twist my head back toward him enough so he could take my mouth.

Giving me his lips.

Giving me his tongue.

Stealing my breath.

Stealing my soul.

The fist in my hair kept me where he wanted me, while his other hand continued to pump my cock.

My hips now rocked forward to fuck his hand, backwards to feel the slide of his erection against my ass.

Back and forth.

In and out.

Then my head got jerked back even farther, straining my neck.

He used the handful of my hair to roll me over as he continued to kiss me. Continued to explore my mouth like he had last night.

Our tongues furiously tasted and tangled as he kept tugging and shifting at the same time until I was completely flat on my back, his weight pinning me down and our erections perfectly aligned.

I stopped myself from protesting when he released my cock, even though it was quickly replaced with the pressure of his own.

His fingers drove into the hair above my ears on both sides of my head, holding me there so he could take the kiss deeper.

I had never been kissed so completely, so thoroughly. Women's kisses always seemed so tentative now that I knew how a man kissed.

Or at least the man currently in my bed.

It wasn't better or worse, it was… different.

Good.

Satisfying.

Addicting.

I couldn't get enough of it. The more intense the kiss became, the faster his hips pumped against me, pulling a groan from me.

Ronan, what are you doing to me?

What is this?

Why am I liking this? Wanting this with you?

Please help me understand.

Please. Because I don't. I don't understand any of this.

The more he thrust against me, the more I thrust back, the cotton of my boxer briefs brushing roughly across the sensitive skin of my cock and driving me to the edge even quicker.

When his hips hiccuped, Ronan shoved his face into my neck and he released a long, low groan as he pumped with excruciating slowness against me one more time and his back arched. A few seconds later, he shuddered and stilled.

Through the two layers of our underwear, I could feel his cock pulsing against mine as he finished spilling a warm wetness between us.

I almost came myself at the thought that Ronan just rubbed one out on me, using our cocks pressed together to do so.

Like the kiss, I wanted to be disgusted because, again, this wasn't me. I wasn't into this. I wasn't into men.

I wasn't.

This was a fluke. A dream.

Nowhere close to reality.

My pulse pounded in my throat as we remained in place, both of us still, the only noise in the room our rapid, ragged breathing. That was when I realized I was holding onto him by digging my fingers into his hips.

As if someone pushed his On button, Roe suddenly moved. But he didn't roll off me, he didn't jump from the bed, instead he slithered his way down my body, heated skin against skin, kissing my chest and stomach along his journey. When he reached the top of my underwear, he continued, pulling the damp cotton—from both his ejaculation and my own leaking precum—along with them, exposing my throbbing cock to the air and also to him.

But it was only exposed for a second because he immediately swallowed it almost to the root. To stifle my whimper, I jammed my fist between my teeth.

I threw my head back and sucked in a harsh breath at the pull of his mouth.

He was like a starving man and my cock was the first food he'd stumbled across.

He sucked and licked, tasted and traced with the tip of his tongue. His own saliva and my precum the lube as he pumped me within his fingers over and over.

My eyes rolled back and my hips rose each time he devoured me. I didn't know how he wasn't gagging with as deep as he swallowed me. Dahlia gagged only partially down.

I ripped that thought out of my head and tossed it away.

This wasn't Dahlia.

This was Ronan.

This. Was. *Roe*.

Tracing his tongue down the thick ridge. Sliding it around the crown to lick off the precum. Kissing along the seam of my sac and then…

Further.

Sucking on the spot where my taint met my scrotum and then moving back up to take my balls into his warm, wet mouth.

"Fuck," I breathed, fisting the sheet beneath me. "Fuck. Fuck, Roe. *Fuuuuck*."

I was losing my mind. Seeing spots behind my closed eyelids.

I opened them and tilted my head to see what I was afraid to see.

Ronan's dark head bobbing up and down my cock, expertly sucking me off.

Driving me to the edge of my consciousness.

Driving me to the edge of my sanity.

Driving me to the edge…

To the edge.

To…

My hips surged up and since he had a hold of my sac, the sharp pull kept me grounded, kept me from floating away. A tightness pulled at my groin. A pressure built in my balls.

And then… Like a geyser, I let loose.

Grabbing two handfuls of his hair, I was semi-aware I was most likely hurting him by ripping on his scalp, by shoving my cock deeper down this throat…

But I…

I…

I was *done*.

A cry bubbled from me when I spilled down the back of his throat. The pressure gone, the tightness gone.

He didn't try to free himself or pull away. He swallowed every drop I gave him. His fingers tightened around my cock to milk it as I continued to come. He made sure to pull every drop from me with both his mouth and his hand.

When I finally collapsed back to the bed, not one bone remained in my body. They had all dissolved into liquid. Not one cell remained in my brain. Not one damn care was left that it was a man, my friend, who just gave me the best head, the most intense orgasm, I ever had in my entire life.

One sole thought flitted through my muddled, tired brain...

I might not care now, but that wasn't going to last. Not when the fantasy was steamrolled by reality. Not when I finally allowed myself to recognize the fact that Ronan *was* a man and I'd been intimate with him.

With my head on the pillow, I continued to stare up at the small crack in my ceiling.

I concentrated on that while I waited for my thoughts and my sanity to return.

I didn't look at Ronan when he released me from his mouth. When he loosened his grip and finally let go.

When he rolled from between my legs.

When he sat up on the bed next to me and, from the corner of my eye, I watched him wipe a hand across his mouth.

He was waiting.

For me to say something?

For me to react because I was disgusted? Ashamed? Embarrassed?

For me to freak out because my closest friend just sucked me off? Or because of Dahlia finding out? Or *anyone* finding out?

Was he as worried as I was about ruining our friendship? Ruining my relationship with Dahlia?

Or me getting angry with him? *Hell*, with myself?

Or all of it?

I struggled to swallow the lump lodged in my throat as the blood slowly receded from my erection.

Nothing but our breathing filled my room as the bed shifted and he climbed off the mattress.

I thought he might address what just happened between us, but instead he said, "Do you have underwear I can borrow? I need to clean up and…"

I could only imagine the mess in his boxer briefs. To put his jeans back on and walk back to campus like that would be miserable.

Without looking at him, I answered, "Dresser. Top drawer."

I listened to him move around my room. Gathering his clothes, grabbing a pair of clean underwear from my drawer, then shutting himself in the bathroom.

The water ran. The toilet flushed.

While he was in there, I forced myself to sit up.

I needed to get up. I couldn't spend the day in bed, even though I was spent. Emotionally and physically.

I needed to function like it was any other day, as much as I didn't want to.

I only got as far as sitting on the edge of my mattress, before I dropped my head into my hands and dug my elbows painfully into my thighs to support it. My head felt heavy and it throbbed. Possibly still from my hangover, more likely from what we just did.

And the fact that I liked it.

I *really* fucking liked it.

None of it made sense.

As soon as the bathroom door reopened, a soft "Tate" reached my ears.

I shook my head slightly. I couldn't look at him. Not yet.

I didn't want to hurt him with my reaction. It had nothing to do with him and everything to do with me.

This went way beyond kissing.

This morning couldn't be chalked up to a drunken mistake because I was now sober. I had no damn excuse other than just like the kiss last night, I *wanted* it to happen.

Bottom line, I didn't want what we did to ruin our friendship. Ronan meant too much to me to lose him over being self-indulgent.

Maybe that right there was the answer I needed. But, where did we go from here?

It was best if we simply forgot about the whole thing. Moved forward like it never happened.

Yes, that was a good plan. The only plan.

"We're never talking about this again." My voice was scratchy and raw. And though I did my best to hide it, it contained a slight shake.

For what had to be at least two minutes, I didn't get a response.

But I could feel his eyes on me. Searching. Wondering. Maybe even hoping our friendship wasn't ruined, too.

"Yeah, okay." Those two simple words were heavily coated in disappointment.

After a few more seconds, I finally heard his footsteps heading toward the door. Again, another hesitation, but I still could not make myself look at him.

"I'll let myself out."

I opened my mouth to stop him, but all my words disintegrated before they were formed.

When the door closed behind him, the soft click might as well have been a slam.

CHAPTER 8

I'D GROWN up with a financial disadvantage.

I never would've gone to college if it wasn't for earning scholarships, grants and a lot of hard work.

My father worked his ass off to provide for his family, to put food on the table and a roof over our heads. Especially as an immigrant from South Korea. He came to the States for a better life and went after it with gusto to provide for me and my brother.

He was the kind of man who never gave up until he got what he was working for.

Including my mother. He saw, he came and he conquered. He swept her off her feet and in turn, she helped him improve his English. Together they created a home and a family.

But, in the end, he worked himself to death.

A heart attack killed him when he was only forty-one during a double-shift at the factory where he had worked his way up into management.

Even though his life was cut short, I wouldn't be where I was if I hadn't learned from him. I wouldn't let his goal to live the American dream go unfulfilled. My brother and I wanted to make him proud even if he was no longer around to see it.

We wanted to make our mother proud, too. Between the two of us, we bought her a newly-built home in a fifty-five-plus community in a much warmer climate than Pennsylvania and moved her out of our cramped childhood home. Declan and I both continued to make sure she was taken care of.

My brother gave her grandchildren. I didn't. My brother made sure the family name lived on. I didn't.

My father didn't know I was gay when he died. My mother didn't find out until after I graduated high school. She found out by accident. A slip of the tongue on my part. Thankfully, she was supportive. So was my brother and his family.

They still were.

I loved and missed them. I thought many times about moving closer to them in South Carolina.

Even beyond college, I'd worked damn hard to get where I was currently. I sacrificed, I scrimped, I saved. I studied successful investors very closely. I learned, I emulated, I manifested.

Because of that, I was no longer poor. I had built a quickly growing, very successful empire. It also helped that I surrounded myself with good, trustworthy people.

But that was in my business life.

In my personal life, I was alone.

Money couldn't buy me love or companionship.

Well, it could buy me the second, but for the most part, that was illegal.

Anyway, I preferred someone willing to spend time with me because it was their choice, not someone who was obligated to because I was paying them with money or gifts.

That choice meant I stood alone in front of the stretch of windows with a bottle of Penn Pilsner dangling from between two fingers, while looking out over a city chocked full of people. None of them belonging to me.

Tonight was tougher than normal. Loneliness ate at me. Normally, I didn't let it bother me, but I currently struggled to tuck away that emptiness. Actually, it wasn't just tonight, it started the moment I first saw Tate checking his mailbox in the vestibule. Him living a few floors below didn't help, either.

Because now he was constantly on my mind.

I needed to do something about the void inside me. Filling it with alcohol until I fell asleep wasn't an acceptable solution.

I tipped the bottle to my lips and the smooth pale lager slid easily down my throat. It pooled in my gut to join the previous bottle I drank earlier while eating cold, leftover beef *bibimbap* from a local take-out joint.

My favorite Korean meal now sat like a brick at the bottom of my stomach.

I needed to find something, or someone, to distract me from Tate being so close. From being so accessible.

I sank onto the sectional that faced the night-time view of the city, balanced my beer on my thigh and swiped my phone from the black marble coffee table in front of me. Sighing in disgust at my own self-loathing, I propped my bare feet on the table and crossed my ankles, then stared at my phone for a few heartbeats.

After unlocking it, I stared at it for a few more heartbeats, contemplating whether I was making a mistake or not and already knowing full-well I was.

But of course, I opened the app, anyway, and began to check out Grindr and the vast menu of men available.

I quickly swiped past the twink I brought home the other night and continued to search with mounting dissatisfaction.

Nobody was catching my eye tonight.

I continued through pages and pages of profile pics, available men all within a close radius, finding one reason or another to skip over them. Some reasons valid, some of them not. Some with profile photos that showed their faces, some not.

I kept mindlessly scrolling and exploring the various photos, unable to find even one to make me pause. My finger moved in a constant repetitive motion.

Swipe. Swipe. Swipe.

I paused.

What the...

I scrolled back, thinking I imagined it.

I didn't.

I stared at the picture, then squinted my eyes and dropped my head enough to inspect the profile photo even closer. I checked to see if this man was in the vicinity. The app said he was only a hundred feet away.

So close I could almost reach out and touch him.

My heart knocked against my chest, trying to create its own escape route. I set my beer on the floor next to the couch and pressed my hand over my heart so it wouldn't do just that. I held it there while I clicked on the profile and quickly skimmed the bio to see if I was correct. Unfortunately, there wasn't enough information to confirm who I thought it was.

But... I *knew*.

Even without a face, I recognized that body. I knew every damn inch of it. I'd never forget it even though it had been twelve years and he'd matured over that time.

It also helped that I'd seen it again recently when he came out of the pool. Also when he was on his knees at my feet.

The first name given on the profile was Harris. Not surprising since on the hook-up app, I used Ron instead of Roe or Ronan, to keep my real identity secret.

I decided to message the man, but kept it brief and to the point. If I was wrong and it wasn't him, the person would need to ask for an address. If it was... He would know exactly where I wanted to meet him.

My fingers trembled slightly as I typed. When I was done, I double-checked the message. Once. Twice. Then before I changed my mind, I sent it off out into the wild.

Roof. Door locks automatically at ten. Be up there before then. At ten, drop to your knees. Want you waiting and willing. Otherwise, don't come at all.

My heart continued to pound while I waited for a response. It could come in minutes. It could come in hours. Days. Or not at all.

I didn't even know if he was active on the app. I was actually surprised to see him on there. Did he sign up as soon as he split from Dahlia or had he been on it a lot longer than that?

I was pretty sure I already knew the answer. This was not Tate's first rodeo on a gay hook-up app.

That made me angrier than it should.

Anger wasn't even what it was.

The whole reason why I trembled wasn't from nervousness, it was from rage.

He gave me up for Dahlia. Then he cheated on his wife with other men.

I hoped I was wrong.

I was damn sure I wasn't.

I glanced at the time on my phone. It wasn't even nine yet. Over an hour to go. Even if he didn't respond via message, I'd go upstairs after ten to make sure he wasn't waiting.

Or maybe I should let him wait and not show up at all.

Either way, if I went up and he didn't show or if I didn't go up at all and left him hanging, the app had thousands of other men in the Pittsburgh area to choose from.

I'd hit up dozens of them myself. I'd probably hit up dozens more.

With a growl, I threw my phone on the couch next to me and swiped my beer from the floor, downing half of it in one swallow as I waited for my phone to chirp.

It didn't.

It remained quiet. Dark.

And I remained alone.

～

Ronan (Now)

EVERY STEP I took up the spiral metal staircase was taking a step back in time. All the way back to that first kiss in the dark in Carson. Then it fast-forwarded to the next morning in Tate's bed.

I left him that morning while he was still super confused and I totally understood that. He was straight. Or so he thought. It could be he would chalk up what we did to experimenting.

Or he could chalk it up to being a complete mistake.

Either way, when I left his apartment I figured our friendship had been decimated. The actions of one night—and one morning—had effectively destroyed it.

At the time, I beat myself up for not having the strength to fight the urge to touch him. But I had done it in my sleep, unaware I was spooning the man I considered my best friend.

It didn't help that he didn't push me away, tell me to stop or, *hell,* even punch me. Instead, everything he did encouraged me to continue once I woke up and realized what was happening.

Even though he didn't stop me, I should've stopped myself.

However, for a brief moment that morning, I had a sliver of hope. Hope that he might feel the same way about me.

No matter what, we needed to talk about it and, at the time, I wasn't sure if that would happen since I didn't see him for days afterward. That was unusual. Normally we saw each other every day or at least talked by text and occasionally by phone.

Reluctantly, but also understandably, I had given him some needed space. However, I was worried if he didn't show up for our creative writing class the first Tuesday after the party, he'd land on Dr. Louden's shit list again.

Especially when I arrived and he wasn't anywhere to be found.

Just as the professor appeared about to start his lecture, Tate rushed through the door with that damn overstuffed backpack of his. With a grimace, he mouthed a "sorry" to Dr. Louden, then tucked his head and rushed up the steps.

I expected him to sit as far away from me as possible and was completely speechless when he flopped beside me, a bit out of breath. After flipping the folding desk up into place, he rooted through the backpack now sitting at his feet and began to pull out the stuff he'd need for class.

Not once had he glanced at me. Or given me any kind of recognition.

He had said nothing. As if I was invisible.

So, I said nothing, too.

Dr. Louden said everything for the next seventy-five minutes.

But after ten ticks of the long hand on the round analog clock on the wall above Dr. Louden's head, I sensed when Tate finally settled in. His breathing returned to normal, his knees had spread, his shoulders dropped and he scrubbed both palms down his denim-encased thighs.

Him relaxing helped me relax, too. I was just relieved he didn't detest me.

That I hadn't disgusted him.

That tiny sliver of hope returned.

After two more ticks of the clock's long hand, something brushed the side of my left hand where I had it pinned to my outer thigh.

It happened again. A whisper of a touch.

Then once more.

The last time wasn't so subtle. Tate's pinky hooked with mine under my desk where no one would see it.

I breathed a little easier, my mind cleared and I pressed my lips together so I wouldn't grin like a damn fool, drawing attention.

We stayed like that for the remainder of the class.

Connected.

We weren't holding hands but it was close enough.

And like Tate becoming a habit, that little gesture became one, too. It continued until the end of the semester and we no longer shared a class.

Though, after that, I missed that little secret. It was one secret I didn't mind keeping versus all the rest that eventually came later.

What I hadn't realized that first time or even in those remaining few weeks of our creative writing class, the connection with our pinkies was not only the beginning, it also led us to the end.

Now standing in front of the door at the top of the steps, I dragged myself out of the past and lifted my head. With my fingers curled around the handle, I stiffened my spine along with my resolve, and shoved open the door.

Once I stepped out, I paused for a second, letting my gaze sweep the rooftop to make sure no one else was around. Once I confirmed that, it landed on the man waiting.

Tate was on his knees like I demanded, but not where he was the other night. This time he was kneeling under one of the fabric-covered pergolas. The white string lights cast a soft glow on his bare skin. He wasn't completely naked but wore swim trunks and from where I stood, it appeared his hair might be damp. He must have come up for a swim first.

But what caught my attention was not only was he facing my private door where I exited, but his head was tipped down.

In submission?

We had never been into that. We'd been basic back then. Two guys enjoying exploring and learning about each other.

Or was he bowing his head in forgiveness?

If so, I wasn't ready to forgive him. I wasn't sure if I'd ever be.

The roof was quiet. The only noise reaching my ears was the hum of the pool filtration system and the distant, muted street noise from below.

As well as my own racing heart.

"Why is no one ever up here?" Tate whispered as I took my time approaching him.

I hadn't planned on talking, but even as angry as I was, I'd give him that. "The pool's closed after ten. That means no one should be up here. It's why I come up here when I do. It's also why I told you to come up here before the door locks."

I stepped in front of him and stared down at the top of his dark head for a few seconds before gently tracing my fingertips from his forehead down along the side of his face.

A whisper of a touch. A simple caress.

I tucked them under his chin and tipped his face up with a rough jerk.

A strong reminder.

He didn't resist. Instead, he lifted his blue eyes to mine.

I saw what was in them and I almost took a step back.

Complete submission.

I could do whatever I wanted to him right now and he'd let me.

This was not the Tate I remembered. Nor was it the Tate I had fallen in love with.

"How long have you been waiting?"

His nostrils flared slightly. "Twelve years."

My breath caught and my heart skipped a beat. "Why are you here, Tate? In my building? In my life?"

"I told you, I didn't know you lived here."

"Would you have moved in anyway if you had?"

"I don't know."

"You made a bad decision," I concluded.

"Moving here?"

"That's one of them, but not the most egregious."

His gaze dropped to my feet. "I acknowledge the fact I made a lot of mistakes in my life, Roe. But I would like to fix as many as I can."

"I'm not sure that's possible," I murmured.

He wasn't only talking about leaving me or about marrying Dahlia. One mistake had obviously snowballed into more.

Not unlike telling lies. You tell one, then you need to tell another. And another. Until you either forget what was the truth or the original lie.

Tate made one mistake, then the next until it spun out of control. And he had no way to rein it in until everything in his life imploded.

Our relationship.

His marriage.

Maybe even his career. I hadn't asked and right now I wasn't sure if I even cared.

It was best if I didn't. I didn't want to make that mistake again. Caring about someone who could so easily destroy me.

I had given him everything. He turned around and left me with nothing.

I bit back the questions I had about him being on Grindr. I wasn't sure if I wanted to know that, either. And even if I did, the answers might only infuriate me more.

At this point in time, while on this roof, I only planned on focusing on the here and now. On what was in front of me. On who was on his knees. Waiting and willing.

I still had a tight grip on his bearded chin. "What are you waiting for?"

"I was waiting for you."

"I'm here. Now what are you waiting for?"

Something I couldn't identify slid behind his eyes. "For you…"

I tilted my head. "For me to what?"

"Whatever you want, Roe. If you want to continue to punish me for what I did to you, I'll accept that. If you want to move on from that and give me pleasure instead, I'll accept that, too. Again, I know I made plenty of mistakes and I'm willing to pay for them." He shook his head slightly, not enough to break my hold. "I *have* paid for them. I continue to pay for them. And if this will fix what's broken between us," he paused and his chest slowly rose as he filled his lungs, "then I'm willing to do whatever it takes."

I released his chin and stared down at him. "Whatever it takes," I echoed in a murmur.

His face tipped up a little higher and his eyes now held a boldness that had been missing since the first time I saw him in the vestibule. "Whatever it takes."

I wanted to scream in his face, *"Why? Why now? Is it only because you happened to move into the building I own? Would you be making an effort to fix things if you hadn't?"*

I swallowed all that rage back down and let it simmer in my gut. Because I knew the answer. Hearing it from Tate himself would only fuel that fire and I wouldn't give him that chance to fix what he broke between us.

And I wanted him to. I did. But I just wasn't ready for it. Not yet.

Especially after finding him on the app earlier.

"Tonight you're simply a Grindr hookup. Nothing more."

He closed his eyes and licked his lips. "Right. Nothing more."

I dragged my thumb along his bottom lip, his warm breath rushing over my fingers. "Let me tell you something that has changed since we were college kids. I used to bottom for you. I no longer do that for anyone." I tucked the tip of my thumb into his mouth and opened it wider. "I also no longer get on my knees for anyone." I dipped my head down even further and whispered, "Not even for you."

"I understand."

I shook my head. "No. I don't think you do. But you will."

"I can't apologize enough—"

I cut him off. "I don't want to hear your apologies, *Harris*. I don't want to hear you at all. There's a reason you're on your knees right now and it's not to beg for forgiveness."

He nodded. "I understand."

"Good. Then you know what to do." I removed my thumb from his mouth and waited.

His swim trunks were tented and I was just as hard as he was.

I was fighting what I really wanted to do... Yank him to his feet, kiss him long and hard and take him downstairs to my bed so we could rediscover each other all over again.

So we could start over and do it right this time.

But I was still too pissed to let myself have that or to even give that to him. I was too bitter to give him any softness or leeway.

Right now I needed to take my pound of flesh before I'd ever be willing to give it back to him. Before I'd let him dip a toe back into my life.

He might not even want that, but I needed to fortify my heart behind steel walls just in case he did. This time I needed to protect myself since too much damage had already been done.

I might not survive any more.

"I'm waiting, *Harris*," I growled, not giving him an inch.

He licked his lips again as he stared at the bulge in my jeans, then unsnapped and unzipped them.

My blood was rushing with the anticipation of having his mouth wrapped around my cock.

Back then, I gave him head more than he gave it to me. It took him a bit but he eventually began to excel at it. He also enjoyed it, both giving and receiving. But he had been intuitive and quick to figure out what worked and what didn't. What I preferred and what quickly made me come. And I learned the same about him.

I also taught him what would drive me insane. How to manipulate the prostate to make my orgasms more intense. The best lesson was the night I did it to him for the first time. He learned just how mind-blowing it was.

While it might have been the first time, it was definitely not the last.

I wouldn't demand him to do it tonight but would see if he would on his own. My guess was that if he'd been with other men in the last twelve years, it was something he hadn't forgotten and might have even had plenty of practice doing.

The rage once again surged from deep inside me just thinking about Tate with other men after he walked away from *us*.

I had him for almost two years. I dreamed about him for twelve more.

Prostate massage or not, if I was being honest with myself,

tonight it wouldn't take much more than him taking me into his mouth for me to fill it with my cum.

I wanted this to be quick and dirty, anyway. No lingering. No connection. Because the more time I spent with him, the better the chance those walls I put up would begin to crumble and if they did, it might open the door for me to forgive him.

Something he clearly wanted.

And, again, something I wasn't ready to give him.

Maybe one day, but not today.

I bit back my groan when he took me in his hand, stroking me lightly, spreading the silky drop of precum around the tip with his thumb.

I didn't watch him, instead I stared at a nonexistent spot in the distance. Anything to keep from establishing a connection with him once again.

But when his warm, wet mouth encased the crown, my gaze dropped to him against my will.

One more mistake in a long list of them.

His eyes weren't closed, he wasn't concentrating on what he was doing, he was watching me.

That made me press my lips together and lock my knees. I wouldn't give him any satisfaction. Not even with my reactions from him sucking me deep into his mouth. Or swirling his tongue around the head. Or running the flat of his tongue down the ridge. Or sucking on my scrotum. Pressing on my taint or tugging gently on my balls.

From watching my slick cock sliding in and out of his mouth. The pull from the suction. The circle of his fingers squeezing the base.

He was still good at it. Better than I remembered.

That last discovery was all I needed to recapture my anger and wrap it around me like a protective cloak.

I kept myself from unraveling by standing over him while he was on his knees at my feet.

It was wrong, the satisfaction of watching him with minimal participation on my part. But like when I came all over his face the other night, having him on his knees was a power play I didn't know I needed. It kept me strong, it kept those walls locked in place.

It kept me safe.

It kept me from crumbling and becoming soft. From forgiving him too easily.

Or even giving me hope that there might be a future between us.

At this point there wasn't.

And I wasn't sure if it would ever get to that point.

I reminded myself tonight wasn't about forgiveness. It wasn't about the future.

He was only a Grindr hookup.

That. Was. All.

I was here to get what I wanted from him and leave the rest behind.

My eyelids became heavy as he took me so deep, he gagged slightly. And he did it again.

And again.

Even though he was doing everything right, at the back of my head I kept thinking this was so wrong.

In this moment, I needed to forget about the past. Forget there ever was an *us*.

And just remember why I messaged him.

Keep it at surface level, Ronan. Don't dig too deep. You could tumble into that abyss and never be able to climb back out.

You clawed your way out of that hole once before, don't let it trap you again.

He stopped the pressure against the spot on my taint where just on the other side of his fingers was my prostate and he drove his hand into his swim trunks.

He began to pump his fist over his own erection.

I quickly grabbed a handful of his hair, ripped on it and barked, "No! No part of tonight is for you."

His eyes flicked up from my cock to my face. Our gazes held as he slowly released himself and straightened his trunks.

He'd always taken direction well. Apparently, that hadn't changed.

The more he sucked me, licked me, teased me, the harder it was to keep from closing my eyes, dropping my head back and just letting myself enjoy it. Simply losing myself in what he was doing with his mouth and hands.

I refused to let him see just how much I wanted this.

Still gripping his hair with my right hand, I tightened my fingers, letting him feel the pull. It didn't slow him down, but instead he worked harder to take me to the finish line.

He gently kneaded my balls, swallowed my whole length, and made a cock ring out of two fingers around my throbbing root. Due to the tightness, my veins had popped and my cock had turned a slight purplish-red. My precum also leaked at a rapid rate.

I weaved the fingers of my left hand into his hair. With both hands, I gripped his hair so tightly he could no longer move. Instead, I moved my hips, taking over the pace. Forcing him to take what I was willing to give him.

I held him still and thrust harder, faster, all the way to the back of his throat. Not caring if I bruised him there. Not caring if he couldn't breathe. Not caring if he was choking on my cock.

Not fucking caring.

I punished him. For back then. For now.

For the time in between.

Pretending his mouth was his ass, I railed him until his face turned red, then a slight shade of purple.

But he did not tap out. He did not try to pull away. He did not struggle at all.

He gave me no indication that I should let up or even stop.

He took every inch I gave him.

I saw it for what it was. He was trying to prove to me that he'd do whatever it took for me to forgive him.

I needed to stop. I needed to give him a break. But I couldn't. I kept going. For a moment drowning in my anger, being swallowed by my want, my need.

And, ultimately, for my love for the man on his knees at my feet.

For my hate for that same man.

I loved everything about him.

I hated everything about him, too.

I hated what he did to me.

I hated what he did to himself.

I hated what he did to us.

And hate was just as strong of an emotion as love. It didn't take much to tip it from one side to the other.

It also didn't take much for me to finally come.

I clamped my teeth together to smother my groan as I thrust my cock to the very back of his throat and held it there as I pumped cum down it. Made him swallow every damn drop until I was drained.

It was at the point when he swayed and his eyes began to bulge that I finally pulled back, finally loosened my fingers.

And finally considered forgiving him.

But instead, I fortified those walls around my heart and jerked myself free, releasing his hair, letting him suck in air.

Watching his face return to its normal color.

Watching a string of cum cling between the crown of my cock and his lips.

Panting, he licked it free, then wiped his mouth with the back of his hand.

I turned away while I adjusted my boxer briefs back in place and fastened my jeans. Because the urge to drop to my knees and comfort him was too strong. Too tempting.

Too risky.

Way too fucking risky.

Without another glance at him, I left him there on his knees and strode toward my personal access door to the roof.

"Do you leave all your Grindr dates unsatisfied?" he called out, his voice raspy from me abusing his throat.

His angry words stopped me in my tracks but I didn't bother to turn around. I shouldn't answer but in a moment of weakness I did. "No. Just you."

I continued toward my escape.

"Ronan!" he shouted.

I inhaled a sharp breath but paused again, this time inches from my exit.

"I know it took me too long, but I wanted you to know... It's important that you know, I eventually figured it out..."

I waited, even though I shouldn't. But I wouldn't ask what he figured out because I wasn't sure if I could handle what he was about to say next.

His voice was thick and tinged with agony that clawed at my insides when he confessed, "It wasn't men I craved. It was only you. It has always been you."

My jaw worked violently. My fingers curled into tight fists. It was either that or grind my teeth down to the roots. Or, *for shit's sake*, simply go back and knock him the hell out.

It took everything I had to make sure a shake wasn't detectable in my response. "Too bad you didn't figure that out twelve years ago."

I don't know if he heard me and I didn't care if he didn't. My message had been loud and clear. The only thing I was willing to give him at this point was already coating his throat and stomach.

I yanked the door open and slammed it behind me, but before heading downstairs I made sure my private entrance was secured so he couldn't follow me.

Because if he did...

If he did, I'd struggle to find the strength to push him away.

CHAPTER 9

Ronan (Then)

A POUNDING on my dorm room door made me jump out of the seat at my desk and rush to unlock it. It wasn't normally locked, especially when Dominic was out, but my roommate had headed home for the weekend for some family thing.

While I studied, I tended to lock my door to make sure I wasn't disturbed. I needed to keep my grades up to keep my scholarship. Partying was great, working was great, spending time with Tate was great, but my grades needed to be better than great. They needed to be perfect.

A solid education, and a degree, would hopefully give me a solid foundation for the rest of my life. If I ended up not being successful, I didn't want it to be because of a lack of trying or slacking off. So, I did all my assignments, as well as any extra credit when it was offered, plus I studied. A lot.

Sometimes Tate helped me. But my guess was it wasn't due to his knowledge being greater than mine but because he wanted to spend time with me.

At least, that was what I hoped and allowed myself to believe.

We hadn't made any plans to study together tonight, so I had no idea who stood on the other side of the door. As soon as I yanked it open, my breath caught. It *was* Tate with his *bursting-at-the-seams* backpack flung over one shoulder. A few strands of his dark hair had fallen across his forehead, his blue eyes were bright and his cheeks were flushed.

But then, it was a blustery fall day and he'd probably either hoofed it over to campus from his apartment on foot, or rode his bike.

"What are you doing here?" I asked.

"Dom's gone for the weekend, right?" He nudged me with his shoulder to move me out of the way so he could step over the threshold. As soon as he did, he shut and relocked the door.

"Yeah. He went home. He'll be back early Monday."

He turned back to me and grinned.

"What?" Suspicion colored my question and I narrowed my eyes at him.

He moved past me and set his backpack on Dom's bed, unzipped it and pulled out a laptop.

It looked brand-new. He already owned the most recent model and that one certainly didn't need to be replaced.

"You break your other one?"

"Nope," he answered as he shoved it at me. "It's not mine."

My brow furrowed. "Did you steal it? Whose is it?"

"Yours."

My frown deepened and I stared at the Apple MacBook still in his hands. My chest filled with dread. "I can't afford that."

"I can."

That laptop cost over a grand. That was why I didn't have one. I couldn't even afford a new Windows-based laptop, forget an Apple. That was why I used my old dinosaur and prayed to the computer gods that it kept working every time I opened it. "I can't pay you back."

He shrugged. "Okay."

What? He bought new laptops like it was nothing? "Tate…"

He shoved it into my gut, forcing me to grab it. As soon as I did, he let go and I was stuck holding something I had always wanted but knew I'd never be able to afford.

I held it out to him and shook my head. "I can't take this."

"It's not a big deal. Don't make one out of it."

It *was* a huge deal. "It is."

"Roe…"

"Tate, this is crazy. I can't accept this."

"Yes, you can. You're going to need a good computer for the next four years. Plus, I wanted to do this for you."

"It's too expensive." Even if it wasn't, I couldn't have him buying me a freaking laptop. Like he was my sugar daddy or something. I loved Tate for being Tate, not because of his family's money. I didn't care about that at all.

"It really wasn't."

"For you maybe…"

Tate shrugged again, once again pretending like this wasn't a big deal. "I got it with our student discount. I want you to have it because I want you to do well here. I don't want anything holding you back. Including that old paperweight of yours. It's not going to last much longer." He pulled the MacBook from my hands and set it on my desk. When he turned, a frown marred his handsome face. "How about a thank you instead of fighting me on this?"

"But—"

"No buts. I'm done talking about it. That's not why I came here."

My forehead scrunched together. I'd deal with the laptop again later. "Then why did you come here?"

He stalked back over to his backpack and dug around until he found what he was searching for. I didn't know how he found anything in that damn thing.

But what I was not expecting was for him to pull out what he did.

When he turned toward me again, he gripped the neck of an unopened fifth of Jim Beam and was smiling.

The student residents weren't allowed to have alcohol in the dorms and the university was very strict on that policy. I could risk losing my housing if we got caught.

Maybe even lose my scholarship.

Since we went to parties practically every weekend, we had no reason to drink in my room. Plus, Tate had his own apartment off campus. It made no sense. "Why would you bring that here?"

He licked his lips, most likely out of nervousness. When he began to fidget, it slowly sunk in as to why he brought the booze. I wasn't quite sure what to think, so I'd need to hear it from him. I wasn't going to assume anything.

Hooking our pinkies together this week in class was far different from anal sex. Or even a blowjob. Or frotting, what we did last weekend by rubbing our cocks together and causing that messy explosion in my underwear.

And anyway, we weren't even sure if he was gay, or bi, or... whatever. The label wasn't the important part. We hadn't talked about what happened last weekend at all, which I'd been meaning to do. I was only giving him space and time because I was trying to avoid him freaking out all over again.

I figured him hooking our pinkies together in class—even as small of a gesture as it was—was a good start and if he wanted to build whatever was between us from there, we could.

But did he now want to take the plunge and just dive right in to see if sex with other men was for him?

Was I supposed to be his test subject? I wasn't completely opposed to him having his way with me, but still...

Did he really want to take it further tonight than just getting each other off?

"I," he took a breath, then the rest of the words tumbled out, "want to explore this." He waved a hand between us. "I brought some reinforcement." My eyes dropped to the bottle of Jim Beam in his hand when he lifted it.

"Lube and condoms would have been a better choice," I said dryly, not sure about any of this.

"Well, I figured you had some. But if not, I brought those, too, just in case. However," he lifted the bottle up in the air again, "I need this first."

He needed liquid courage to be with me? That wasn't very reassuring.

And did he actually want to *fuck*? Or did he just want to play like we did last weekend in his bed? He'd been freaked out about that and it hadn't gone as far as being intrusive.

Anal sex was definitely intrusive. *Very* intrusive.

Worse, I hadn't expected this at all, so I hadn't prepped like I normally would. I didn't mind being a bottom for his first time and, of course, that would be easier than if he was…

I shook myself mentally. No, this was too much. I couldn't wrap my head around him wanting to take us to the next step, wanting to *explore,* as he called it.

I was thrilled but worried at the same time.

As much as I loved him, I didn't want to lose him, even if I had to keep him in the friend zone. However, that wouldn't happen if we kept having sex, even if it didn't get as far as doing the actual "deed." Sex didn't need penetration to be satisfying or to be considered sex.

Jerking each other off, sucking each other's cocks, frotting, docking… the list was endless on what we could do.

He placed the bottle on my desk and then went back to Dom's bed to pull two Dixie cups out of his backpack. Being stuffed in his bag had basically crushed the small waxed cups so he worked them back into shape. While he did this, it was hard to ignore the shake in his fingers.

He was totally wired.

Since I knew he didn't do drugs, it had to be because of nervousness. I was nervous my first time, too. It was awkward, messy and almost a complete failure, but I wasn't the only one in that experience who had no idea what they were doing.

It also didn't stop me from trying again and again and finding others with more experience than me to teach me tricks and methods to make it better and more satisfying. I also did a lot of "research" on my own.

I stared at Tate as he took the two misshapen cups over to the desk, cracked open the bottle and filled them to almost the brim with the amber liquor.

When he turned with them in his hand, my gaze dropped to the whiskey before rising once again to his face. When I didn't take the one he offered me, he downed the other one in a single swallow. Then he drank the one that was supposed to be for me next.

He turned, filled the cups again and once again offered me one.

This time I took it reluctantly. "I'm surprised you're not drinking directly from the bottle."

"It's early yet."

"Tate… If you need alcohol to—"

"I just need it to relax a bit. That's all. I feel like I'm about to come out of my skin."

"You look like it, too."

He swept a hand through his hair, pushing it off his forehead. Of course, like normal, it didn't stay put. "It's not you, it's me."

"No shit," I murmured, taking a sip of the Jim Beam. I wrinkled my nose, swallowed the remainder and crushed the cup in my hand before throwing it in my trash.

One of us needed to remain sober if this was going to happen. Actually, both of us needed to remain sober. I'd allow him one more shot before cutting him off. If he needed more than that, tonight was not going to happen.

I understood he needed to calm his nerves, but he also had to remain aware of what exactly was going on.

If I was straight, I certainly wouldn't fuck a drunk chick. Since I was gay, I applied that same principle to guys. Unless we were in a relationship and we were just having agreed upon fun together. But someone trashed? No. No matter who it was.

"Tate, if you get drunk, I'm not touching you," I warned him. "I'm not letting you touch me, either. Not like that."

He glanced down at the full Dixie cup in his hand, then back up at me.

I raised my eyebrows at him. "After that, no more." Tonight, I felt older than him rather than the other way around.

With a nod, he put the cup to his mouth and threw it back, then put the cap back on the bottle and set the empty cup down next to it.

I sighed softly in relief. "Are you sure about this?"

He nodded.

I shook my head and went toe to toe with him, staring at him directly in the eyes. He was only an inch taller than me, so we were pretty even in height. If he glanced away, I would know he wasn't ready.

He didn't. He stared me straight in the eyes with his full of more confidence than a few minutes prior. "If this isn't for me or I have to stop, Roe, please don't hold it against me. I trust you. If I'm gay or bi, or… I don't know what… I trust you enough to let me take my time to figure it out."

At whose expense, though? Mine?

He wanted to use me to figure out if he was sexually attracted to men, but one thing about that worried me. He didn't know I was already in love with him. However, that was my problem, not his.

In that same light, confusion about his sexual identity was his problem, not mine.

But here was the rub, I kissed him first. I felt responsible for causing that confusion. Did I owe it to him to help him figure it all out?

The answer would be much easier if I didn't love him. Didn't want him in my bed or my life.

The truth was, I did. I wanted him completely, but only if he wanted that, too.

For that reason, I was willing to sacrifice a piece of myself to see if I ended up the winner in the end.

I was also fully aware that if it didn't go the way I hoped, I'd be the loser.

It was a gamble. For both of us.

~

Ronan (Now)

I PACED BACK and forth across my living room like a restless caged tiger with my jaw working, squeezing the lowball glass of Johnnie Walker Blue between my fingers so tightly, I was surprised it hadn't shattered.

The whole Grindr thing had already ticked me off, but what aggravated me even more was I had spent years beating back the memories, of reliving that time when I was too young, too stupid to see what was right in front of me.

When love blinded me from seeing the truth.

Now all that had been stirred back up. Every minute of every day that Tate and I had spent together.

After leaving Tate up on the roof and as I descended the steps, I spiraled back into the past.

Tonight it was back to that first weekend we spent together. When things between Tate and me began to tip from friendship to something else...

Like my first time, Tate's first time with me was awkward, uncomfortable, and definitely nothing to write home about. Not that I would. My family was certainly accepting but didn't want to hear about my sexual escapades.

Not that I blamed them. I certainly didn't want the details on how my brother Declan made my nieces and nephews with my sister-in-law.

I grimaced.

I thought about that first weekend together often in the weeks that followed, going over everything to figure out what we could've done differently to make it easier on Tate.

The foreplay had been great. Kissing, sucking and touching each other, a fantasy come true for me. I took my time getting to know Tate's body up close and personal. I got familiar with every inch. I laid on my back and he did the same with me, then flipped me over. I somehow kept my patience as he tentatively explored my whole body from the top of my head all the way to my toes by tasting and touching.

By the time he was done, I was horny as hell, hard as a freaking rock and ready to burst. But I forced myself to take things slower than I normally would.

When it came to sex, patience wasn't my strong suit.

I explained things as we went. Any question he asked, I answered to the best of my ability. Had I had a lot of anal sex? No. I was only nineteen, and with being gay, I didn't get the chance to have a lot of sex in my teens. It was difficult since I wasn't out at the time, afraid I'd become a target of bullying. By other students, by parents, even by teachers. Plus, I wasn't out to my family yet, either, and didn't want them to find out from someone else.

Like Tate, I wanted to be absolutely sure of my sexuality before announcing it to the world.

Okay, maybe not quite announcing it, but at least being out in the open.

But to be sure about what I wanted and what I didn't, I had to look outside of school. Eventually, I found another kid about my age much braver than me and *was* out. Once we connected, we fooled around a lot. Including doing "the deed" for the first time.

Unfortunately, it had been way more awkward and messy than Tate taking my ass for the first time because I had a whole slew of knowledge by then.

Even though having sex with a man was all new to Tate, he was open to learning. It was no surprise that he didn't last long, but in the end we both had intense orgasms due to all the foreplay and prep. The anticipation alone had drove us both to the breaking point.

While he wasn't put off by having sex with me, I could tell his emotions flip-flopped back and forth. When they did, when he began to question whether he wanted to have sex with me—or any man—we slowed down. During those times, I had to dig even deeper to find my patience because I didn't want to rush him.

I didn't want to ruin the experience for him.

I wanted him to want it as much as I did. I also hoped that if this first time went well, he'd want to do it more.

With me, of course. That was a no-brainer. The hell if I was going through all this for him to go do it with others.

That first night in my dorm room turned into a whole weekend together. We only left my room occasionally to grab food. If anyone asked, we told them we were working on a paper for creative writing together.

By late Sunday night when he finally left me and my bed, I was actually ready for a break. The more we fooled around, the more Tate wanted to try new things.

Normally I'd be all gung-ho about that. However, I wasn't used to bottoming and I was starting to feel the results. But it was too early for me to ask Tate about switching. I would eventually, *if* this continued, since I preferred to top but in the meantime, I needed to stay patient while Tate got his bearings.

He hit the Jim Beam a few more times that weekend but not as much as I thought he might. He only took a shot or two here and there to take off the edge and loosen up a bit.

Even though the whiskey didn't end up being a problem, one major, unforgettable issue remained with what we were doing. Tate was still officially dating Dahlia. And I had no idea what excuse he told her about where he was that weekend.

His relationship with her either needed to change or he would have to stop using me to explore his sexual curiosity.

Were we exclusive? No. At that point we were still only friends.

Friends with benefits, I guessed. But I wanted to head toward something more serious and I hoped he did, too.

If he did, he needed to break things off with Dahlia. Like pronto.

Or, I would tell him he needed to stop coming to my dorm room whenever Dom was away. Or stop inviting me to his apartment whenever his roommates were out.

The fact he didn't want witnesses made it clear he preferred to keep what we were doing a secret.

Maybe he wanted to keep his attraction to men—or at least to me—a secret, too.

I wasn't one for secrets. Especially potentially harmful secrets like that. They usually ended up infecting everything it touched like a festering wound.

In the meantime, we had to pretend we were only friends and nothing more. Even though every time we hooked up, not just as friends but lovers, I could feel the shift in our relationship.

We got tighter. We got more bold in bed. And during the down times, we would lay next to each other and talk about everything under the sun, important or not.

Those were the times I cherished the most. We weren't just sexually attracted to each other. It went much deeper than that.

Even when we sat next to each other in creative writing, we'd spread our thighs enough so they touched. His pinky always found mine and we kept them hooked together for the hour and fifteen minute long class.

Many times, we'd try to concentrate on Dr. Louden's lecture with both of us hard, counting the minutes until we could find a private moment together. I never clock-watched so much in my life.

When it got bad, I would sometimes breathe, "Tate." Unsure if I could sit in that chair a second longer without dragging him down the steps and into the nearest utility closet so I could do more than touch his pinky or brush my thigh against his.

He had a stronger resolve than me. He'd continue to sit and stare at our professor and only give a slight shake of his head. I would try to collect myself by concentrating on Dr. Louden as he scribbled away on the whiteboard, his voice droning on endlessly as the long hand on that damn clock moved in slow motion.

All I could think about was Tate. Every second of every day.

His touch.

His scent.

The way his pinky hooked with mine under our desks.

How our warm, bare skin felt against each other. How our lips met. How our breaths mingled and our moans blended. How he stretched me and filled me. How we took the time to discover new things about ourselves and each other.

But before the end of the semester, I was done "exploring" with Tate until he broke up with Dahlia.

It wasn't fair to her. And it certainly wasn't fair to me.

He needed to get that done, even if he didn't want anyone to know about us yet.

When I finally put my foot down, he assured me, "I'm going to talk to her."

"Tate…"

"I promise."

Dragging myself out of the past, I stared down at my lowball glass still full of whiskey. Much more expensive than the Jim Beam we drank back in college.

I began to raise it to my lips but stopped halfway as the past bubbled up like an erupting volcano.

"Fuck!" I screamed and whipped the glass across the room with every bit of strength I had.

The impact against the window sounded like an explosion.

Leaving behind a fractured view of the dark city beyond.

CHAPTER 10

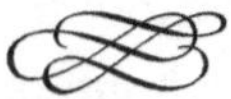

Tate (Now)

I STARED at the bottle of The Macallan Ronan had left behind the first time he found me on the roof. Ever since then, it had been sitting on the counter in my small kitchen. A reminder in more ways than one.

I meant to give it back. I should've taken it up with me the other night since it wasn't mine to keep. But then, what was?

Everything I've ever had, I'd lost.

Ronan.

My wife.

Even my children.

In truth, I had no one to blame but myself.

That also meant that I had to be the one to make it right.

Or at least try to.

I couldn't fix everything. Some mistakes were unfixable.

Being unhappy with myself or my situation was no excuse for the damage I had caused the people in my life.

Sometimes the only thing to do was to acknowledge, apologize, move on and do better in the future.

I was currently at that point in my life.

139

Everything had crumbled around me. Now it was time to rebuild. Starting with myself.

I did that by finally coming clean with Dahlia.

I didn't do it back in college. When I broke up with her, I told her it was for a reason that wasn't true to try to soften the blow.

If she saw through my lie, she didn't say.

I loved her and didn't want to hurt her, but I did anyway. And I continued to hurt her throughout our marriage, even though it wasn't my intent. She was an excellent mother and a decent wife.

It was the old adage: *It's not you, it's me.*

I tried to fight the urges, the ones I had buried deep and wanted to forget. But I couldn't. All it did was eat at me and make me unhappy. My being miserable affected my whole family.

When I saw how it was affecting my children, I knew something had to change. And it had to start with me.

I would not destroy their lives because I had destroyed my own. I owed them that much. I knew they would be upset with me—possibly even hate me—for leaving and of course, they were. I was to blame and I accepted that.

It started a little over a year after we married. A little over a year after I graduated from Duquesne. A little over a year from when I walked away from Ronan. From when I walked away from who and what I was, trying to convince myself I was wrong with my discovery, when deep down I knew I was right.

I ignored it until I couldn't ignore it anymore.

That led me to late night random hookups with nameless men.

In sketchy motels, dark parks and filthy bathroom stalls.

Quick, dirty and anonymous.

But I beat myself up after every time. Did that make me stop? No.

I had an unreachable itch I kept scratching.

Worse, not once did I find real relief. It was a desperate attempt to remember who I lost. What I lost.

Who I walked away from.

A desperate attempt to recapture what I missed and who.

It failed every time.

But I kept trying. If nothing else, to punish myself. To prove I had made a mistake, chosen the wrong path.

I convinced myself that meeting these random men in random locations was nothing. That I was hurting no one but myself.

I was wrong.

I hurt Dahlia.

I hurt my kids.

I destroyed my family by not being true to them or myself.

No matter what, I loved my children. They were my heart and soul, and I would never regret having them.

However, I regret what I did to them. To us. To my family.

To the woman who bore my children. Who stood by my side for years even though she sensed something was off.

There came a point I had to come clean.

It was either that or jump off a bridge and take my secret to my grave.

But I owed my children better than that. Even if it took them a while to forgive me. Eventually they would when they were older when I could explain and they'd be mature enough to understand.

It was difficult to break up with Dahlia in college. It was even more difficult to do it over twelve years later when I had so much more to lose.

We sent the kids to her parents and I flayed myself open.

I could see it on her face. She already knew.

Of course she did. She knew back when we were at Duquesne. She ignored it then. She pretended the truth was a lie.

But I wouldn't let her ignore it now. No matter what she said. No matter what she did.

"Tate, don't do this," was the first thing she said when I sat her down. Her face was pale, her throat rolled when she swallowed.

"I think... No, I know... I'm gay. I've always been gay. I never wanted to admit it out loud. I saw how others were treated. I didn't want that. I thought I might outgrow those feelings, those urges. I convinced myself I was experimenting, even though I knew I was lying to myself. I was wrong. And I'm tired of living a lie. I'm tired of lying to myself. To you. To the kids. To..." I sucked in a breath, unsure of what to say, unsure of how to soften the blow. A hit she had to know might be coming for years and exactly why.

Silence filled the space across the living room where she sat on one couch and I sat on another.

Finally she shook her head, once again ignoring what was clearly in front of her. The whole reason why it made it easy to continue to live the lie. "You're not gay."

"Dahlia..."

"No, Tate! Gay men don't have sex with women."

She was so, so wrong.

"At most you're bi. You always acted like you enjoyed sex with me."

Acted was the key word.

But I was tired of acting. I was tired of the charade. The lies. The denial.

Hiding who I was on the inside, making what I looked like on the outside my whole personality.

Wearing a skin that was not mine. And maybe never was.

I played the part I was given. By my parents, by Dahlia, even by my employer.

How could I teach my own children to be true to themselves if I wasn't to myself?

I couldn't. I didn't want to fail them. I had failed Ronan. I had failed Dahlia. I had failed myself.

Many times I wondered if Ronan hadn't been a part of my life, hadn't awoken what was inside of me, at what point would I have discovered it on my own?

Would I have been miserable and just not known why? Would I have not been able to pinpoint the problem?

Dahlia also told me I needed therapy that day in the living room. I agreed. I did.

Right now, with the divorce and the child support, the move back to Pittsburgh and the new job, I just couldn't afford it. Maybe after my benefits kicked in.

But she mentioned therapy because she thought it would convince me I wasn't gay. That it would prove I had only been in love with Ronan and not because I was attracted to men in general.

It was possible she was right. That it wasn't just any man I wanted. It was only one.

The one I fell in love with. The one I could never get over.

The one I had carried with me in my head and my heart for the last twelve years.

Moving into the same building where Ronan lived dropped an unexpected opportunity in my lap to be able to fix what I had broken all those years ago. But he had to be willing and open to it.

I wasn't sure if he was.

He might not ever be.

It was worth a shot. If it failed like everything else, I could look back on it that I at least made an effort, instead of hiding.

Instead of ignoring.

I was taking that shot. Even if it wounded me beyond repair.

I didn't have his number. I didn't even know what unit he lived in. I had only one way to contact him.

My gaze landed on my phone.

I forced myself to walk slowly over to where it sat on the table next to the couch. If I didn't, I'd sprint. I took those few moments to check myself. To make sure I was making the right decision.

I flip-flopped with every step I took.

Should I? Or shouldn't I?

Was it too early for us? Or was it too late?

I focused on that phone and once I stood over it, I stared at it instead of snatching it up.

I counted to ten in my head. Then out loud to twenty.

I took one deep breath. Two.

Fuck it.

I swiped it off the table before I changed my mind, woke it from sleep mode and double-checked the time on my phone.

After opening the Grindr app, I scrolled through my messages until I found the string with Ronan. I hit Reply and typed out a short message. *Can you meet me on the roof at ten?*

I almost added a "please" but didn't want to sound as desperate as I felt.

I also wanted privacy, so I wanted to wait until the door to the roof was locked and we wouldn't be disturbed.

Plus, if I ended up groveling, I didn't want anyone else to witness it. It would be bad enough that the two of us would.

Time ticked by slowly in my head as I waited for his response. Even if he saw it right away—and he might since by the looks of his "date" last week, he was very active on the app—he could purposely make me wait for his answer.

In truth, he might make me wait until only minutes away from ten o'clock. Almost two hours from now.

I wasn't sure I could hang by the thin thread I was clutching until then.

Luckily, I didn't have to wait. His answer came almost immediately.

You know what to do when you get up there.

Another message popped up before I could respond to his first one.

Otherwise, find someone else.

That was the rub. There was no one else. I could delete the app because no matter what happened between us tonight, tomorrow, months or years from now, now that I found Ronan, I doubted I'd ever use it again.

I only previously downloaded and used it out of desperation.

I hoped I had no reason to use it again because whatever he wanted from me, I'd give him.

Whatever he wanted from me, I wanted, too.

Even if he wanted to humiliate me, I'd let him.

I deserved it and owed him.

Any and all of it.

No matter what it was.

I opened my eyes as soon as I realized I had them squeezed shut. I typed out my reply. *I'll be waiting.*

"But please don't make me wait too long," I whispered to my empty apartment.

~

Tate (Now)

LIKE THE OTHER two times I met Roe on the rooftop—one planned, one not—I dropped to my knees to wait.

And wait.

I had grabbed one of the lounger cushions this time and placed it under my knees. Yes, I only recently turned thirty-five but my knees and the pool were two of the reasons I sublet an apartment in this building. I hadn't run in a few years because of them. Swimming was easier on the joints than running and right now I couldn't afford both rent and a gym membership.

Ronan and I had run together all the time in college. I continued for a while after that to stay in shape until it began to take a toll. The last two times I was on my knees at his feet I had to hide the discomfort from my face.

It was also why last time I had chosen to kneel under one of the pergolas. The wood was slightly easier on my knees than the concrete.

But if Ronan asked, I would kneel on the damn concrete until my knees bled. And then I'd keep kneeling even longer.

Whatever he wanted, I was willing to give him.

All I asked from him was his forgiveness.

I wanted Dahlia's, too. But that was a whole other painful situation in itself.

I had a lot of work to do. Not only on myself but with my relationships. Even so, I was determined to get it done.

I refused to bow my head this time when the side door opened. I was curious to why Ronan always used a different, unmarked entrance. Was there a back way up to the roof? A service entrance maybe?

Right now that wasn't important. What was important was the man coming through that door with his dark brown eyes locked on me as he strode across the roof to where I waited.

I couldn't look away if I tried. As always, he stole my breath just the same as he'd stolen my heart.

He was so much broader than when he was in college. Muscular. Mature. He had aged well.

I didn't know the extent of his tattoos, but figured he had a lot more than what I could see. From what I *could* see, his left arm was a complete sleeve. And sometimes when his shirt sleeve pulled up as he walked, I got a peek of more on his right bicep. Possibly a quarter sleeve.

How many more did he have hidden?

Seeing that body ink drove home how far he had come from being a college student. Ronan was now a man.

Even his stride was determined as he took his time closing the distance between us.

Back in school, we had worked on our physique together. But now, he clearly had taken it farther than the average person.

Every sculpted inch of him was solid. Powerful. His waist was trim, his thighs thick, his biceps bulging. His neck corded.

He had even grown facial hair. A goatee of sorts. In college, he had given it a shot and it ended up being sparse and splotchy, so he shaved it all off. Especially after I teased him about it and even went so far as to brag about how I could grow a thick beard my senior year in high school to bust his balls.

For a moment, the memory of his laughter that day filled my ears.

Tonight, he wasn't laughing. He wasn't even smiling.

I would give anything to see it again.

Absolutely anything.

I fell in love with his smile before I realized I was in love with the man it belonged to.

He stopped in front of me, his face an unreadable mask.

"Roe..."

His gaze raked me from my head to my bent knees. "You're fully dressed."

"I didn't come up here for sex."

His dark eyebrows pinched together. "Then why the hell did you message me?"

"I was hoping for a chance to talk."

"About?"

He was purposely being obtuse. No surprise that he would make me work for it.

Little did he know I was willing to do that. I was willing to do more than work for it. I was willing to fight for us.

No matter what it took, I wanted a second chance.

A chance to heal the break.

Even if it was a slow and painful road to travel.

Even if I had to get on my knees every damn night.

If I had to beg for his forgiveness.

Seeing him that first time downstairs had cracked me open all over again. I know it did the same for him, so I hoped he'd give me the opportunity to repair that crack. Maybe even fix it to the point it would be unbreakable.

But I wasn't foolish enough to think it would happen tonight.

Or tomorrow.

Or even next week.

It would take time and patience. It also might hurt along the way.

Someone else might not think the battle would be worth it.

I did.

I could only hope Ronan would, too.

If he allowed it, tonight could be the start of that battle. The beginning of that war.

I was ready and had donned my armor in preparation. No matter what, I would not lie down and accept defeat easily. "I want us to sit and talk, Roe."

He tilted his head to the side with the corners of his mouth tipped down. "And what good would that do, *Harris?*"

I inhaled a calming breath and whispered, "Don't call me that."

"It's the name you're using on your *fuck-me* profile. You messaged me on Grindr and I planned on treating you like a Grindr date."

I was going to do my best not to argue with him. I continued as if he hadn't baited me. "I think talking will do a lot of good. Not only for me, but for you and if you say otherwise, you'd be lying." I visualized my spine becoming wrapped in steel. "I'm getting off my knees now and I'm going to sit in that lounge chair," I jerked my chin toward the one to my left, "and you're going to sit in that one and—"

"That's not what I came up here for."

"I know." I slowly rose to my feet, wincing slightly at the ache in my knees. I grabbed The Macallan I had set on the ground next to me and held it out to him. "I also brought this back for you. You left it behind the other night."

He stared at it. "You can keep it."

"I don't want it. It's yours."

His nostrils flared as he snagged it from my fingers. "You were mine, too. Remember?"

Only too well.

"Roe, please… Just… sit. I'm only asking for a few minutes of your time. That's it. I need you to hear me out. In exchange, I'm willing to listen to whatever you have to say to me. Good or bad."

"I already heard it all. Not only that, I heard it on repeat over and over in here." He tapped the side of his temple.

I waved my hand at the lounger next to mine. "Sit. Please."

He dropped his head and stared at his feet.

He was barefoot, which surprised me. He only wore a pair of

well-fitting jeans and a snug Linkin Park T-shirt. It was probably tight because I remembered him wearing it in college and his chest and arms were so much bigger now.

I continued to stare at him, drinking him in. Eventually he sighed and sat, but his expression made it very clear he wasn't happy about this change in plans. He probably had come up hoping I'd let him use my mouth for his pleasure again.

I wasn't against it, but only if we got to talk beforehand. I wanted something from him first, if he wanted something from me.

We didn't recline on the loungers, instead we sat along the sides, facing each other with maybe three feet separating us.

Close but still so far apart.

I hoped to close that distance. And not just physically.

"Talk, then. I don't have all night."

"Are you going to actually listen?" I asked. "Or discount everything I say? You're probably doing that right now before I get a chance to speak."

"Do you blame me?" His face twisted slightly before he quickly smoothed it out. "You broke my heart, T."

"You don't think mine broke, too?" My words were thick with regret and sadness. He needed to understand I hurt back then as much as he had. I still did. Unlike him, I wasn't going to hide it.

"You fucking *crushed* me."

I closed my eyes for a second because, while I had regret in my voice, his was full of pure torment. And him hurting like that hurt me, too. Since I caused that agony, I wish I could simply erase it. "For what it's worth, I'm sorry. I can't take any of it back. No matter how much I wish I could. I wish I had the knowledge back then of what I do now. But then, I'm sure most people wished the same. No matter what, we can't go back. We can only move forward. Or move on."

"I moved on, Tate. You left me no damn choice."

"Again, I'm sorry, Roe. It was the biggest mistake of my life. The only bright spot in all of it are my children. Without Dahlia, I wouldn't have them."

A sound caught at the back of his throat. His eyes became as sharp as knives. "You could've had children with me. I never said that was off the table. I never told you once I didn't want kids."

"The problem was, I didn't know what *I* wanted, Roe. My head was fucked up because I'd never been in a relationship with a man before. As you know, I definitely had never been intimate with one. Sex aside, I'd never been in love with one, either. I was confused. Spooked. Unsure of my choices. One minute, I thought I knew and in the next I questioned everything. I was also pretty damn sure my family wasn't going to handle it well... I... The truth is, all of my insecurities back then made me feel overwhelmed. Like I was drowning."

"You hid all of that from me."

"Not all." I did hide a lot of it, hoping it would work itself out. Even though I tried to be as open with him as I could, it hadn't been enough.

Again, my fault, not his.

"Most of it," he corrected. "But despite all that, what you did..." He shook his head. "What you did in the end was unforgivable."

"I know. I made it worse by telling myself it was only sex between us. Exploration. Two boys figuring things out in a safe place."

"Boys? Hardly. Only sex?" He shook his head again. "No, it wasn't. You can try to convince yourself of that now to help make swallowing the guilt a little easier, but that's a lie that you don't even believe, Tate. You know it and I know it. We were together two fucking years. Or I thought we were. Now that I look back, I question that."

"We were."

"Then, tell me... How did Dahlia get pregnant, Tate?"

"I explained what happened."

"Yeah," he huffed. "You explained all right. Explaining doesn't change the fact of what you did. You fucked us both, Tate. Both me and Dahlia. And I'm not talking about sex."

I opened my mouth to apologize for the hundredth time, but I stopped myself. I've told both Roe and Dahlia how sorry I was more times than I could count. Sorry didn't cut it. Action would.

That was why I was sitting across from Ronan and facing my past. Facing *our* past.

If nothing more, I hoped to at least cleanse away the bitterness he held for me. The bitterness I held for myself. And help us both heal.

"At the time, I tried to convince myself I was doing the right thing. Even though deep down, I knew," I blew out a breath, trying to relieve the massive knot in my chest, "I *knew* it wasn't. But I felt like I was on a path I had no control over, a path I didn't know how to step off. My mistake was taking the path of least resistance."

"You could've been there for Dahlia without leaving me."

"I could've but I already had been selfish enough. I was trying to fix that."

"And here you are, trying to fix things now."

"Yes. I don't want you to hate me."

He scraped his fingers over his short, dark hair. "Too late for that, Tate. That ship sailed a long fucking time ago."

"I also want to stop hating myself. It's not good for my children."

He stared at me. "Speaking of children. Where's your other kid?"

Shit. I couldn't avoid this, either. As much as I wanted to.

"The older one," he continued as I scrambled to compose my answer so I wouldn't completely shut down. "Wouldn't he or she be about twelve now?"

"Eleven."

"Was it a boy or girl?"

"A boy."

A heaviness suddenly filled the air between us enough to compress my chest, making it feel as if I was being held underwater before getting a chance to take a big breath of air first.

Maybe this had been a bad idea. I should've just let this be. We could've simply ignored each other and gone on about our lives.

I was beginning to worry that I'd messed up again.

But then, that was nothing new.

CHAPTER 11

Tate (Now)

"So, what happened to that kid? The excuse you used for marrying Dahlia because she got pregnant *after* you broke up with her? Neither of those kids I saw you with were close to being eleven, Tate. Was the reason you used to leave me a lie, too?"

This was the last place I thought tonight's conversation would go. I figured in the future what happened would need to be discussed but not tonight. I expected anything but this. "It wasn't a lie."

"Then?"

I struggled to take my next breath. "The baby was still-born."

He drilled his elbows into his thighs and leaned forward, closing the gap between us slightly. "What?"

Of course he hadn't heard me. The words I spoke were both silent and deafening at the same time.

I cleared the rough from my throat and tried again. "He was still-born."

I rarely talked about it because it still tore me apart like it happened yesterday. It was a day I'd never forget.

I pressed my thumbs into my eye sockets to ease the sting.

"Tate…"

I shook my head and lifted a hand so he could give me the moment I needed. To gather myself. Because if I didn't, I'd shatter and I wouldn't be able to continue.

While it was an important discussion, I didn't want to derail the whole reason I wanted to meet Ronan on the roof.

Surprisingly, he remained quiet and waited, but I was afraid to look at him. I didn't want to see any pity in his eyes.

Or maybe I was afraid I wouldn't see any empathy at all. I feared I would discover that Ronan Pak was heartless and cold and I never really knew him.

Instead, I slipped my fingers around the black chain I always wore and pulled the pendant from where it was hidden under my shirt. I pressed the black pendant between my fingertips and held it tightly for a few more seconds before lifting it between us.

"This is my son…" I risked a glance at Ronan.

His brow furrowed as he stared at what I held. "I don't understand."

I flipped the circle of life symbol over, set it on the center of my palm and stretched my hand out as far as the long chain allowed. "We named him Connor."

Ronan lifted the round pendant from my palm and leaned forward to read Connor's name and the date of his birth I had engraved on the back. The writing was small but no one really needed to see it but me.

And now Ronan.

"It's actually an urn that's filled with some of my son's ashes. I never remove it."

His dark eyes flicked from the pendant in his fingers to my face. "Never?"

"I've never had a reason to. Not yet. I wear it so he's always with me."

Ronan rubbed the pad of his thumb back and forth over the tiny engraved letters and numbers as he stared at it. His face not giving away anything.

But watching that gesture…

I was just glad I was already sitting because I might have fallen to my knees.

When he was done, instead of simply releasing the pendant and letting it fall back to my chest, he stretched forward and placed it back where it belonged. Near my heart.

I wanted to touch him when he was that close, but I refrained and waited for him to sit back and get settled again.

The pendant was still warm from his touch when I picked it up and dropped it back under my shirt. Then his lingering warmth touched the skin of my chest.

"I'm sorry for your loss, Tate. I am. It had to be devastating and I'm not sure if anyone can fully recover from that kind of loss, but…" He paused as if he was carefully considering his next words. "You asked me to come up here tonight to hash things out, right?"

That was true. "Yes, I was hoping to."

"Then I'm going to be brutally honest. Even after what you just told me."

"That's all I want."

He nodded. "I'm going to give you what you want. Brutal honesty."

I struggled to swallow.

Ronan had been out of my life for twelve years. I didn't know what happened to him between then and now, so I wasn't sure how brutal he could get. But, again, I was willing to do whatever needed to be done.

Even if it meant him slicing me open.

I mentally prepared myself by taking a long, deep inhale, planting both hands on my thighs and making sure my feet were flat on the ground. I nodded, signaling that I was ready.

"If you only married her because she *accidentally* got pregnant... I understand staying for a while after a loss that great, but... And this is where it doesn't make sense to me... After supporting and helping each other grieve, you *stayed*. You stayed long enough to have two more children. *Two*, Tate. Two who I assumed were planned. I could be wrong but I bet I'm not."

"I know you can't understand it, Roe—"

"You're right, I don't."

"Tell me how I could have left after that? We were both devastated. It was a huge loss that crushed us both. What made it worse was that she carried our baby to full term. Only to... Only to..."

"Again, if I look past the reason you married her, the reason you stayed after the loss of your son, that's where I have a hard time wrapping my head around it."

"Guilt. Expectations. The list is endless, Roe. Why does anyone stay? Did I love her? Yes. Did I love you? Of course. Did I love her more than you? No. But I made a vow to her and I really wanted to keep it. Truthfully, it wasn't just my guilt that made me stay, it was the fact I wasn't convinced I was strictly gay. I convinced myself I could live a straight life and be happy. I was wrong." I tried to live my life in accordance to the expectations of the people around me. My family. Dahlia and her family. My job.

When I was desperate to do right, I ended up doing more wrong.

"Yes, you were wrong because in the end, you didn't keep your vows, did you?"

That blade he wielded was sharp and sliced right through me. "You're right. I didn't keep my vows."

"Vows you shouldn't have made in the first place. Yes, I'm being harsh. And I'm not going to apologize for it... Because, Tate—again, keeping with being brutally honest—for years, I suspected her pregnancy wasn't an accident back then, either. That made it even worse for me."

The blood drained from my face. Of course, I knew the truth. But

I never held it against Dahlia, even though I should have. However, no matter if she trapped me or not, the baby she'd been carrying inside her was mine. I was responsible for it. And in turn, felt responsible for her.

"I didn't plan it."

"Not you."

I stared at him and after a few seconds nodded. "Unfortunately, your suspicion is correct."

"You didn't have to marry her, Tate."

"At the time, I did what I thought was right, Roe."

"Right for who?"

"For me, Dahlia and the baby."

Roe nodded and whispered, "Yeah."

That soft *yeah* might as well had been a direct punch to the chest.

He felt discarded. My decision to do the "right thing" turned out to be wrong. I hurt him badly. I understood that.

I had broken up with Dahlia to be with him. Then I turned around not even two years later and broke up with him to go back with Dahlia.

I gave us both whiplash.

But I never stopped loving him.

Never.

And I wanted to show him that now. To make up for what I did to him. He didn't deserve any of it.

"You loved Dahlia enough to marry her. Have more children with her. Willingly, Tate. Not because you were tricked the second and third time she got pregnant."

"You're right."

"Of course I am. So, you should be able to understand that makes it even worse for me. After you grieved the loss of your son, after you began to heal, you didn't come looking for me. You stayed right where you were. Why? Because it was easier. Having a wife, fitting in with your family's expectations and society's standards were damn well easier than being gay and having a husband, wasn't it?" He lifted a hand. "You don't have to answer that. I already know the answer. Do you know why? Because once I turned eighteen, I decided I wasn't going to let anyone stop me from being who I am. I was true to myself. You were not. Here's the kicker… I would've been there for you. I would've helped you. Would it have been easy? No. Is it easy now? No. But you know what?"

He surged to his feet and I quickly followed.

"At least I'm not lying to myself or anyone else." His voice broke when he said, "I loved you. You can't say you didn't know because I told you those words so many times. But for me, they weren't only words, I meant them. You said those three words back to me countless times and I believed them, Tate. I fucking *believed* them. I thought we'd be together forever. I was wrong for believing that and I was wrong for believing in you." He shook his head and walked away, his long stride quickly taking him away from me and the conversation I wanted to continue.

This conversation wasn't over. It couldn't be. Not yet.

"I did, Roe. I still do," I shouted to his retreating back. "I'm willing to do whatever I need to. Just tell me what that is!"

He suddenly spun on his heels and took two steps back in my direction with his face a mask of rage. With his hands curled into fists and his shoulders rigidly drawn back. "Answer me this, Tate. Would you have searched for me if you hadn't accidentally moved into my building? Would you have looked for me to fix things between us if the opportunity hadn't fallen into your lap?"

I wasn't going to lie to him. Not ever again. So, I gave him the truth now, even if it hurt my chances to fix us in the future. I swallowed to try to relieve the tightness in my throat. "I don't know. Maybe not. I honestly didn't think you'd ever want to see me again."

"And you would've been right." With a stiff nod, he turned and strode back to that side entrance.

I rushed after him. I needed to stop him. I didn't care if he punched me. At that moment, I didn't even care if he threw me off the roof or drowned me in the pool.

The only thing I cared about was the man trying to escape.

"I also thought I was protecting you by staying away!"

From over his shoulder, he sneered, "Protecting *me*? Or yourself?"

"I realize now by staying away I did the exact opposite. That I hurt you even more."

I made it to him just as he pulled his cell phone out of his back pocket and waved it in front of the card reader next to the door. I reached past him and slammed my hand against the door to prevent him from opening it and disappearing.

I took the easy route too many times in the past. Now I needed to take the challenging one. The one that would hurt.

"The truth is, Roe... I was also scared. I was scared to learn that you might've found someone else to love as much as, or even more than, you loved me. That you could find happiness with someone else other than me. Even though you deserved every fucking bit of that love and happiness. So, yes... Maybe I was protecting myself, too."

He froze as I molded myself against his back, the heat of our bodies blending, and put my mouth to his ear. "Roe, I'm willing to do whatever you want. I'm willing to fight for forgiveness. To fight for *us*."

Neither of us moved for a heartbeat. Then two.

Ronan gradually turned to face me. I had him blocked in with my body and my arm braced against the door. Even though we were similar in height, he was much more powerful than I was and he could easily push me out of his way. Or knock me down.

With excruciating slowness, he tipped his head and put his mouth to my ear. "I'm... not."

His warm breath across my ear made me shudder and a soft hiss slide from between my lips. I did not hide any of that from him. I wanted him to know how much he still affected me. How much I still wanted him.

And, eventually, I hoped he would realize how much I still loved him.

But my reaction was not because of what he said. It was the fact he was lying. I saw it in his eyes as he struggled to hide it. His erection began to grow between our pinned bodies. He also had to feel mine caused from us being pressed together. From inhaling his scent. From our lips being only inches apart.

His lip pulled up as he snarled, "Fuck. You."

It was in that moment I was done.

I was done letting him control the narrative. Letting him continue to treat me like he was.

And for being so damn stubborn.

I found my self-respect. My strength. My courage. And donned it like a cloak.

Yes, I was willing to fight and I was about to show him how hard I'd battle for *us*.

Using my chest, I bumped him backwards until he was sandwiched tightly between me and the door.

I reached up, grabbed his face and crushed my mouth against his.

I did not beg. I didn't even ask.

I took what I wanted.

I saw what had been behind his eyes and I was going to prove that I knew he was lying.

Yes, he was still pissed at me, but deep down... He also still loved me.

I *saw* it.

I also saw how him still loving me made him furious, too. But that gave me the slightest hope that he'd be able to get past that anger. And once he did, I'd be waiting for him on the other side of it.

While at first he didn't fight the kiss, he also didn't participate.

I was not giving up that easily this time.

I moved my lips against his, brushed my tongue across his. Continued to explore his mouth, a groan slipping from me and getting caught between us.

Our erections now raged and I moved my hips the slightest bit so they brushed. A reminder of what we used to have. What we could have once more.

I did it again and again, getting bolder each time.

Until finally…

Finally…

He broke. With a growl, he shoved my tongue out of his mouth and plundered mine instead. If he wanted to lead this dance, I'd let him. For now.

But the second he stopped cooperating, I'd take it back.

As our tongues tangled and our lips moved, I reached between us for the button on his jeans. Lightning quick, he clamped a hand around my wrist in a tight, painful hold, stopping me.

I pulled back, breaking our kiss.

His eyes were closed, his lips parted slightly. His panting as rapid as mine.

I waited, hoping I didn't just screw everything up by pushing him too far too quickly.

When he finally opened his eyes, his pupils were dilated as he stared at me.

Anger was no longer in those dark brown eyes, anguish had replaced it.

Maybe even a touch of fear.

"I can't do this again," came out on a broken whisper. With that, he slammed his palms against my chest, shoving me back a step. I hadn't been prepared for it.

While I caught my balance, that gave him just enough time to spin around, unlock the door again with his phone and disappear behind it before I could stop him.

The door slamming shut echoed across the roof like a gunshot.

But I wasn't giving up. Not now.

I now had hope and I'd cling to it until I could no longer hold on. Until it no longer existed.

I yanked on the door handle. "Roe!"

Of course, it was locked.

I pulled my keycard from my own back pocket and swiped it. The light flashed red.

Fuck.

This wasn't over. Not even close.

No, this was only the beginning.

A start of our second chance.

I was sure of it.

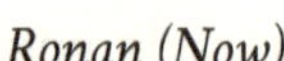

Ronan (Now)

I SLAMMED my back against the door and slid down until my ass hit the floor. I folded my arms across my knees and dropped my head into them.

I couldn't stop trembling.

I couldn't catch my breath.

Squeezing my eyes shut did nothing to stop the burn. Or to stop a few hot tears from sliding down my cheeks.

I was stronger than this.

I was.

But Tate had swung a freshly sharpened sword and cut me off right at the knees.

The pounding on the steel door could be felt against my back.

My name being yelled still managed to slip through.

I stopped myself from covering my ears.

But I couldn't move to escape.

I couldn't descend the spiral steps back to my empty penthouse.

Not yet.

Where I sat was in the middle. Between the past behind me and the future ahead of me.

I needed to decide whether to go down the steps or go back out to the roof.

I did neither.

I remained paralyzed where I was.

Eventually my name faded away and the pounding stopped. But when it did, I was both relieved and disappointed.

Empty and lonely.

Angry and scared.

Worried I'd forgive him too easily. Worried I might never forgive him and I would let this eat at me for the rest of my life.

Tate wanted to fight for us.

He wanted me to give us a second shot.

He wanted to take us back to a time when things were different.

When I had hope.

When I had dreams.

Of a future.

Of a family.

Of a forever.

He was trying to give me hope that I could still have all of that.

That this time everything would work out.

But the fear of allowing that and then losing him all over again swallowed me whole. I couldn't risk it.

I lost a piece of myself when I lost him the first time. A piece he had only been capable of filling. But a piece he hadn't been willing to give me in the end.

When I think back, maybe it was something he'd never been willing to give me.

Maybe neither of us knew it at the time. Or we ignored the obvious signs. And what happened with Dahlia was the perfect excuse for him to walk away.

I needed to remember what he did. What he was capable of. How much he could hurt me, even when he insisted he didn't intend to.

I needed to protect myself by steel-coating my heart and guarding my feelings.

Being cautious.

Not easily breaking to forgive him for something I always considered unforgivable.

I could pretend he was someone else that night I came all over his face.

I could pretend he was someone else the night I fucked his mouth.

But tonight, when he had pressed against me, when he had kissed me, I could no longer pretend.

CHAPTER 12

Ronan (Then)

"YOU NEED TO TELL HER, T. It's not fair to her." It wasn't fair to me, either. It was like he was only keeping Dahlia in his pocket for "just in case."

Or he was keeping me in his pocket. Just in case.

I shouldn't be number two in his life. Neither should Dahlia. Even though she had never warmed up to me, that didn't mean I wanted her to be hurt.

But if he was going to be with me, he needed to let her go. Or be with her and let me go. He needed to stop straddling that fence. Or I'd have to push him off it myself.

"I will."

I bit back a frustrated sigh. "When?" It had been over a month since that night in his bed after the party. I'd generously given him over four weeks to choose.

"As soon as I figure out what to say. I want to break it to her easy, Roe. We've never fought. There's never been tension between us. She's not going to understand why I'm breaking things off with her out of the blue. Especially when we've discussed a future together."

I stopped walking. We were headed back to my dorm room after our run. Fall was in full swing now, with the leaves dropping and the cooler air swirling around us.

The other day it had even flurried and it wasn't even Thanksgiving yet. That was another discussion I wanted to have with Tate. Thanksgiving and Christmas breaks.

From what Tate had mentioned, Dahlia had planned on going home with Tate for Thanksgiving next week and then he planned on going to Dahlia's parents for Christmas and New Year's. That meant he had to break up with her soon.

"How about telling her the truth?" I asked him.

He got quiet.

I didn't like that quiet. It worried me.

It also pissed me off.

I hadn't pushed him hard before now because I recognized the fact he was still very confused and I'd been trying to be patient. Things between us were still very new as well as him discovering he was attracted to men.

Or at least one man. Me.

While I would still try to be understanding, I was done with being patient.

Since he had stopped beside me on the wide sidewalk, I stepped in front of him so I could face him. This was a serious conversation and we probably shouldn't be having it where we were.

I should have waited until we were in the privacy of my room since Dom was off visiting his girlfriend until tomorrow, but it had been bugging me. Plus, I was worried that if I got him up to my room and we got naked, I'd let it go once more.

I couldn't. Not any longer.

The problem was, all I thought about while we ran side by side through the streets and pathways in and around campus was how Tate hadn't done it yet.

And why.

Tate's gaze swept the immediate area to make sure no one would overhear us. An obvious sign before he even opened his mouth that he didn't want anyone to know what was going on between us, that we had slipped from friends to lovers.

"Can we just keep this between us for now and let me ease into it? I'm not ready to take any slack from my family or my roommates. Even our classmates. It's not new to you but it's new to me and I'm not ready to come out and be labeled yet. I'm not even sure what that label should be, Roe. I want to make sure I have things figured out before I come out, if that's even what I need to do. I've never been attracted to other guys before. And if I have, I hadn't given it much thought."

And there it was, the most worrying part: *If that's even what I need to do.* That meant he was thinking about possibly denying who he was. Because I knew who he was whether he denied it or not.

Men had been known to renounce their true selves their whole lives, even go as far as marrying a woman and having children to convince themselves *that* was who they were, and then they ended up living a miserable life full of pretending.

Some even ended up going so far as committing suicide because of it. They couldn't come out of the closet and they also couldn't stay locked inside. They relieved their agony in the only way they knew how.

I knew who I was for years. But in the beginning, I questioned my thoughts and feelings, too. I was also wary to come out at first. I knew it was a risk because once I stepped out of that closet, it would be hard, if not impossible, to step back in. I had to be either in or out. Stepping one foot out while keeping one foot in just wasn't realistic.

Right now, that was what Tate was doing. He had one toe in my world and a whole foot in the other.

But if he didn't plant both his feet on one side or the other, or even one foot solidly on both sides if he was bisexual, he'd eventually lose his balance.

While I understood where he was coming from by being cautious, I also didn't like it because that meant we couldn't be "out" together as a couple. We had to hide behind closed doors. We had to hook fingers under desks. We had to pretend we were studying when what we were actually studying wasn't in our textbook.

I also understood we all had to travel our own path of discovery, in our own way and time, and I wasn't going to force him to do anything he wasn't comfortable with.

However, him not telling the truth to Dahlia was the biggest issue I had with all of this. What was between us, while maybe it had started out as experimenting for him, was now long past that. The sex had gotten more serious. Our bond had also grown a lot stronger. We were now inseparable.

Tate and I spent more time together than he did with Dahlia.

"Tate, I'm okay with giving you that time, but I'm not okay with you stringing Dahlia along. And that's where I'm taking a stand. We're not having sex again until I know you've broken it off with her. And if you don't want to do that, then *we* need to break it off."

One of my worries, something I thought about too often, was that if he could lie to Dahlia, he could lie to me just as easily. That concern was why I was no longer going to sit back and let him do it.

If he wanted to keep his sexuality from everyone else for now, fine. But at the minimum, he needed to stop stringing Dahlia along, letting her think that everything was okay between them.

It wasn't.

I had to dig deep to give him my ultimatum. "So, instead of you coming back to my room, you need to go back to your place and figure out what you're going to tell her and break it off with her tonight. If you don't want to do that, let me know now."

I held my breath as I waited for his response.

"Roe..."

I blew out my held breath and shook my head. I couldn't take any more indecision from him. "I can't let this continue the way it is. As much as I want to be with you, I can't until you decide who you want to be with. If it's not me, I'll understand. But I don't want to get any more invested than I already am, Tate. The deeper this gets, the harder it'll be if you decide you don't want to be with me and want to be with a woman instead. Whether that's Dahlia or not."

I opened my mouth to tell him I loved him, but I hadn't told him that yet and I didn't want that to weigh heavily on his decision. He needed to decide what he truly wanted and not let what I desperately wanted to influence him.

So, I kept that to myself.

The only hope I held onto right now was that all signs were pointing to him falling in love with me, too. Of course, he hadn't said those words, either.

Instead of revealing how much he meant to me, I whispered, "If you're not going to do this for you or Dahlia, please do this for me. I can't let this keep going on the way it has. I either want all of you or none of you, Tate."

He nodded, his expression not giving me much of anything. "I'll tell her at dinner."

I took that as a sign he would finally break up with her after all the times he assured me he would. But until it happened, I wasn't holding my breath.

We stared at each other for a few quiet moments, both fully aware that we stood in the middle of campus. I wanted to reach out but I knew if I did, it would be obvious that we were more than friends.

Instead, I curled my fingers tightly into my palms and watched him as he turned and walked away. I clenched my jaw so I wouldn't call out to him to tell him to forget everything I just demanded.

I didn't. But I did stand there until he disappeared from my sight.

And with every step he took, I had to fight even harder to stop him.

~

Ronan (Then)

I CHEWED on the pen cap as I sat staring at my notebook. I was supposed to be reading two chapters in my Business Law textbook. A required class if I ended up picking Entrepreneurship as my major.

It was my first choice since Duquesne had a great business school and programs, but like Tate trying to figure out his sexuality, I was still undecided.

However, I had time. Tate did not.

I glanced down at the spiral notebook empty of any notes. Instead, the page was full of doodles. Not even good ones. Mindless squiggles and shapes filled the lined paper.

I spit out the decimated cap, sighed and threw my pen down before I used up all the ink doing nothing productive.

When a pounding began at my dorm room door, I jumped out of my seat. Like normal, I had locked it to get some studying done. I failed, of course, because I couldn't keep my mind off Tate and the conversation he might have had with Dahlia earlier at dinner.

It had to be him at the door. Especially after I got a text from him a couple of hours ago telling me, *It's done. Will call you later.*

I had been relieved, excited and worried all at the same time. I was also anxious about what had been said and how it had been received.

I hadn't lied to Tate about not wanting to hurt Dahlia. She was an unfortunate participant in this whole thing.

But the guilt every time Tate and I had sex... It had eaten at me. I had been selfish with someone already taken.

I wouldn't want it done to me. I didn't want it done to anyone else.

I hoped with him finally letting Dahlia go meant that our relationship could progress the way it was meant to be.

He might not be ready to go public with it and I was okay with that.

For now.

I could wait until he was more comfortable.

With a huge smile on my face, I unlocked the door and swung it open.

Then swallowed the words I was about to say.

It wasn't Tate on the other side of the door.

It was Dahlia.

Shit.

My heart began to thump even faster in my chest. And I was frozen where I stood. At least until Dahlia shoved me with all her strength, making me stumble backwards into my room.

She followed me and slammed the door shut.

Shit.

If anything, I expected her to have a red-tipped nose and bloodshot eyes from crying, not be wearing a mask of rage. I scanned her hands to make sure she didn't have a weapon.

"Dahlia—"

"I didn't waste over a year of my life being dedicated to Tate to lose everything I'd been working toward to *you*, Roe. Not to you. Tate isn't gay and you've done nothing but confuse him and twist him inside out and upside down. He's mine. So, back the fuck off," she snarled with her expression twisted.

I stared at her. Everything she'd been working toward? What the hell did that mean? I'd heard rumors that some girls went to college hoping to land a husband, but was that actually true? Did that really happen in this day and age?

"You stole him from me. He's mine and I want him back." When she took a step toward me, I took a step back. "He's." *Step.* "Mine." *Step.* "So." *Step.* "Back." *Step.* "Off."

As she approached, I retreated until I backed into my desk chair.

Had she lost her damn mind? What happened between her and Tate?

I swallowed to try to loosen up my throat. "My goal wasn't to steal him from you, Dahlia. That was never my intention. My goal was for him to be my friend. Things just... happened. It wasn't planned."

"You are such a liar. I saw the way you looked at him. I *see* the way you still look at him. Friends don't look at each other like that, Ronan. *You* led him into temptation. *You* corrupted his soul. You've stolen his will to say no to you."

I had no idea I was that powerful or convincing. In my head, I was just a nineteen-year-old college kid who happened to fall in love with a junior.

I didn't come to Duquesne to find a husband, I came to get an education. Unlike the woman fuming in front of me, apparently.

"Just to be clear, Dahlia, we can't convert straight guys. No magical rainbow glitter exists that I can sprinkle on a man to turn him gay. If he wants me, it's because he's always had those tendencies and just ignored them. Or didn't recognize them for what they were," I shook my head, "*are*. Nothing will make him desire another man without him wanting that for himself. It seems I'm proof that he does."

She jabbed a finger in my direction, coming uncomfortably close to my chest. "Give him back to me. I want to spend the rest of my life with him. You can't say the same."

I *could* say the same but wouldn't since Tate and I hadn't known each other that long.

No matter what, I didn't want to fight with her, but I was getting annoyed at her viewpoint. "Tate's not an object in a store, Dahlia. I can't simply give him back like I'm returning an item. He has emotions and desires. He needs to *want* to go back to you. If that's what he wants, nothing I can say or do will stop that. But if he doesn't, nothing that you can say or do will make it happen, either."

She glared at me with her lips tightly pressed together for a few seconds before she sneered, "We'll see about that."

Shit. The determination in her brown eyes worried me. "You're right. We will. But just remember, you can't change who he is. If he's gay, or even bi, you'll have to accept it because *that* is who he is, Dahlia. Whether you like it or not."

She leaned forward and screamed, "He's not gay!" in my face. "He only pretends to be gay for you! This is all your fault. *Yours*, Roe. You infected him."

You infected him.

That stung. Way more than it should even though I knew she was only striking out because she was upset and hurt.

As calmly as I could, I said, "I'm not a disease."

"You are," she snarled, spun on her heels and jerked open the door.

With my stomach twisting in knots, I continued to stare at it after she slammed it shut. I had no idea what Tate had said to her or how he handled the whole situation, but I needed to find out.

I had a really bad feeling about this. Really bad.

Dahlia wasn't done with Tate.

Even if he was done with her.

CHAPTER 13

Ronan (Now)

I STABBED the button for the ground floor and once the elevator doors closed, the car jerked into motion.

I was mentally drained because my brain kept dragging me back to the past, almost making it impossible to concentrate on what I had to do today or what I had to plan for the upcoming week.

I always had some sort of deal on the table but I was struggling with my latest. I decided to go into the office this morning to see if a change of location would help cleanse my brain. Being holed up in my penthouse was unhealthy.

I already decided that when I got home later, I'd go for a long run to help clear away the cobweb of memories clinging to me. I'd considered swimming some laps after the posted pool hours but I was afraid I'd run into Tate.

Like a zombie, I stared sightlessly at my feet and listened to the dinging as each floor passed, hoping it wouldn't stop along the way.

I had slept like shit because the silent nights seemed to drag out even more memories. Like the memory about the night not long after winter break my freshman year. The night I'd never forget when Tate and I first said we loved each other. I still saw it crystal clear in my mind like it happened only yesterday.

We'd been lying in my dorm room bed since Dominic was now staying with his girlfriend practically every weekend. And when he did, Tate had gotten into a habit of staying with me from Friday night until Sunday night or even early Monday morning.

Even though he wanted to keep our relationship a secret, it certainly wasn't. Him staying in my room so often pretty much guaranteed everyone in my residence hall knew. Plus, Dahlia didn't hesitate to tell others why her and Tate broke up.

In fact, she made a point to bad mouth me as much as she could. Of course, that got back to me several times. Whether it got back to Tate, he didn't say and I didn't ask. I figured it was better to try to be the better person and ignore it. In exchange, I didn't say a bad word about her. Not once.

Tate and I had both been in the wrong for starting a relationship —even if it had only been sexual "exploration"—before Dahlia and Tate's ended.

I didn't blame her for being angry. I would be the same. But I figured she'd eventually have to let go and move on. I only hoped it would be sooner than later before it caused any major issues.

That particular night, when Tate weaved his fingers through mine under the covers and whispered, "Roe?" I *hmm*'d sleepily.

I was spent, satisfied and feeling lazy after what we'd just done...

Which was each other.

"I think..." His words drifted away. When he spoke again, he still sounded tentative and his fingers twitched within mine. "I think I'm in love with you."

My eyes sprung open at the tumble of words and I turned my head on the pillow to stare into the endless depths of his bright blue eyes. They sucked me in every damn time. "You think?" I sort of teased, even though I was thrilled at that unexpected admission.

I wanted to tell him it was cute the way he said it, but clearly he was still unsure about everything in his life right now. Especially about being open with both his sexuality and our relationship. I hadn't pushed him but was trying my best to be patient.

I studied his profile since he wasn't looking at me, but had turned to stare up at the ceiling instead. When he finally turned his face back toward mine, we locked gazes.

"No, I don't think, I know." He inhaled deeply and on his exhale, stated, "I'm in love with you."

His words warmed me from head to toe and made my heart expand in my chest. The fact that he stared me right in the eyes when he said them the second time with confidence...

It was what I'd been hoping for. Waiting for.

That time was finally here.

It was now.

Tate loved me.

And not in the way friends did. It was way beyond that.

I grinned. "About time you caught up."

His eyebrows rose and his eyes widened a bit, showing off those breathtaking blue orbs. "Wait... You love me?"

Why did he sound so surprised? I might not have said the actual words before but I certainly didn't hide how I felt about him when we were alone. And actions were so much more "real" than words.

Words could be empty and meaningless.

I cupped his jaw and swept my thumb over his bottom lip. The man had some skills with his mouth, but this moment was far from about sex.

I confessed, "For a while now. I'm not sure of the exact moment when I fell in love with you but I realized I was already in deep that day we took the spin class and then spent two hours talking under that tree. That was when I really *knew* and there was no question."

"That was like... toward the beginning." His forehead scrunched up and he lifted his head slightly. "You didn't say anything."

I shot him a look and jerked my shoulders slightly.

He read that unspoken message, nodded and then settled his head back on the pillow with our faces only a few inches apart. "You didn't think I'd handle it well."

"It wasn't about handling it. First and foremost, I didn't want to screw up our friendship. I valued it too much. I also didn't want to make things uncomfortable between us. Plus…" I gave him another easily readable look.

"Dahlia."

"Yeah."

I hadn't wanted to bring her up while we were lying in bed after just having some awesome sex. He was much more confident in that department now, too. That stemmed from me letting him do whatever he wanted to me to build that confidence. And we'd tried just about everything. Except for him bottoming for me. I hoped one day he would.

When I thought he was more comfortable, I'd approach that subject.

We lay there quietly for a while longer, letting the fact sink in that we both loved each other and that love wrapped a sort of cloak around us both.

At the time, I was stupid enough to assume our love would protect us. Of course, also at the time I didn't know how wrong that would be.

"I've been thinking…" he started.

"Haven't we both?"

He ignored my ribbing and finished, "About this summer."

"What about it?" Truthfully, I wasn't looking forward to us being apart. I certainly couldn't go home with Tate since his parents still had no idea about him or us. I also didn't know how they'd take it once they did. He'd already broken the news to them about Dahlia, but didn't tell them why he broke it off. They'd been extremely disappointed since they thought she'd been a perfect match for him. Tate also hoped Dahlia wouldn't tell them out of spite before he was ready.

Personally, after what she spewed in my dorm room the night

Tate broke up with her, I wouldn't put it past her to make trouble with them. He had a lot more faith in her than I did. But then, he had loved her and I didn't.

But as much as I loved him, I wasn't sure I could live with spending months away from each other. Maybe he felt the same way and that was why he was bringing up our summer break.

I had no firm plans whether to stay in Pittsburgh or head home. I needed to either find a better job or continue to work at the Power Center, *if* I stayed and was allowed to remain living on campus. I wasn't sure yet if I could since I wasn't enrolled in summer courses.

However, staying on campus would be cheaper than trying to rent an apartment on my own. I had planned on looking into it until Tate released my hand and rolled onto his side to face me.

"I applied for a summer internship at KDKA."

I blinked and let that sink in since KDKA was a local television station and not in his home state of Virginia.

"And if you get it?" I asked, rolling to my side, too, so it was easier to read his face.

He smiled. "I already got it."

I didn't smile back because he'd kept it a secret from me. "Why didn't you tell me?"

"I am."

"I meant tell me that you applied," I spelled out.

"Because I didn't know if I'd get it and I didn't want to disappoint you if I didn't."

"How would it have disappointed me?"

"Because I hoped…"

I raised one eyebrow as I waited for his explanation.

"I plan on getting my own place. Our current lease doesn't cover the summers, so I'm going to find another apartment near campus. Once I do, you can stay with me."

"For just the summer?"

"Until I graduate."

"Without Thom and Jack?"

He nodded. "With you instead."

My heart thumped. He wanted us to live together for both the upcoming summer and his senior year? Was I awake or was I dreaming?

While I was excited he wanted to take that step... "You know I'm required to live on campus my first two years, Tate." Reality quickly smothered any eagerness about living with the man I loved.

"Well... you *will* be officially living on campus during the school year. You just won't be spending a lot of time in your dorm." He winked.

My stomach sank. "T, you know I can't afford both room and board on campus, as well as half the rent and expenses of an apartment. I barely can afford my room and board. Without my scholarships and grants and—"

He pressed a finger to my lips to stop me. "I got it."

I jerked my head away. "You got what?"

"The rent. The expenses. You worry about your room and board and I'll worry about the rest."

Whoa. "Tate, no. It was bad enough you bought me a damn MacBook. This is way bigger than that. It's too much."

"I don't care."

"I do!" I shot up in bed and stared down at him. Anger was beginning to bubble to the surface and I didn't want us to have our first fight. "I'm not a charity case."

He sat up, too. "Of course you aren't."

"I don't want to feel like you need to support me."

"I don't want you to feel like that, either. I'm just... I just..." He frowned. "I want to spend our summer together. I don't want us going our separate ways. That's all. And with the internship I need to get another place anyway, so I figured..." He scraped a hand through his dark hair and I watched that unruly lock fall across his forehead. "Were you planning on going home this summer and staying with your mom?"

"If I have no other choice."

He shrugged. "Well, now you do."

I shook my head at what he was suggesting. "I can't let you pay for everything."

"Then just pay me what you can. I'll pick up the rest."

I rubbed at my forehead. I wanted to be with him but I hated being broke. "Tate…"

"Roe, don't say no. At least think about it first. We can stay in Pittsburgh this summer while I do my internship. You can look for a temporary full-time job somewhere and," he shrugged, "we can see how it goes…"

The doors sliding open after the elevator reached ground floor pulled me out of the past and back to the present.

I was relieved the car hadn't stopped on the sixth floor. It would've been my luck for Tate to get on the elevator with me when I was trying to avoid him.

I blinked and stared at Tate staring back at me.

Shit.

Before I could stop myself, my gaze raked him from head to foot like I was perusing a gourmet buffet.

He wore a crisp, well-fitted dark navy suit along with shined dress shoes. His beard appeared freshly trimmed and groomed, unlike the last time I saw him. But his hair didn't match his sharp attire. It was mussed like he'd been dragging his fingers through it.

His beautiful blue eyes—the ones I had stared into for countless hours—were marred by having dark half-moons under them.

I guessed I wasn't the only one who had lost some sleep.

Did I take pleasure in that? Maybe a little.

But then, with the memory that kept me company on the ride down from the penthouse, I was currently feeling pretty damn petty.

He waved his hand between the two elevators doors to keep them from closing. Of course, with me still standing inside the car like a dummy.

I mentally sighed and forced myself to step out.

Once I did, I held the doors for him since I assumed he was

heading up to his apartment. However, I was curious as to why he was coming in dressed like that instead of going the opposite direction and leaving for work.

Maybe he was working nights at some local news station.

Maybe it was best if I didn't care.

After the elevator dinged a couple of times at me for holding the door and Tate still stood there not moving, I pulled my hand away and let the doors close. The car would remain at lobby level unless a resident pushed the down button on their floor.

I tried to ignore how utterly fucking delicious he looked in his crisp suit that hugged his thighs and waist, and the jacket that made his chest and shoulders look even broader...

While me? I was headed into my office wearing a much beloved Pittsburgh Pirates T-shirt, worn black jeans with a few in-style, strategically placed rips and my favorite pair of broken-in, black Timberlands.

Very professional, of course.

Truth was, I wasn't out to impress anyone. I normally didn't deal directly with the public and my employees didn't care what I wore. I also didn't care what they wore. I trusted them all to make the right decision for the right situation when it came to their wardrobe.

If it was a day they could get away with dressing casual, they did. If it was a day they had a face-to-face meeting, they dressed for success. I did the same. If I had an important meeting with outsiders, I'd break out my dreaded dressy attire and play the part of the successful businessman and investor.

Unlike today, when I had dressed to try to simply make it through the day.

The growing silence between us became awkward, so I finally said, "All right, well..." Then I stared at him for a few more seconds before turning to head to where I parked my vehicles.

I jerked in surprise when his hand snaked out and snagged my forearm to stop me. "Roe..."

Shit. Shit. Shit.

I didn't want to talk about two nights ago. I didn't want to talk about twelve years ago. I didn't want to talk about anything with him.

I stared at where he held me for a second, then lifted my eyes to his face.

When I tipped my head at his hand, he quickly released me and asked, "Do you have jumper cables?"

Jumper cables? I wasn't expecting that to come out of his mouth.

"My car won't start." He drove his fingers into his hair and instead of only being tousled, some of the strands now stood on end. I fought the urge to smooth them back into place. "I don't want to be late only two weeks in at my new job."

My new job.

Was that why he returned to Pittsburgh? For a new job? What happened to his old job? Did he fuck that up like his marriage?

I pinned my lips together so I wouldn't ask all the questions I didn't need answers to. I shouldn't care.

I shouldn't.

"Get an Uber." I turned and walked quickly toward the maintenance door at the back of the lobby.

"I... can't," he called out.

"There's an app for that," I said as I kept moving.

"I can't afford it."

He didn't say it loud, but I heard it, and it stopped me in my tracks.

His family had been rich. Maybe not billionaire type of rich but definitely upper class and living an easy life type of rich.

What the hell happened that he now couldn't afford a taxi-service?

He had helped me out financially so many times during college...

I blew a breath through my nose.

I shouldn't care.

I shouldn't.

However, I considered his admission. I'm sure it was difficult to tell me he was struggling financially. Especially with how I'd been treating him.

I slowly turned around to see he was still standing where I left him. He wasn't looking at me but somewhere beyond me. As if he was embarrassed.

I chewed on that for a few seconds, then finally said, "I think the maintenance staff keeps a set down in the basement."

"How do I get down to the basement? Do you think there's anyone down there now who I could ask for assistance?"

Shit. Shit. Shit.

I didn't want him to know that I had free access to the basement and the maintenance area. I especially didn't want him to know the reason why I had it.

"Do you know anyone who works in maintenance?" I could hear the plea in his voice. The actual hope.

Somehow it had wormed past the steel coating I had used to seal my heart.

Son of a bitch.

Normally, I wouldn't hesitate to help any of my residents. I shouldn't treat Tate any different simply because we had a past.

"Fuck," I muttered under my breath, then said, "I do," loud enough for him to hear me. I strode back toward him. "Come with me." I tipped my head toward the vestibule and outer doors.

I didn't wait for him, instead I walked like I was a man on a mission. Which I was.

If I took him the normal way down to the basement, I would have to use the app on my phone to electronically unlock the door. A typical resident of the building would not have that. Instead, I led him outside, through the side alley and to the rear of the building where there was a wide concrete ramp, an oversized garage door and a regular person door.

I hoped at this hour the door would be unlocked. However, I had no idea if anyone was down there right now. I didn't keep track of the maintenance crew since I had someone else do that for me. I also had no idea who would be assigned to River View Heights today. My crew was large and they rotated through all of my properties. They went wherever they were needed.

I tugged on the door and was relieved when it opened so I wouldn't have to use the keyless entry app, especially with Tate on my heels.

All the overhead lights were on and the door was open to the large room where the maintenance tools were stored.

"Wait here," I ordered, went inside and grabbed the set of jumper cables hanging on the pegboard.

When I came back out, I shoved them in his direction. He took them and then simply stared at the cables in his hands.

"You know how to use them, right?" I asked. Was it possible he didn't?

"I do. But…"

"But?"

"They need to be hooked up to another vehicle to work."

Damn it. "Yep, that's how they work," I said dryly, then sighed. "I'm heading to the office anyway. I can jump you."

I ignored the catch in Tate's breath. "You mean my car."

"That's what I meant," I muttered and headed toward my Range Rover. I parked both my vehicles down there. It was one of the perks of owning the building I lived in.

When I stopped in front of my Range Rover Evoque, I heard a soft whistle behind me. I glanced over my shoulder to see Tate had paused at my GranTurismo and was staring at it. "Damn," he whispered. "The Maserati's sweet. I can't believe anyone in this building can afford to own one."

I wasn't sure if any of them could. "It's the owner's," I said in a dismissive tone, hoping he'd drop it so we could get moving. Especially if he was worried about being late for his new job.

"Owner?" He circled my car, admiring the sleek lines. I loved taking that car out on the Turnpike to open it up and let the horsepower kick in.

"Of the building."

He glanced up and his eyes narrowed on me. "I thought the building was owned by a real estate corporation."

"It is. But he's the head honcho." I jerked my chin toward my SUV and pulled the fob from my pocket to unlock the door.

When the horn chirped and the parking lights flashed, Tate's gaze flicked from my Rover to me. "This one's yours?"

The surprise was thick in his voice but I got it. When he knew me in college, I was practically dirt poor.

I was far from that now.

"Yes. Get in." I hopped into the driver's seat and pushed the Start button.

He went around to the passenger side and slipped in beside me, settling into the leather seat. "It's nice."

Of course it was. It was practically new. I had planned on taking the Maserati this morning but I didn't want to risk the electrical system by using it to jump Tate's vehicle. Plus, I didn't want Tate to know I owned it. Or the building.

If he was surprised about me owning a new Evoque, he'd most likely be shocked about all the rest.

As Tate belted himself in, I put it into Drive and pushed the button under the rearview mirror to open the garage door. By the time we reached it, it was open enough for me to drive through. I quickly closed it behind me and pulled into the back alley, heading toward the parking garage a half block away.

"I assume your car's in the garage down here."

Most of my tenants who owned vehicles parked there since it was close. However, the monthly parking permit wasn't cheap. The garage was convenient but costly.

"Unfortunately."

Twenty minutes later, after failing to get his old Toyota Corolla to turn over, we finally gave up. His car was deemed dead and Tate's hair now looked as if he'd stuck a fork in an electrical outlet.

I could see his desperation and frustration growing by the

minute. But no matter how much he willed his car to start, the piece of shit needed a lot more than a simple jump. Truthfully, it needed to be junked and Tate needed to get a more reliable ride.

I had hidden my shock when I first saw what he was driving and now was more than curious about why he was so damn broke.

My guess was it had to be from the divorce and Dahlia's lawyer taking him to the cleaners but I refused to ask. I didn't want to feel sorry for him. I actually preferred to not feel anything at all.

"I'll have to get Triple A to tow it to a shop," he finally said after pacing and releasing a long string of curses with his hands clamped on his hips.

"It'll take hours for Triple A to arrive," I mentioned.

"It'll also take money I don't have for repairs."

That meant he needed to get to work soon since he couldn't afford to lose his new job.

Shit. Shit. Shit.

As much as I wanted to deny it, I still loved the man as much as I hated him. I didn't want to see him continue to crash and burn. And right now he was dropping as fast as a meteor about to plummet to Earth.

"Let's go," I ordered after rolling up the jumper cables and tossing them behind the driver's seat.

"Go where?"

"To wherever you work. I'll give you a ride. You can deal with this," I bit back what I really wanted to call his ancient Toyota and ended it with, "later. But you need to get to work, right?"

Relief filled his face. He didn't bother answering me but instead immediately climbed back into my SUV without another word.

As I paid the ridiculous parking fee for the short time I was there, I asked, "Where we going?"

He rattled off an address and I quickly plugged it into my GPS system before pulling out onto the busy street and heading toward I-579 and Veterans Bridge that crossed the Allegheny River.

Since we were going north of the city, I figured he'd been hired at the local television station, WPIX, which was in that direction.

Before I could confirm that, he said, "The owner of River View Heights… You know him well enough for him to let you park down there, too. Does that mean you two are close?"

What was he getting at? "We are."

"I'm going to ask you something I wish I didn't need to, but unfortunately, I do. Would you think the owner would mind if I parked down there, too? The monthly parking fee at the garage… It's…"

I said nothing and let him struggle to get it out. To ask me for a favor he really shouldn't be asking. Because, again, I was exhausted and feeling extra petty today.

"I'd be willing to pay him something, of course."

"As you saw, he doesn't need your money, Tate."

"Obviously. I know I'm nothing more than a tenant and I shouldn't expect a benefit that the rest of the tenants don't get, but…"

"But you're asking for that anyway," I finished for him.

"Maybe you can put in a good word. As a favor for me?"

"You ask friends and family for favors. I'm neither of those, Tate. I'm not your anything," I reminded him. And also myself. Because I feared the steel coating around my heart was beginning to develop holes just like the rusty spots on his Corolla's fenders.

"I get it, Roe. I do. I was only asking for a simple favor, that's all. I understand if you're not willing to put yourself out there for me… Just forget I asked."

Did he miss the part where I was already doing him a big favor by taking him to work?

I clenched my teeth together to prevent me from telling him he could park below the building. He wasn't getting any special treatment from me. Instead, I concentrated on the traffic as we headed north on I-279 and toward the Summer Hill area.

For a few awkward minutes, the Range Rover was only filled with the annoying GPS lady barking out orders.

As we got closer to our destination, my attention was pulled from the road to Tate's knee bouncing like crazy in the passenger seat. Then it was drawn to his long fingers spread over his left thigh. I noticed his nails were neatly trimmed and taken care of.

He might be broke but he still made an effort. But my guess was he likely sat at the news desk at wherever he now worked, so he had to keep up with his appearance.

I wanted to put my hand on top of his. To lessen his jitters about whatever he was nervous about and... quite frankly, simply to touch him.

I missed the feel of those hands and fingers.

I missed—

I mentally shook myself to rid myself of that next thought. I couldn't go back down the rabbit hole of memories. So, when I finally opened my mouth to prevent that, I asked, "In front or behind?"

I glued my eyes back on the road when his head twisted toward me. "What?"

Then it hit me how that question came off and I groaned under my breath. In the past, I would have turned it into playful teasing. Not this morning. "The camera. Are you in front of or behind it?"

"Oh. Uh... Behind. I have to earn my spot to sit at the news desk."

That statement surprised me. Toward his senior year at Duquesne he had decided he wanted to do some investigative reporting first but eventually be in front of the camera, not be in the background.

I want to be the star, Roe, not the supporting actor.

I swatted that memory away. "You didn't already earn that elsewhere?"

After he graduated, I never followed his career. If I had seen him on the evening news, I would've smashed my television.

From the corner of my eye, I noticed his bouncing knee abruptly stop and his fingertips dig into his thigh. "This isn't elsewhere."

"You're right. It's not," I murmured. I turned where the annoying female voice told me to turn and pulled up to the curb in front of the building to drop him off at the entrance.

He opened the passenger door. "Thank you."

I didn't respond. I was busy reading the large sign over the glass doors as he climbed out.

The Burgh Media Group.

"For everything, Roe," he added, his voice thicker than normal. With what? Regret? Sadness?

My gaze dropped from the sign to him where he stood outside my vehicle. He simply stared at me like he was waiting for me to say something.

For shit's sake. It hit me that the man probably had no way to get home.

I kicked myself as I asked it, but did it anyway. "What time are you done?"

My question stopped him from shutting the passenger door.

Tate leaned into the car with his hand braced on the door frame. "After the six o'clock news. Usually around seven or so."

"I'll pick you up then. Eat early."

Tate blinked twice as he stared at me. "Why?"

"Because I don't want you to get sick."

His head tilted and his brow furrowed. "Why?"

I simply gave him a look that he should have no problem understanding. We had communicated a lot back then simply using pointed looks and body language. It was one way to keep our secret safe when we were around other people.

With nostrils flared, he gave a single nod and slammed the door shut.

I twisted my mouth so I wouldn't grin, stomped my foot on the accelerator, and pointed my Rover back toward the city and my office.

CHAPTER 14

RONAN DIDN'T PICK me up like he said he would. However, he didn't leave me hanging, either. When I walked out of the building, I expected to see the Range Rover but a car service was waiting for me at the curb instead.

When I climbed into the back, I found a note left on the seat. Even after all these years I recognized his handwriting.

Ride's paid for. Get yourself ready, then at nine, be on the roof waiting.

I crumpled the slip of paper into a ball and my heart raced all the way back to River View Heights.

He wanted me on the roof at nine when the door was still unlocked? When anyone could intrude on us?

He didn't say if he wanted me on my knees and Ronan had never been shy about letting me know what he wanted. So, this time I planned on waiting for him while standing on my two feet.

Once I got back to my apartment, my fingers trembled from a mix of nervousness and anticipation the whole time I prepped myself. Like he told me, I had eaten a light lunch a little later in the day and skipped dinner completely.

I kept going back and forth wondering if we were having dinner together or sex. I assumed the second one, but with Ronan, it could go either way. One minute he seemed to hate me and wanted to punish me for hurting him, the next I would see glimpses of the old Ronan. The one I had fallen in love with.

The man I still loved despite everything.

I sighed.

My nervousness stemmed from never bottoming before. Not with him or with any of my anonymous Grindr hookups.

Back in college, Ronan had wanted to switch and had showed me what to do to get ready. He was thorough and wasn't shy about any of the details. While we had been working toward us switching, I always tensed up too much when it came time for me to try to be the receiver instead of the giver.

Except for when it came to head. Every chance I could I took Ronan with my mouth. I loved how it had driven him out of his mind. I loved having that power over him.

Back then, he had a lot of patience with me. Something I truly appreciated. And I did promise I would bottom for him one day.

Apparently, that day was today. Only, I wasn't sure if I was ready.

But if it took us one step closer to him forgiving me...

I already told him I'd do anything for that to happen and that wasn't a lie. I'd do anything to fix our relationship.

Now I needed to stick to my word and not back out no matter how much it turned me into a ball of nerves.

I only hoped he didn't take out his anger for me on my ass. I clung to the fact that he'd always been a considerate lover and hoped that was still true.

When I stepped out onto the roof, darkness had already fallen. Even though the pool wasn't officially closed for the night, only the lighted pool and the white string lights strung around the perimeter and along the pergolas kept the roof from being pitch black.

For two people in love, the atmosphere would be romantic.

For two people simply having sex, it was only background aesthetics.

Right now, we were the second but I hoped we'd get back to the first. It would take time and patience, but I was willing to work at it. But again, the man already waiting for me by the pool would need to want the same.

I was surprised to see him there since he had instructed me to wait for him on the roof.

Only a pair of dark silky shorts clung to his thick, powerful thighs. He wore nothing else.

I sucked in a breath at seeing his bare chest for the first time since... forever. My guess that he had more tattoos than the ones previously peeking out of his shirt sleeves had been correct. In addition to his arms, a variety of tattoos covered his chest, his shoulders and even his ribs.

I couldn't make them all out from where I stood but hoped to have the opportunity to explore them closer at a later date if I didn't get the chance tonight.

What I could see was he had built up a lot of muscle and I was wrong about how much. He was freaking ripped under all that ink. He looked like the ultimate bad boy. He could be a biker, a rock star, a boxer or even an MMA champion.

Any and all of the above.

I realized then that I had no idea what he did for a living since we hadn't gotten too personal. Unlike long-time friends, we hadn't spent time catching up for "old times' sake." But owning a new Range Rover like he did, he had to be doing at least okay.

Unless he was living above his means.

However, if he still had the mindset now as he had back in college, he would be very cautious with his spending. Back then he had to be.

I could have easily googled him and done some investigative research. What I did at the beginning of my journalism career and still occasionally did when I had the opportunity, simply because I enjoyed it. But, would it really matter what he did?

I wanted the man himself. His job, whatever it was, did not define him.

Unlike Ronan during our time at Duquesne, I really never gave money much thought because I'd always had it. Until now.

Currently, I was broke. I couldn't fault Ronan if he still was, too.

Though, I'd be disappointed if he was since I had always wanted better for him. I figured once he found his footing in life, he'd go far and be super successful.

I kept my thoughts to myself as Ronan came over to where I stood near the main door. He stopped in front of me, his eyes dark and intense as he scanned me from head to foot.

He'd already seen me in only my swim trunks. This wasn't checking me out because of curiosity, he was doing it as a power play.

I'd give him that because, while it might be a power play for him, it was foreplay for me. Having him take his time and explore my body, even with only his eyes, caused blood to rush to my cock, quickly thickening it from being semi-erect to a full-blown hard-on.

Since he carried no food, I was right about this solely being about sex and nothing to do with sitting down with me for dinner. Seeing him in those clingy short shorts that were tented, I was quite okay with that.

Dinner could wait.

Ronan would not.

"You stated you'd do anything for me to forgive you. Are you sure?"

Both his words and the deep rumble behind them sent sparks of electricity shooting through me, making me break out in goosebumps. My nipples tightened under my T-shirt and my cock flexed in my loose cotton shorts. "Yes."

He cocked his head to the side and met my eyes. "What if I can't promise that?"

Without blinking, I held his gaze to show him how serious I was about fixing things between us. "It's a risk I'm willing to take."

He considered me for a few more seconds, his expression giving away absolutely nothing.

"Whatever you want, Roe," I whispered.

"Whatever I want," came his soft echo.

"I just ask one thing…"

His eyebrows jumped to the top of his forehead.

"Not on the rooftop. I've never… I've never bottomed and I know that's what you want from me."

"Never," he repeated, his expression once again tightly under control.

"No."

"I'd be your first." Like with his face, he also gave me nothing in the tone of his voice. No surprise. No excitement. Nothing.

"Yes."

When his eyes slid to the side to avoid mine, I knew he was hiding something. Because I watched him closely, I didn't miss it when his jaw shifted the slightest bit.

It might be absurd, but in that exact moment, because of that reaction, I *knew* he still loved me. While it gave me some hope and something to work with, my biggest obstacle would be convincing him to forgive me. We could not move forward without that.

Tonight could possibly be the first step in that direction.

Jesus, I hoped so.

After a few long minutes of staring past me, he finally sliced his eyes back to me. "You're willing to do that for me." Again, it wasn't a question but a surprised statement.

"I said anything, Roe," I reminded him. "I meant it. But please, just not up here."

Some of the tension I'd been holding onto disappeared when he nodded.

When I automatically moved back toward the main door, Roe stopped me with a sharp noise at the back of his throat and tipped his head toward the unmarked door he disappeared through the other night. As soon as we got close enough, the lock clicked and after he opened the door, what I assumed were motion lights illuminated a narrow stairwell.

I watched my footing as I followed him down winding metal steps and directly into what was a massive residential space. It took my brain a few seconds to register where we were and what that meant.

One of the neighbors had ridden down the elevator with me one morning and casually mentioned that the top floor of River View Heights only consisted of one penthouse and the building's owner lived in it.

If I hadn't seen him with a date the other week, I would have mistakenly thought Ronan lived in this space with the owner.

I now realized *he* was the owner.

Ronan owned the fucking building I lived in.

He lived in a penthouse that had to cost...

I shook my head.

A fortune. I didn't even know what a place like this would cost. Or even what a whole apartment building would cost. I had never been into real estate. The only property I'd ever purchased was the house Dahlia lived in with my kids.

The impact of this discovery hit me. He'd been scraping by in college and now this?

That also meant he not only owned that Range Rover, he owned the Maserati, too. He had purposely kept me in the dark for the last couple of weeks.

I didn't blame him, but it still stung.

After I graduated from Duquesne, I had no idea just how differently our lives would turn out. He'd been scraping by back then, now it was me.

The person in the elevator had been right. I could easily see that the penthouse took up the whole top floor, since the floor plan was open concept. Nothing like the apartment I leased on the sixth floor.

I swore my place would fit in what might be considered his living room. It could be considered a "great room" due to it being so massive with no walls separating it from the kitchen, a cozy sitting nook to the side with a huge TV, and a dining area.

From where I still stood at the bottom of the spiral staircase, I took in everything I could see. From the exposed brick accent walls in contrast with the earth-tone colored drywall, to the huge leather sectional that faced a long line of windows where one could sit and appreciate the twinkling lights of the city beyond.

"*You* are the building's owner," I said, still in shock.

"I am."

He had hidden that fact from me. On purpose.

I tried not to let that eat at me as I walked through the large chef's kitchen fitted with all stainless steel Viking brand appliances. Those were quite the investment. I wondered if he ever used them since they looked spotless. Not a smudge to be seen. "That's quite an achievement."

I'd never been in a place quite like this. Admittedly, it was stunning and perfectly decorated. Neat and tidy with zero clutter and nothing left out on the counters, unlike the average American home. Definitely too neat for a single man living a bachelor's life.

It was also very modern. Everything screamed quality. From what I could see, the interior design and decor weren't overdone but done right. While the wealth needed behind it was easily recognizable by someone like me who grew up around it, it was also both subtle and tasteful.

I even spotted a few art pieces. Again, all of it unpretentious and all in good taste.

"Ronan... You've done well for yourself." I was having difficulty wrapping my head around this whole thing.

"You sound surprised. But," he casually lifted and dropped one shoulder, "I work hard. Or I used to. I don't have to work quite as much anymore. Or as hard."

My brow furrowed. "Why? What does that mean?"

I wasn't sure if he'd explain since it meant telling me details he apparently hadn't wanted me to know.

"I bought my first house not long after I graduated. It needed a lot of work, of course, to be in my price range. I had to do most of the rehab myself, along with help from a few good friends, to save money and make it habitable. Once it was done, I immediately got an offer on it I couldn't refuse, unless I was a fool. I accepted the offer and ended up making a nice chunk of change in profit. After that, I bought another fixer-upper because I had learned a lot with the first one. I flipped the second house, took that money and invested it into a larger, multi-family house. When I flipped that, I invested in my first apartment building. A smaller one I lived in for a while and still own. Now I buy run-down apartment buildings—mostly foreclosures and short-sales—throughout the city and surrounding areas, rehab them from top to bottom, then rent the units out or turn them into condo co-ops."

"You're good with your hands." Among other things.

The last thing I expected Roe to do out of college was go into construction. By the end of his sophomore year he had picked Entrepreneurship as his major.

I figured once he graduated, he might go into the tech business, which had been quickly growing at the time. Instead, it sounded like he turned flipping homes into a business. So, maybe he was using his degree the best way he could.

"I no longer do the work. I now have a full crew on the payroll for the rehabs. They also do maintenance and repairs on my occupied buildings. They're highly skilled and reliable because I pay them well for their expertise, whether it be electrical, carpentry, HVAC or plumbing. If they can't handle a specific job, I hire a subcontractor. I no longer buy single- or multi-family homes. I stick to higher capacity buildings. Like this one."

While I listened with interest to him tell me about his start in business, the whole time I was not only thrilled with his success, but the fact he was actually opening up to me when I didn't think he'd tell me anything at all.

I considered this another step forward. I needed to keep him talking. As an experienced journalist and newscaster, asking questions was my forte. But I decided to throw softball questions at him so he wouldn't shut me out. "Is this your largest?"

"No."

"Then why do you live here?"

Whether he realized it or not, I was also engaging him in small talk to put off the sex—the whole reason he brought me down to his penthouse in the first place—even if for only a short while. I desperately wanted to reestablish the connection between us and this could be the start of that.

If I could tie that snapped thread together again, the sex could possibly strengthen it.

"Location. Plus, the top floor in this building was perfect for a penthouse. It had good bones, plus opening up the existing smaller apartments gave it a lot of windows and light. I designed it myself and I love it. The view can't be beat for this area and it's conveniently in the heart of the city."

Yes, the city we both loved so much. Once I left, I missed it. But I knew if I stayed it would only remind me of Ronan and what I couldn't have.

While he'd been talking, he'd poured a finger's worth of The Macallan into two glasses that had been sitting waiting on the black granite counter in the kitchen. That meant he had planned on us not staying on the roof tonight, but bringing me down to his place. I hadn't even needed to ask.

With the two glasses in hand, he came over and offered me one.

I could really use it to take off the edge. When I took a tentative sip of the rich amber liquor, it went down smoothly and warmed my insides.

"Except for the Range Rover, of course... To look at you, I never would've guessed you ended up so successful."

"I never expected you to hit rock bottom, either."

Touché. I scraped the back of my thumb across my forehead as I contemplated the man standing before me. "I deserved that."

"Life happens to the best of us. Some things we can control, some we cannot." He shrugged and tipped his glass to his lips. When he was done, he continued, "The way someone looks or dresses isn't a measurement of success. I actually prefer to be seen as the average Joe."

"The average Roe," I teased, even though there was nothing average about the man standing less than four feet away from me.

He tipped his head in agreement.

"So… You never wear a suit?" I didn't know many successful businessmen who didn't. If I had the money, I would pay to see Ronan in a perfectly tailored suit.

"For weddings and funerals mostly."

"But not for business?"

He barked out a dry laugh. "I'm at the point in my life where I no longer need to fall into the trap of 'dressing to impress.' I now rely on my own successes to create more and to build financial bridges. I don't answer to anyone and no longer hide who I am for anyone, either."

That last part was said with intention. It was duly noted.

"While I don't flaunt it, I can proudly say I'm a gay businessman who might dress casually but can easily afford to buy a city block. With cash. If someone can't accept me as I am, then I prefer not to do business with them."

With cash. My knees wobbled a little.

Holy shit. I was lucky if I had a wrinkled ten in my wallet right now.

It was like our lives had done a complete swap.

With anyone else what Ronan said would sound like bragging. But his words were filled with passion, not dripping with arrogance and one-upmanship, like some of the people I had grown up around. My parents had plenty of friends and acquaintances who looked down their noses at others less fortunate than them. They dismissed anyone they didn't consider on their level.

Just like they now dismissed me. A broken man who broke up his family and was now financially broke to boot. I was no longer worthy of their time or attention.

I didn't care.

My children were who made me wealthy, not money. I valued them above all else.

I didn't care how poor Ronan was back in college. It also made no difference to me how rich he was now.

Again, my interest in him was only about the man under the tattooed skin, not the money. Back then, I had loved him for who he'd been, not what material things or comforts he could provide.

Ronan had come from very humble beginnings. And that humility remained today even though he had to be a multi-millionaire. One who wore ripped jeans, old T-shirts and decorated his body with lots of ink.

He was living his life the way he wanted to, not the way he was expected to.

I needed to tear a page out of his playbook and follow it.

"Wearing a suit did not make my success happen. Dressing a certain way did not teach me how to invest and grow my portfolio, whether it be stocks, bonds or real estate. It took hard work and good business sense. Dedication and determination. If I wanted to be strangled with society's expectations, I would've followed the unspoken rules. But rules were meant to be broken. Unlike my heart."

I tried not to let the small digs bother me because in the larger picture he was opening up to me. In time, I hoped the sharp digs would lessen and his openness with me would increase.

It would take bucket loads of patience and very thick skin, but, at this point, that was all I had.

"Once I built a small real estate portfolio, I put together a small management team because I could no longer handle everything myself. As my real estate portfolio grew, so did my team. Now it not only manages my buildings, it manages both commercial and residential real estate for others."

"You're a collector of buildings and businesses," I summarized to keep him talking.

"I collect a lot of things."

"Men? Like the one in the elevator the other week?"

"Investments are for my future. Men are just my…"

"Toys."

"An outlet. I keep what makes me money. I get rid of what doesn't."

I took another sip of the pricey scotch. That should've been an obvious sign.

The Range Rover. The Macallan. The fact he used a different entrance up to the roof than the rest of the building's residents.

Maybe my investigative skills were slipping since, at the last television station I worked for, I rose up the ladder to the point where I was simply given news copy to read in front of the cameras. None of it produced from my own legwork.

With my new job I was back in the trenches. It was harder work for less money than sitting behind the nightly news desk as an anchor.

No matter what, I was willing to put in the time and effort to get back to where I was previously. A "pretty" face in front of the camera with a fatter paycheck to help pull me free from the mountain of debt I currently was buried under.

"So, you gave up your dream of getting into the tech industry."

"That was never my dream, T. It was only a direction. I drifted off that path when I found a better one."

"Drifted," I repeated softly. That wasn't the word for his career path.

He shrugged. "I smashed the accelerator pedal."

I wanted to tell him how proud I was of everything he'd accomplished but I wasn't sure if he'd be open to compliments or kudos from me. He probably didn't want anything from me besides sex. An outlet, as he put it.

I'd work on changing that. One step at a time.

I finished off the eighteen-year-old scotch, placed the empty glass next to the bottle that probably cost half my month's rent, circled my hand in the air and asked, "May I?" unsure if he'd like me wandering around his home.

Ronan hesitated for a few seconds before nodding.

I headed toward the long hallway on the far side of the "great room" eager to see the rest of the penthouse.

Surprisingly, he didn't follow me, but let me explore on my own. I took that to mean he had nothing to hide.

As I wandered through the penthouse way too big for one person, I scanned for signs of other men—whether past or current, other than Grindr dates—around his home.

I found nothing.

I flip-flopped between pleased about that fact and also sad. Pleased for me. Sad for him. I wondered if I had been his last and only serious relationship.

I had always wanted him to be happy. I took full responsibility for crushing his happiness all those years ago.

The only photos I spotted—mostly in his large and well-equipped home office with a view as impressive as his living room—were of his parents back from when his father had been alive and what looked like more current ones of his mother, as well as some of Ronan and his brother. Even a couple of Declan with his family.

The massive main bedroom had a California king and was done up in shades of grays accented with white and black.

Classy.

Like his vehicles. Unlike how he dressed.

He certainly was an enigma.

I was thrilled for his success and even happier to see him doing much better than I ever thought he would.

It also drove home the fact I hadn't been there for him. I hadn't been by his side as he built his business and his success.

But then if we had stayed together, maybe he wouldn't have reached quite this level of success. Maybe his life would've been different. He might not have pushed himself as hard.

I wasn't taking credit for his success in any way, but I also speculated on how my life would've been different if I hadn't made the choices I had.

CHAPTER 15

Ronan (Now)

I LEANED a hip against the counter in the kitchen and sipped on my scotch as I waited for Tate to do a self-tour through my place.

I couldn't believe that Tate Harris was walking through *my* penthouse, *my* home, after all these years. And I was letting him.

Even crazier, we were about to have sex.

Never once did I expect we'd be back to this point in our lives.

His questions had been an obvious delay tactic—not because I didn't think he wanted to have sex, maybe not bottom, though—but because he wanted details about my life and for me to drop the fortress walls I had built around me.

While I gave him some details—the ones he could easily research online if he cared to—I didn't give him all.

He'd have to earn them. He couldn't simply walk back into my life and expect me to act like he never left.

Because he did.

And in a way, I had a hard time forgiving him for it.

Ultimately, that was what he wanted from me. Forgiveness.

It wouldn't come easy, if it came at all.

He might want a new beginning, but I wasn't sure I could ever get over the last ending.

As I waited for him to return, I reflected on the success I've had over the years. Would I have been as successful if Tate and I had stayed together?

Would I have been as driven? Would I have fought as hard to make my way in the world? To prove everyone wrong? That someone like me could claw their way to the top?

Maybe not. Back then, Tate had an easy life. Maybe I would've slipped into that easy life along with him.

I guess I had Dahlia's calculated scheming to partially thank for how determined I was to create my own path in life.

She knew how rich his family was and really didn't want a career. It turns out, she only went to college to find a good husband who would let her be a housewife. Or trophy wife. Her major in college had been husband-hunting. And once she had set her eyes on Tate, she had her target.

Only, a freshman came along and screwed that up for her.

She had Tate within her grasp and I had pulled him free, without that even being my intent. She considered all the time she had put into Tate wasted when he broke up with her.

As graduation closed in and she realized she had no excuse to avoid finding a job since she didn't land a potential husband, she began to panic and resorted to tricking Tate into sleeping with her again.

Most likely her original intent was to convince him he wasn't gay or even bi. To show him he was only confused and she could prove to him he was straight.

Even worse, by convincing him that I had only messed with his head. That it had been me who'd been out to scheme, not her.

However, the method she used to prove all of this ended up being way more effective.

And changed the course of all our lives.

~

Ronan (Then)

EVEN THOUGH TATE'S graduation was still a few days away, I was already feeling the loss. Unless he landed one of the jobs he applied for in Pittsburgh or the surrounding areas, we'd be apart for the next two years until I graduated.

Yes, we'd have this summer together, as well as the next, and my breaks between semesters, but that would never be enough time for us.

We could also text, call and email, even Skype, but it wasn't the same as climbing into bed with him every night and waking up next to him every morning.

I hoped we'd at least have this summer together in the apartment we now shared. Since this would be my last year required to live on campus, if he got a job locally, I could finally give up the dorm room I paid for, but rarely spent time in, and "officially" move in with Tate.

However, if Tate moved too far away to start his journalism career, I'd be securing another dorm room on campus for my junior and senior years. It would be more affordable and convenient for me.

It sucked, but I kept telling myself I needed to have patience when it came to our relationship. The time I was investing now, with both Tate and school, would pay off in the future.

Graduating from college and also being on the Dean's list every semester was as important to me as Tate. He encouraged me to stay and finish getting my degree.

I was now majoring in Entrepreneurship, a path I hadn't even thought of before my advisor happened to suggest it. My ears had perked up and I bugged him for all of the details.

I pictured someone asking me, "What do you do for a living?" and answering with, "I'm an entrepreneur," in a matter-of-fact tone. It kind of sounded snobby and that made it even funnier for me who right now was barely scraping by.

But what really caught my attention was when my advisor told me about a program at the university where I could get the opportunity to build my very own micro-business and the school would actually invest the seed money.

I knew I couldn't pass that up even though it seemed too good to be true.

But if I started a micro-business and it actually did well, then I was already on my way to becoming successful.

I was all about seizing opportunities.

Including the guy who sat beside me in class my first semester at Duquesne.

I was waiting for that guy to walk through the door of our apartment any time now.

He had texted me earlier when he arrived at KDKA. He had gone to meet with management there hoping to snag a permanent paid position. The odds were pretty decent he would succeed since he'd spent all of last summer interning at the TV station and learning the ropes firsthand on what went on behind the cameras.

However, that meeting had been scheduled *hours* ago.

I didn't want to text or call him in case his meeting had been delayed or had gone long. I hoped good news was the reason for him being gone for so long.

Maybe he had even stopped on the way home to pick up stuff to celebrate.

My mind spun with all the possibilities.

I wanted him to land the job at KDKA more than anything. That meant we could both stay in Pittsburgh, which we now considered our "home." Better yet, we could stay together and continue to build our relationship.

I sprung off the couch and my body began to hum with anticipation as soon as I heard his keys jingling in the hallway.

"How did it go?" burst from me as soon as the door opened and he stepped inside.

Immediately, I sensed something was wrong and my stomach dropped.

His face appeared too serious and his vibe was off. By now, Tate was usually greeting me with one of his handsome smiles while demanding a kiss, one that sometimes led to more.

I swallowed down the lump stuck in my throat and tried to ignore the dread filling my chest.

"Ronan..."

My heart squeezed, then began to crack at the way he said my name. Not only did he use my complete first name, I'd never heard him say it like that before.

With caution. As if he was preparing me for the worst.

I had to be simply imagining things. Or being over-sensitive since I'd been so invested in him staying in Pittsburgh with me.

I took two steps toward where he stood by the door. He hadn't even put his messenger bag down yet. He usually dumped that right away since, like his old backpack, it was so packed full that it was bulging and heavy.

"Did the meeting not go well?" My heart was knocking in my chest.

Thump.

Thump.

Thump.

"It went okay, but..." He pressed his lips together.

"But you didn't get it," I concluded.

He shook his head.

"Shit," I muttered. "Well, maybe WPIX will still come through. There are so many news organizations and radio or television stations in and around the city and I'm sure—"

"Roe, I got a message this morning from WGAL. They offered me a spot at their station in Harrisburg."

Harrisburg.

He paused for a few seconds to let that news sink in, then

finished with, "I called them back after…," he shook his head, "my meeting at KDKA and accepted."

I was trying to remain positive. I knew this could be a possibility. I had prepared myself for it. "Is it a good position?"

He nodded, but he didn't look happy about it. In fact, his face now looked ravaged. It didn't make sense.

"As an investigative journalist to start."

Just what he wanted to do. "And the salary's good?"

He nodded again, licking his lips. He was ghost white.

He was hiding something.

Whatever it was…

I shrugged like it was no big deal for me, when that was farthest from the truth. "Harrisburg isn't that far away. Only about three hours."

Since Tate was off to bigger and better things, it could be nerves making him look like that. Or the fact he didn't want us to be apart once my summer break was over.

I shrugged again, trying to hide my devastation. "I'm sure I can easily find a job in Harrisburg for the summer and I'll just sign up for campus housing again come fall. We'll make it work."

He still hadn't moved.

The only time I'd seen him look so sickly was last winter when he got the flu and he couldn't stop throwing up.

But unlike then, he was quiet. Too quiet.

Until he wasn't.

"Ronan…" His next words tumbled out in a rush. "You can't come to Harrisburg with me."

What? "But that was our plan, to spend the summer together, no matter where you got a position."

"I know…" He sounded like what he had to say next would be torture.

No. Whatever it was had to be bad. I braced.

"Ronan…"

No.

"There's more."

More? He was leaving me, what more bad news could there be?

"My parents came to Pittsburgh early to surprise me."

Shit. His parents were expected to arrive tomorrow to attend his graduation, not today. He had planned on sitting them down and telling them about us. About him being gay, too. Finally laying everything out on the table since he was graduating and moving on to the next chapter in his life.

With me.

We had even gone over several times what he would say and how he would say it. He even practiced because he'd been nervous.

I'd been crawling out of my skin because he wasn't sure they'd be accepting. Of him being gay or of me being in his life.

My guess was, if he wasn't sure, then they probably wouldn't be.

I wasn't liking where this was going. Not one bit.

Especially when he had to take a huge inhale to tell me what spilled from him next. "When I got out of my meeting at KDKA, they were already waiting for me outside. They wanted to take me to lunch. I figured I'd just tell them today what I had planned on telling them tomorrow, but..."

"But?" I echoed. My own voice sounding like I was standing at the bottom of a deep well. I swore I was going to throw up. My stomach was cramping and my head was spinning. I just needed him to get it all out. And soon.

"On the way to the restaurant they told me they had a surprise for me."

I wasn't liking this at all.

"It wasn't a surprise, Roe. It was an ambush."

"What do you mean, an ambush?"

"When we got there, Dahlia and her parents were already at the table waiting."

What?

"That was the surprise."

"Okay... So you ate with—"

He shook his head and, "Dahlia's pregnant. We're getting married," tumbled out.

I blinked, not understanding.

Then those words hit me like a ton of bricks.

No. No. No.

Those were two things I never wanted to hear. Never expected to hear.

My throat began to close. My eyes started to burn. My heart stopped beating.

What he said couldn't be possible. They had broken up two years ago. We'd been together ever since.

Unless...

They had never broken up and Tate had lied to me?

Or Tate had lied to Dahlia?

Or he lied to both of us?

No. Dahlia confronted me the same day he broke up with her, so I know he went through with it. Tate and I even talked about it afterward and he told me everything.

He told me the details of that whole conversation with her.

So...

None of this made any sense. Even worse, he wasn't explaining any of it.

Why the hell was he so damn quiet?

Maybe he was just pranking me. "This is a joke, right? You're messing with me." When he still didn't say anything, I stared at him, willing him to start laughing. "Tate, you're messing with me, right? Tell me this is all a sick joke."

His Adam's apple worked its way up his throat, then dropped like a rock. "I wish it was."

I pinched the skin on my arm because this had to be a nightmare. I was going to wake up and everything would be the way it was supposed to be. Not what was currently happening.

"I don't understand. How could this happen? You broke up with her. That's what you told me. You broke up with her, Tate!"

"I… I did."

"Then how the hell did this happen? And in the last few months?" None of this was making any sense. "We've been together for the last two years. I *thought* we were only fucking each other. You lied to me."

"I didn't. We were. It was a mistake—"

"I just can't wrap my head around what you're saying. Or why you would even sleep with Dahlia again. I thought you loved me."

"I do love you, Roe. More than anything." He blew out a breath. "What happened had nothing to do with love."

"Apparently," I ground out. I slapped a hand to my forehead and spun on my heels, taking long strides to put much-needed space between us. When I got to the end of our living room, I spun back around to face him. The dread I originally swallowed down now rushed back up as rage. "I knew it! I knew if you could do it to Dahlia, you could just as easily do it to me."

His brow furrowed. "Do what?"

"Cheat!"

"It wasn't like that, Roe. I didn't… It wasn't… She asked me… She was trying to… Fuck!" he screamed. "Fuck, Roe. I didn't plan it. I didn't even want it. I was… confused and it just happened."

I ignored everything he just said because I instantly lost all trust in him. Every damn bit of it.

"Even worse, you said *nothing* to me about it. *Nothing*, Tate. I never would've known what you did if she hadn't gotten pregnant."

His nostrils flared and he finally had the audacity to look guilty. "You're right, I wouldn't have said a word because I didn't mean for any of this to happen. But it did and now I can't take it back. I can only try to fix it."

"I know how to fix it," I ground out.

"I…" Tate shook his head. "I can't do that and it's too late for that, anyway. She made sure of it. She also sprung the news with my parents sitting at the table. She told them she was keeping it a secret because she wanted to surprise me as a graduation present."

Graduation present?

"She knew for the last few months and waited to tell me in front of my parents. She knows they love her and that they'd pressure us to get married. She even told her parents before me."

On purpose, no doubt. *Conniving bitch.* "Tate, you can still support your kid and not be married to the mother you don't love." It happened every day. Plenty of people co-parent successfully.

"Roe..."

He still hadn't explained how this happened. Only that he'd been "confused" and it had been a "mistake." "Did she trick you? What did she say to convince you to have sex without protection?"

"She didn't have to convince me."

My jaw hit the floor. "You did it willingly?"

He blew out a breath. He was holding back on the details. There had to be a reason. There was something so off with this.

"Can we sit down so I can—"

"No, Tate. We're not sitting down and having a cozy chat about it. I want to know details on this so-called mistake. Like... When did this happen?"

"Winter break."

My brain rewound.

He had gone home for Christmas to spend some time with his family. I had done the same to spend time with my mother and my brother's family for the holidays.

Even though it had been two years, Tate still hadn't come out to his family. They still had no idea we were together.

Two damn years later.

The whole reason why he was finally going to tell them tomorrow!

This was what I got for being patient and understanding. I got fucked up the ass in more ways than one.

"But you don't even live near each other," I forced up my throat. "How were you together on winter break?"

He needed to start talking and he needed to do it now. The

patience I had for the past two years was quickly crumbling. And I wasn't sure I'd ever be able to get it back.

His expression turned grim. Just like my damn future. *Our* future. "My parents invited her and her parents over New Year's. As you know, my parents always loved her. They were upset that I broke up with her. Over the holidays, our parents were trying to be matchmakers and get us back together. I was completely blindsided, Roe. They surprised me."

Another fucking secret. "You said nothing to me about it."

"I didn't want to upset you. It wasn't important. I figured they could matchmake all they wanted but no matter what, I was always coming home to you. I love *you*, Roe."

"But somehow your dick ended up in Dahlia."

He didn't want to tell me the details. Why? Why did he keep putting it off?

He closed his eyes and swayed slightly, the knuckles on his fingers gripping his messenger bag had turned white. When he opened those blue eyes I loved so much, I saw the defeat in them.

For a second I felt sorry for whatever he was about to say. I felt sorry for him being in the situation. Then I quickly realized whatever happened to him had turned me into a victim, too. And he hadn't warned me or protected me.

He actually thought I'd never find out about what happened between him and Dahlia.

"It was New Year's Eve and I got drunk. She slipped into my room. I didn't..." He shook his head. "I didn't mean for it to happen, Roe, but it did. I woke up the next morning and found her in my bed. I was pissed and kicked her out. I wanted to forget the whole thing... I *hoped* to forget the whole thing."

Karma was shrieking with laughter right now.

"Forget? Just like you forgot to tell me?"

Here I'd been anxiously waiting for him to come home and he was off having a lunch and planning a damn wedding with his parents and Dahlia's family.

What the fuck!

"Are you sure she's pregnant? She's not tricking you?"

"She showed me a sonogram picture."

"It could be fake."

"She's already showing."

"She could be getting fat."

"Ronan..."

"You don't know if it's yours." I was grasping at any straw I could. This couldn't be my life right now.

"I pulled her aside afterward and insisted on a DNA test before we get married."

I couldn't believe everything I was hearing. "This was a trap, Tate," I whispered. He stepped right in it. And he was letting her get away with it.

That was the part I didn't understand.

I was always afraid she would do something like this. I had hoped she'd be the bigger person. Apparently she wasn't.

"She trapped you. Don't you see it? It's right in front of your fucking face. You don't have to marry her. Even if she has this baby. You can still be a father without being with the mother." I didn't even attempt to hide the desperation in my voice.

Even though Dahlia was a conniving bitch, that didn't change the fact that he never told me what happened. He went on about life like it hadn't.

Life had other plans for him. And so did Dahlia.

Now he couldn't ignore it. Life was slapping him right in the face.

It was slapping me in the face, too.

"I can't with you. I can't with *this*." The sting from that slap was getting sharper by the second. "I hate your parents. I hate that fucking bitch. And you know what, Tate?" I sucked in a breath to cool the fury burning inside of me, but it didn't work. It exploded from me, instead. "I fucking hate you, too." I didn't want to hear any more excuses. Or any more explanations. None of them made sense, anyway. I couldn't wrap my head around any of this. I jabbed a finger toward the door. "Get out."

"Roe… Please… I'm sorry. I didn't mean for any of this—"

The words got caught in my throat but I forced them out and cut him off. "I need you to leave while I pack my stuff."

"I live—"

"Get out, Tate!"

"I'll pay the rent for the apartment. You can stay here for the summer."

"Unlike Dahlia, I don't want your fucking money, Tate! I wanted you!" I yelled, making him wince.

"I'm sorry. Roe, I'm so fucking sorry…"

My pulse pounded in my temples. The blood rushed in my ears. I couldn't hear. I couldn't see. I could only continue to scream, "Get out! Get out! Get out!" until my throat was raw, my tears dried up, my heart no longer beat.

And until…

Tate was gone.

CHAPTER 16

Ronan (Now)

I HAD SKIPPED Tate's graduation. Skipped saying goodbye.

I never saw him again.

Not until that day he walked into my building.

Now here he was, wandering through my penthouse, acting as if those years in the time between never happened.

Even if it had been a mistake—one he couldn't erase and one I couldn't forget— he'd handled the whole situation badly.

In the end, Dahlia had won. I had lost.

That day I packed my things, moved out of our apartment, and decided I would never let myself lose again. That was the day I hardened both my heart and my resolve.

Dahlia had gotten what she wanted and was happy. Her parents were happy that their daughter was marrying into the Harris family. Tate's parents got the daughter-in-law they wanted, too.

The two people who ended up not happy in the equation were me and Tate.

In spite of that, I had moved on as best as I could. While Tate had remained stuck in that hell.

But then, that was the choice he made and had to live with for over a decade. A decade of waking up next to a person who had deceived and manipulated him on purpose.

While I woke up every morning alone.

Before I could see him, I heard Tate coming back down the hallway. I thought about telling him to turn around and head back to my bedroom, but I needed to keep the sex as impersonal as possible. That meant keeping him out of my bed.

As soon as he reappeared in the living room, he said, "Your place is... impressive, Roe. You've done well. I'm..." He paused. "You probably don't want to hear this, and coming from me it might not mean a thing, but... I'm proud of you."

He was wrong. I did want to hear that from him.

And that "want" floored me.

While I didn't *need* any of that from him, his validation meant a lot more than it should.

I responded with, "Wait out here. I'll be right back."

As I walked past him, I pressed my hands to my outer thighs to keep from grabbing him and dragging him back to my bedroom.

When I returned with the lube and condoms a few minutes later, Tate was standing in front of the wall of windows, looking out over the city.

When he heard me approach, he said softly, "It's perfect."

So was he. Still.

I just couldn't let him worm his way back into my heart.

For my own mental well-being, I had to keep this strictly sex between us.

This way, even if he walked away again, I'd have this.

This extra moment in time.

But would this memory be something to trash or treasure?

Would it bolster or break me?

Unfortunately, there was only one way to find out.

Back then, I had wanted forever. Unexpectedly, he only gave me "for now."

Now he wanted a second chance for the forever we missed out on. But I wasn't sure I'd ever be willing to give it to him.

However, I *was* willing to carve out this time for him. For us. After that...

I couldn't think about what would happen after. I had to wait to see what happened first.

He kept his back to me as I set the lube and condoms nearby and stepped into his personal space. The scent of his soap or whatever he was wearing—maybe even whatever he used to prep—filled my nostrils.

When he slowly turned and his blue eyes met mine... I knew right then how dangerous all of this was for me.

It wouldn't take much for him to crush my heart and soul all over again.

I knew better than to do this, but was about to do it anyway. I was once again being stupid when I should've learned my lesson the first time.

I hated the fact that in the time in between, no one could ever replace him. No matter how hard I tried. No matter what I did. No matter *who* I did.

Whether he knew it or not, Tate was my soulmate. He was also my obsession.

One I was never able to recover from.

I had lived with it for all these years, hoping one day I'd wake up and it would disappear.

Just like him.

And similar to an addict, I tried to convince myself that one more hit wouldn't hurt. It would just give me some temporary relief and I could easily quit tomorrow.

I closed the gap between us until our bare toes actually touched. I leaned in until our mouths hovered. Neither touching or moving away. Just an exchange of warm breath over parted lips.

With each inhale, I stole his oxygen. With each exhale, he stole it back.

However, my thoughts kept interrupting me.

Warning me I shouldn't do this again.

Reminding me that I already had a permanent hole in my heart. If he broke it again, there might be nothing left to heal the second time around.

I shouldn't kiss him at all. Kissing was far too intimate.

But when he whispered, "Roe," I focused on his mouth. Then I crushed it with mine.

The impact was so hard, he stumbled backwards until his back hit the window behind him, shaking the glass. But I stayed with him, keeping us connected. Pillaging his mouth. Warring with his tongue.

Battling those doubts invading my mind.

Trying to convince myself that what we were about to do meant nothing. No different from a Grindr date.

Even though, I knew…

I knew deep down that wasn't true.

And when he touched me… His long fingers gripping my jaw, encouraging me to take the kiss deeper…

His mouth greedy. And needy.

Familiar.

Like returning home after a long trip.

His fingers trailed down my chest, skimming over my nipples and stroking the trail of hair leading from my navel to my aching cock.

His touch caused a current to snap and crackle along my skin. The same as when I was a child and foolishly stuck a fork in the electrical outlet, even after being told not to do it.

Would this be a similar lesson I'd need to learn all over again?

He didn't stop the drag of his warm fingers at the waistband of my shorts, he pushed them down as he went until he circled his hand around me. His breath caught at the back of his throat.

I deepened the kiss when he began to pump me. Softly at first. Tentatively. Then each additional stroke became bolder, more aggressive.

If he continued as he was, I'd shoot cum all over us both. But I didn't want that. My plan was to take his ass and make it mine. Even if only for tonight.

I ripped my mouth from his so I could find my breath, gather my wits. Not just drift away, lost in his touch.

But I wanted it. I needed it.

And, *fuck me*, I had missed it.

It caused an ache in my chest almost as great as the day I lost him.

Grabbing his wrist, I freed his hand from my cock, then pulled his shirt up his torso and over his head, leaving that unruly lock of hair of his falling across his forehead.

I ignored it but what I couldn't ignore were his eyes.

Darker than normal and full of heat and desire.

If I looked in the mirror, I was sure mine would be the same.

But I read the pleading in them, too.

For forgiveness or for the sex?

Maybe both.

"Fuck," he whisper-groaned.

I planned on it. Long and hard and fast.

But we needed to get there soon, before my protective walls completely collapsed around me. They were already beginning to crack and crumble with pieces landing at my feet.

With his mouth parted, he panted slightly. I leaned in again, snagging his bottom lip within my teeth and giving it a firm nip. I then ran my tongue over it and took his mouth again.

No. *My* mouth. Right now it belonged to me.

It only lasted for a moment. Because like his touch, I could easily get caught up in kissing him. I could kiss him all night.

That reminded me of a time when we used to snuggle together under a blanket in bed or on the couch while watching TV or studying. We'd make it a competition on how long we could kiss without one or both of us getting naked.

A challenge of who could hold out the longest.

I yanked myself out of the past and once again ended our kiss.

Shoving his shorts down, I released his very tempting erection. Pleased to find he wasn't wearing anything underneath.

The bobbing length, the broad crown slick from precum, caused saliva to pool in my mouth, from remembering the taste and feel of it against my tongue.

I was tempted to drop to my knees and experience that all over again.

Not tonight. Stick to the plan. It's safer.

Of course, I was lying to myself, but that lie was one more in a slew of them I decided to ignore.

Taking my time, I slid his shorts down even farther, purposely not touching him at all. I kept my grip solely on the soft cotton until they dropped to his feet. He stepped out of them and kicked them aside.

I needed to do the same with the memories that kept creeping in.

I focused on Tate in the here and now, standing completely naked in front of me, for the first time in what seemed like a lifetime.

Did I want to explore and learn every inch of his body all over again?

Yes.

A million times yes.

Did I? No.

Instead, I spun him around until he once again faced the window, afraid of what might happen if I looked into his eyes while we did this. Afraid it would feel too intimate and he'd see things I didn't want him to witness.

Like how vulnerable I was currently. How weak he made me.

I stepped back and gave myself one more thorough inspection from the dark, full hair on his head, down his spine, over his ass, along his lightly-furred legs and finished at his bare feet.

He jerked when I called out, "Alfred, lights out!"

My smart home "butler" acknowledged my command with an echoed, "Lights out," and the room instantly went dark.

The only light anywhere in our vicinity was a small one in the kitchen behind us that I used in case I needed to head there in the middle of the night.

And, of course, the lights in front of us from the city just beyond that window.

"It's like we're floating in the air," Tate whispered. "I bet you can see the fireworks display perfectly."

"I can." Those fireworks were nothing like the ones currently exploding in my center.

"You can probably hear the roar of the crowds from the stadiums."

"From the roof."

More small talk. His attempt at making this more personal.

He wanted to talk? Fine.

"Did you prep like I told you?"

"Yes."

"Just like I taught you?"

"Yes."

"Did you think about me while you did it?"

The last "yes" sounded strained.

"Did you get hard while you did it? While thinking about me and about what was going to happen tonight?"

"Yes."

"Did you make yourself come?"

His breath hissed from him along with his answer, "Yes."

My cock flexed from hearing that. "Stay right where you are. Don't move. Not an inch."

I headed over to the side table and grabbed the condom, ripping the wrapper open and taking my time to roll it on, the whole time keeping my eyes on the man waiting obediently for me by the windows.

When his head began to turn in my direction, I barked, "No. Don't look at me. Look at the city that used to belong to us."

With a nod, he turned back toward the window. But his eyes remained on me, this time using the reflection in the glass.

After making sure the condom was seated properly, I snagged the Lubido from the table and headed back over to him, unscrewed the cap on the tube and squeezed out a generous amount onto my palm.

Using the lube, I coated my latex-covered cock, more thickly than normal, since this was his first time being a bottom and I wasn't going to take much time to help stretch him.

I stroked myself, partially to evenly distribute the Lubido along my length and partially for my own pleasure. Reaching past him, I held the tube in front of Tate's face. "Prepare yourself."

His body jolted in response to my demand. That meant he had expected me to do it for him. That wasn't how we were playing this.

After reluctantly accepting it, he squeezed some on his fingers. I once again backed up to watch when he reached around, tipped his ass up, pulled one ass cheek to the side and used his slick fingers all around his hole.

A heady feeling came over me since I would be his first. He was trusting me over all the men in his past with this monumental step.

Both a blessing and a curse.

Another chunk of my crumbling wall fell to my feet.

"Inside, too," I instructed, scrambling to patch that wall.

His breath caught as he inserted one finger, then two, into his canal, working the lube inside and out.

My cock was rock hard and throbbing within my hand as I continued to slowly stroke it from root to tip.

When he was done, I wiped the Lubido off my hand and onto my shorts before dropping them to the floor and stepping closer.

I caged him in by planting my hands against the glass on either side of his head.

I planned on taking this as slow as I could until I couldn't resist any longer.

Tate (Now)

WITH HIS HANDS braced on the glass, Ronan slowly leaned in and ran his warm breath from the top of my neck to the bottom. His lips never touched me. Nothing did, only his exhale as it swept over my heated skin in a ghostly caress.

I dropped my head forward and tensed to fight a shudder.

When he did it a second time, I accepted defeat and my body quaked with its reaction, spreading goosebumps along every inch of my heated skin.

A whispered, but shaky, "Roe," escaped me when he separated my cheeks, ran a finger down my crease and across my anus. On his way back up, he paused on his target, pressing his fingertip against the tight ring of muscle, which I swore had its own heartbeat.

After slowly working one finger inside me, then a second, he slid them in and out, distributing the lube more thoroughly and stretching me slightly.

My breath seized and I once again tensed when he added a third digit and began circling and scissoring.

"I'm bigger than that, Tate." His words whispered across my skin. "You can still say no."

My voice had a shake to it when I insisted, "Keep going."

I blew out a long, slow, controlled breath as I breathed through the initial stretch and discomfort.

Three fingers were only the beginning and I told myself to relax. It would be uncomfortable and I wouldn't enjoy it if I didn't.

I had never bottomed with Ronan back in college because I hadn't been ready back then. I wasn't sure if I was ready now.

Because of my unease, I had always topped Ronan. If he didn't finish before I did, I'd make him come by using my mouth or hand. Or by massaging and milking his prostate. Something he'd taught me long ago and we both perfected by watching porn and doing endless amounts of fun practice.

I also got away without bottoming during my numerous random, nameless hookups in bathrooms, bars and truck stops. Even in parking lots and deserted parks.

I fought the shame that washed through me whenever I thought of all the times I cheated on Dahlia with random men. Every time I had to get my fix elsewhere.

If I didn't get my fix, I was afraid of what I'd do.

And no matter what, my children needed me. I needed to be there for them. So, I did what I had to do to survive.

The ugly truth was once I discovered I preferred men over women, Dahlia was never enough for me.

Eventually, I realized she never had been. I never knew why until I met Ronan. Until he opened my eyes and let me see and be myself.

That was the *real* truth.

Did I suffer overwhelming guilt about what I did to Dahlia? Absolutely.

Overwhelming regret? Of course.

I beat myself up every time I met a stranger somewhere in a dark, isolated corner, vehicle or wooded area.

Every time I did, I'd close my eyes and replace the stranger's face with one more familiar.

Even with that, I was never fully satisfied.

Not with Dahlia. Not with random hookups.

Nothing and no one could change the fact there would only be one man for me.

The man I screwed over.

The man I screwed up.

Because of that, I'd give him this tonight.

I told Ronan I'd do whatever it took.

I meant it.

The second his fingers slipped from me, the slick crown of his cock was dragged from my taint up my crack and back, the same as he'd done with his fingers.

I mentally prepared, once again telling myself to relax. To push out when he pushed in. I drew on the knowledge he taught me so long ago but was never brave enough to follow through on.

Tonight, I wouldn't back out like I had so many times in the past. Every time feeling guilty, but also relieved.

If it caused pain tonight, I deserved it.

If I hated it, I would suffer through.

I would do anything to get Ronan back.

Absolutely anything.

Jesus fucking Christ, this man owned my soul. And I owed him mine.

Even if he forgave me, I don't know if I could ever make up for what I did to him, intentionally or not. But I would try. If it took until the day I drew my last breath, I would damn well do my best.

"Give me the lube."

I didn't even realize I was still tightly gripping it. Luckily, it hadn't squirted all over my hand and the floor. I passed it back to him, grateful he would use more.

When he dropped the tube to the floor, I reminded myself once more to relax. To loosen my muscles, to let Ronan lead.

He knew what he was doing and I trusted him.

The pressure, the stretch and the tightness was followed by the fullness as he pushed forward…

"Push out," he breathed.

I pushed out as he slowly pushed in.

He groaned. "You're so damn tight, T."

Of course I was, even though I was trying not to tense up.

Halfway in he paused and let me adjust to him. His breath beat against my neck, his fingers gripped my hips, holding me still. Maybe even in an attempt to hold himself from moving, too.

He was probably fighting the urge to thrust, to take me like he wanted. To take me like I was one of his Grindr boy toys.

When he pulled back, the sensation was unexpected. But he had told me all this. I knew all this. He had made sure I was prepared all those years ago.

It was only one more thing I never did for him. One more thing that disappointed him. Even though he never came out and said it. Even though he pretended like it hadn't.

At the time, it was because he loved me.

Also, because he thought we had all the time in the world.

I thought so, too.

Ronan slowly pushed forward again, then slightly retreated.

A small step forward, a small step back.

Then a larger step forward, an even smaller step back.

He could've forced it. He could've hurt me. He could've taken me quickly and gotten it over with.

He didn't.

He took his time. He kept his patience.

And despite him acting like I was nothing but an anonymous fuck, his actions showed me that was the farthest from the truth.

I glanced up and into the window. What I saw behind me was the old Ronan, not the one from the lobby. Not the one from the roof.

I concentrated on *him*. And before I knew it, he stilled, fully seated inside me.

"I'm okay," I answered.

"I didn't ask," he got out around gritted teeth.

He was struggling. Whether it was because he was trying to hold off on coming or because he was suddenly regretting this whole thing, I didn't know.

"Yes, you did," I countered.

He turned his face away so I could no longer see it clearly in the reflection.

I took that as a positive sign.

"I still love you, Roe. No matter what, just know that I still love you."

"Tate, don't." The crack in his voice was another sign.

"I'm going to tell you every day for the rest of my life. Whether you're around to hear it or not. Whether you *want* to hear it or not. Every damn day, Roe. Even if only the universe hears it."

"You had a funny way of showing it."

"I'm going to show you every day, too. Whether you see it or not. You can listen to what I say and you can watch what I do. Or you can ignore it all. Either way, just know I love you. I regret the past but I will *not* regret where we go from here."

"Stop."

"I won't. I'll never stop."

CHAPTER 17

Tate (Now)

HIS ORIGINAL INTENTION with sex tonight most likely was to punish me, to make me hurt the same way I caused him to hurt.

But he had to realize I'd also gone through that same pain and loss.

Even worse, I lost the very son I gave up Ronan for.

It was a double hit that crippled me emotionally for a very long time.

I would never get over losing Connor but I could make up for losing Ronan. I hoped tonight was a first step in that direction.

I could already feel his walls crumbling around him, now I needed to take a sledgehammer to them. At least to the point I could slip through a crack and finish breaking down those walls from the inside out.

Every step I took toward that goal had to be prudent so he didn't slam them back up and freeze me out. Maybe even for good.

Presently, he wasn't slamming anything but his cock into my ass now that my body had adjusted to his length and girth.

For the most part, anyway.

My own erection bounced wildly with each thrust. Both his actions and low grunts near my ear caused precum to gather rapidly at the tip and start to fall.

Ronan had never been dominant and I still didn't think that had changed, despite how he treated me up on the roof the two times he had me on my knees.

Even so, I was proceeding with caution and didn't want to do anything to undermine the power he currently held and I currently gave him. I wanted him to lead us in the physical sense and, in turn, I hoped to lead us emotionally.

For that reason, as much as I wanted to touch myself, as much as I wanted to encourage him with words, I refrained.

I had no idea if my thinking would work to bring us back together, but I was willing to try. And truthfully, I didn't have a better plan.

"Fuck your hand while I fuck your ass," he ordered in a strained voice.

Finally.

I'd been on the verge of begging him to jerk me off while fucking me despite the fact I was trying to let him lead.

I spotted the Lubido on the floor nearby. "Hold on," I said between clenched teeth as I attempted to bend over to pick it up.

He did not "hold on" in the way I asked, instead he held on to me tighter so he could continue to rail me.

Air rushed out of me every time he hit bottom.

Even with stretching out my fingers, the tube of lube was just outside my reach. If Ronan wasn't going to pause to let me grab it, then I would just go without.

Unexpectedly, he kicked it closer with his foot and as soon as I snagged it, he took a handful of my hair and yanked me back up.

One second he'd be gentle, the next he'd be rough. My assumption was he was fighting an internal battle.

He hated that he loved me and would rather love to hate me.

I got it.

I did.

But at least I was now starting to experience more of the gentler side of him than the rough.

I squeezed some of the Lubido onto my palm and dropped it back to the floor near my feet in case we needed it again. My hips jerked back against him when I circled my fingers tightly around my aching length.

I quickly found a rhythm to match Ronan's.

I continued to stroke and twist, the lube making my cock slick enough to easily slide through my fist. I worked myself as Ronan worked me. It also helped me stay loose, making his cock up my ass more welcomed and wanted.

He'd push in, I'd slide my hand back.

He'd pull back, I'd slide my hand forward.

I switched my grip from underhanded to overhanded.

Tightened it. Loosened it.

I imagined it was Ronan's hand instead of my own.

And in those moments of intense pleasure, everything changed. I was no longer *letting* Ronan fuck me. I was encouraging him to fuck me. I *wanted* him to fuck me. And I wouldn't have it any other way.

Everything fell into place and it seemed as if we picked up where we'd left off. Back to when we would do everything we could to make sex pleasurable for both of us. To drive each other out of our minds.

To the point when we were done, we'd collapse on top of each other, panting, sweating, sighing, smiling, laughing. And after we caught our breath, we'd kiss until we lost it again.

It had been good between us, so *right* between us...

Was Ronan remembering that, too?

Or was he trying to keep me a nameless, faceless fuck?

Either way, I knew deep in my heart that we could have that again.

The only difference being who was doing whom.

Tonight he surrounded me. I could see him in the glass in front of me. I could feel him behind me. His warm breath beat against my skin. His heartbeat pounded against my back.

His fingers dug harder into my hips, adjusting me into the perfect position.

Every thrust became calculated. Targeted. Even though he continued to pound my ass with no mercy.

I had no doubt I'd be uncomfortable sitting tomorrow, but I didn't care. I just didn't want him to stop.

No matter what, I was seizing this second chance to fix what I had broken.

My head dropped forward and my chest heaved as I struggled to pull air into my lungs.

With what he was doing to my prostate, I had no doubt I would come soon.

The smooth, methodical twists and pulls of my own hand on my cock become erratic. It got to the point I couldn't concentrate on what I was doing. I was on auto-pilot. My main focus was on the drag of Ronan's cock over my P-spot.

The stretch and pull had turned from discomfort to pleasurable. I was relieved with how damn good it all felt despite me being worried that I couldn't handle it.

I could.

And I wanted more.

I wanted Ronan forever.

I slid my fingers forward until I gripped my cock at the end, only leaving the crown exposed and, instead of pumping, I began to squeeze and release, squeeze and release.

The pressure built inside me.

Flames licked at my lower belly.

And just when I thought he would slow down and turn it from a simple fuck to more of an intimate connection, his demeanor changed again.

He released my hips and snagged both of my nipples within his fingers, twisting them so hard I had to bite back a whimper. I slammed against him, spearing myself on his cock, driving him impossibly deep.

His raw, animalistic grunt filled the air around me.

Keeping a hand on my nipple, he slid his other up to clamp it around my throat. He paused there for a few seconds before sliding it higher until it caught under my jaw, forcing my head to tip up.

With his teeth bared, our eyes locked in the window's reflection.

I was now pumping my cock so quickly, the movement became a blur.

Each slam of his hips against my ass took us one step closer to the edge. Like I was about to tumble out of that window and free fall to the ground.

I was done. I couldn't take anymore.

The ring of my anus pulsed and my balls pulled tight. I groaned as cum shot out of me with an extreme force in the most intense orgasm of my life.

I painted the window with thick, white stripes that immediately began to slide down the glass, turning my cum into an impressionist's painting.

In that moment, I saw stars.

I saw our future.

I saw everything I'd ever wanted in the man standing behind me.

But he wasn't done and I wasn't sure I could take any more without simply disintegrating into a million particles of matter that would float away on the slightest breeze.

I swore Roe's cock swelled even more inside me and made my channel an even tighter fit.

With another low grunt, he drove forward one more time, tensed and stayed buried deep. His cock pulsed as he spilled inside me and a few more drops of cum dripped from my slit to the floor at my feet.

I'd made a mess in a mess-less penthouse.

After one last shudder, his damp forehead pressed to the top of my shoulder.

His chest heaved against my back.

Our sweat mingled, but our choppy and rapid breathing was out of sync.

He might not realize that he was holding me. Practically wrapped around me with his fingers still clutching my throat and his palm still planted on my pumping chest. His hips and sac still smashed against my ass.

Even though I knew it was impossible, I wanted to stay like that forever. Because of that, I wouldn't move until he did.

The fingers gripping my throat finally loosened, then traced down the length of my neck, while he dragged his other hand across my damp chest.

A caress he didn't want to be seen as one.

He lifted his head from my shoulder and once again, our gazes met in the window.

It was us in the reflection, still connected, as well as our city beyond.

A turning point? I sure as hell hoped so.

An actual moment of softness? It seemed to be.

But in a flash, it was gone.

He had slammed every wall back up in place and sealed them with concrete.

I tried not to let the disappointment swallow me as he anchored the condom with his hand and slowly pulled out.

Before I could turn around, he was already heading toward the kitchen.

I glanced back at the window and the mess I left on the glass and floor. Nothing new since I always seemed to leave messes behind.

"I'll clean that up."

"Leave it."

"Roe, I can—"

"I want it as a reminder."

I frowned at his answer as he dumped the full condom into a stainless-steel trash can at one end of the long center island. I knew I'd regret asking, but I did it anyway. "Of?"

"What could've been. What you threw away."

Fuck.

Even though he was back to being distant, it was obvious I had put some more cracks in his walls. With every opportunity he gave me, I would keep chipping away with my sledgehammer.

I would not give up easily. This time I would not walk away. After what just happened, I was more determined than ever.

"We could have that now, Roe." Despite trying to hide it, a sharpness colored my words since my frustration with his attitude was now at level ten.

He wanted to ignore the way we reconnected. The long buried feelings it stirred back to the surface.

I wouldn't let him.

But I was done with his stubbornness for tonight. I was mentally exhausted and extremely disappointed. I knew better than to expect a miracle, that things would change for the better so soon.

But, like a fool, I did.

Again, my mistake.

My fingers shook in a combination of anger and frustration as I snagged my shorts off the floor and jerked them up my legs. I should clean myself up first, but I wasn't asking him for that opportunity.

I'd do it when I got back to my own space.

A space free of Ronan.

A space free of me being emotionally whipped.

A space free of Ronan's emotional damage.

Despite me wanting to get out of there before I released those frustrations, I didn't make it in time. Words erupted from me like an active volcano. "Why am I letting you do this to me? To use me like this. To treat me like I'm simply one of your boy toys."

He glanced up from cleaning himself off with a damp paper towel. His dark brown eyes narrowed on me. "Because of your damn guilt. For fucking me over, Tate. That's why."

I snagged my T-shirt and yanked it over my head. Once it was in place, I said, "I didn't mean to do any of that."

"But you did it anyway."

I closed my eyes while I pulled in a breath. I was already tired of this fight and it had only just begun. I was letting him get to me when I knew better. "I didn't want to do that to you."

"But you did."

I said it slowly and emphasized each word to make sure he heard each and every one, "I had no choice."

His jaw shifted and his face turned sharp. "We all have choices. It was also your choice to allow me to do this to you."

Matching his energy would only make things worse. I needed to be more understanding until he was the same.

I sighed. "You're right. We all have choices. I'm sorry I keep making the wrong ones and that those choices affected you and still do." With that, I strode toward the door.

Just as I reached it, a loud, "Tate!" made me pause.

I didn't want to get my hopes up. That he might apologize for being a dick. Or that he might ask me to stay.

Or just the opposite, he could tell me to go get fucked and not in a sexual way.

"Did you get your car towed?"

My chin jerked back at that unexpected question.

My mouth was bone dry and if I opened it, I was afraid of what I'd say next. I didn't want to destroy the small steps we *had* made tonight, despite how he was currently acting. So, I simply shook my head while still staring at the door and my escape.

I needed to get out of there since I was on the verge of breaking down. I didn't want Ronan to see how easily he could break me.

When I reached for the door handle, something flashed in front of my face.

A small cream-colored card.

I'd been so intent on getting out of there, I hadn't even heard him approach.

"Text me when you need to leave for work tomorrow. I'll give you a ride." His tone was softer but still very guarded.

I stared at the business card. I could make out the name Pak Property Management, Inc. in a maroon font on the front. A phone number was scribbled in black ink across the top.

With a nod, I plucked it from his fingers and crushed it in my fist as I stepped out into the tiny vestibule .

Since I couldn't bear to wait for the elevator, I took the stairs back to my apartment, instead.

~

Tate (Now)

I DEBATED about whether to text Ronan or not. I was restless all night going over what happened and what could have been said differently.

Basically, I was overthinking something I couldn't change. However, I could learn and hopefully improve on the way I would handle it in the future.

He offered to take me to work when he didn't have to. I couldn't say no. A half hour before I had to leave for work, I made the decision to text Ronan instead of calling a car service. I really couldn't afford one since I'd need every spare dime to fix my Toyota.

Earlier in the morning I had called AAA and met the tow truck driver in the parking garage, giving him my keys and telling them to take it to a shop within my covered towing distance, only a measly five miles. He gave me the name of a shop and their number and while I stood watching the Corolla be towed away, the cement block in my gut became even bigger and heavier.

After going back to my apartment and taking a long, hot shower, I texted Ronan, letting him know what time I had to leave. When he didn't respond after a half hour, I began to worry that he was going to ignore me and I'd need to find another ride.

But just when I was pulling up my bank account to see what was left, my phone vibrated and Ronan's text popped up, instructing me to meet him out front at ten-thirty. I had to be at work by eleven for the noon, five, six and six-thirty newscasts, even though I wasn't an anchor. My manager wanted me to be around to watch the production in case something happened to one of the anchors and I needed to pinch-hit since I had the experience.

It was one reason I wore a suit every day. Unfortunately, dry cleaning could get costly. Thankfully, I already owned an extensive suit collection from my years at WGAL and could put that off for a bit.

As he said he would, Ronan picked me up outside the entrance of River View Heights, this time in the black Maserati with the heavily tinted windows. The car was sleek and smart, but didn't fit Ronan. I could see him in something more rugged than an overpriced luxury coupe. Even so, the car was a magnificent and powerful piece of machinery.

He jerked his chin up at me in greeting once I slid into the passenger seat. And when he hit the accelerator, the horsepower pinned me back in my seat. It also purred like a well-fed lion and still had that new-car scent.

Unlike the rotten food stink that permeated my old Corolla.

If I was smart, I'd just junk it. But I couldn't afford decent transportation, which was why I sold my former fancy gas guzzler with the higher insurance premiums and bought the Toyota in the first place.

I was also still making payments and paying for the insurance on Dahlia's Lexus LX, the one she insisted we buy. More because of optics, not because of reliability or affordability. Unfortunately, I couldn't afford to pay for both of our newer vehicles.

She had always wanted to impress and be the perfect "trophy" wife. Unfortunately for her, she picked the wrong man to get her there.

Like Ronan both loved and hated me, I felt the same about Dahlia.

She was a great mother. She had been a decent wife. But deep down I could never get over what she did to become that wife.

Trickery did not make a trusting relationship. She learned that the hard way. Especially when I finally confessed to meeting up with random men because...

Well, the list why was long. And none of the reasons were acceptable.

Not unexpected, she immediately tossed me out of our home, and while she was still furious—not because I was cheating on her with men, but because I had finally gathered enough strength to leave her —she went about destroying my career at WGAL.

I ended up being "reluctantly let go" for everything she told them, some of it she made up. She caused drama that the station didn't want any part of.

Because of the stench left behind, I couldn't find another job around the greater Harrisburg area. That was how I landed back in Pittsburgh and, this morning, in Ronan's car.

I had needed a fresh start with my career in a city that still felt like home, and ended up unexpectedly pursuing a fresh start with Ronan.

The only issue with being back in Pittsburgh, I was about three hours away from my kids. That was the most difficult part.

Since I was still paying for the divorce, alimony, the mortgage, her car payment and for just about everything else, the nest egg I had built was quickly depleted.

However, not arguing over covering almost all the expenses in trying to maintain Dahlia's lifestyle at least softened her hatred toward me to the point she became cooperative with the kids.

She'd usually meet me on the Pennsylvania Turnpike at the Sidling Hill Service Plaza. It was a little more than halfway for her but it was a sensible and safe, easy-on, easy-off meeting spot to exchange the kids for the weekends I had them.

I only hoped she'd follow the custody orders and let me have my allotted time with them this coming summer. Before I left Harrisburg to start my job at Burgh Media, she had, but that didn't mean she'd continue to remain agreeable. She knew I didn't have squat to hire an attorney to fight her if she decided to go against the judge's visitation orders.

My goal was to recover financially with this new job, even if it was a slow climb. I planned on working my ass off and doing a great job so I could climb the ladder as soon as possible.

One of the news anchors was slated to retire this fall and if I played my cards right, when they hired me they said I had a good chance of taking that spot.

Unfortunately, I'd have to deal with living on a string budget until I saw fatter paychecks. I should also consider getting a second job once I got a reliable vehicle or found something within walking or biking distance. My work hours kind of messed up my day, though, so it might be tough.

Right now, I needed to concentrate on getting my feet securely under me at Burgh Media.

I had been so deep in thought and since Ronan didn't say a damn word the whole time, he pulled in front of my place of employment in the blink of an eye.

I shook my head at myself when I realized I had wasted the time during the drive I could have used for conversation and getting him to open up.

I needed to do better if he offered again. But then, without much sleep I wasn't on my game this morning.

"Text me what time you want me to pick you up."

"Roe..."

"Text me," he repeated more firmly.

I stared at his profile since he wasn't looking at me but straight out the windshield.

"Roe," I tried again. I wanted to tell him he didn't have to go out of his way, but, honestly, I was relieved he was willing to do so. And I took it as another small step forward.

"Or don't."

Shit. "Okay, I will."

He pursed his lips and I thought he would say something else but instead, he only nodded. My attention was drawn to his fingers flexing on the steering wheel. Squeezing and releasing, squeezing and releasing.

A sign I recognized from "before" that he was struggling to keep a hold of his emotions.

I wouldn't push it or him. "Thank you. I know you don't have to do this, but I appreciate it."

As I unfolded myself from the Maserati, the pill bottle I had shoved last minute into the pocket of my suit pants fell onto the seat I had just vacated.

Holy shit.

Before I could lunge for it, his hand struck out like a snake and he got it first. "What are these?" He held it up in front of his face and squinted at the bottle of anti-depressants as he turned it and read the prescription label.

Shit. "Nothing."

I leaned into the car and tried to snatch the container from his fingers but he switched hands and put it out of my reach. I would have to climb back into the car and get into a tussle with him to retrieve it.

But really, it was already too late. The name of the prescription was one he'd recognize. And the reason I needed them.

Yes, if I wanted a future with him, he would eventually find out anyway. Only, I had hoped to put it off until we were way beyond where we were currently.

His dark eyes turned to mine, where I still leaned into the passenger side, waiting for him to say something.

When he didn't, I said, "As you know, my life didn't turn out like I'd hoped."

"It's not over yet."

Many times I had wished it was. Hence, the medication. But that was a conversation for another time. Not when I was standing in front of my place of employment.

Without warning, he tossed the pill bottle at me and I barely caught it in time.

"Don't forget it was a life you chose, Tate. You have no one to blame but yourself."

I shoved the container deep into my suit jacket pocket. "You're right. I accept the blame but that doesn't mean damage wasn't left behind. Can we get past that now and move forward?"

"I won't make promises I'm not sure I can keep."

"I'm not asking for a promise. I'm just asking if you'll at least try."

I held my breath as he considered me. "I thought long and hard last night about what you want from me…"

I forced down the lump in my throat as I waited for the other shoe to drop.

This was where he would suggest we only remain civil to each other since we lived in the same building. He'd want to remain strictly neighbors and nothing more.

I was completely floored when he finally said, "I'm willing to try."

What? I grasped the open passenger door to keep from collapsing right there on the pavement. To keep myself from curling up into a ball and begin crying in relief.

I blinked a few times to lessen the sting in my eyes and I pinned my lips together to help keep my composure.

"Roe," managed to work its way up my closed throat.

"Eat early." I waited for him to tell me I'd have to prep again, but instead he finished with, "We'll grab dinner after I pick you up later."

"I… Uh…"

He arched one eyebrow at me. A warning not to fuck this up.

I nodded. "Okay."

"Now… close the door, Tate."

I shut the passenger door and remained at the curb as the GranTurismo sped away like a rocket.

A smile that was actually genuine for once curled my lips. I closed my eyes and lifted my face toward the late morning sun.

It was bright and warm.

I hoped my future was the same.

CHAPTER 18

Ronan (Now)

LYING IN BED, I stared at his profile, wondering if he hadn't done what he did and we had stayed together back then, would we still be together now? Or would our relationship not have withstood the sands of time anyhow?

We'd never know, but either way, here we were…

Two months later from the night I fucked him against the window, taking it day by day. Even hour by hour.

In that time, we kept moving forward. We had stumbled a few times, but so far, we hadn't fallen backwards.

It might have been touch and go in the beginning, but progress had clearly been made. Not only with me, but with Tate, too.

He groaned and stretched next to me. "I'm going to go shower."

Once he rolled out of bed, I watched him move across my bedroom toward the en suite bathroom naked.

His body trim but with muscle definition from almost daily swimming and me making him eat healthier than the cheap junk food he'd been trying to sustain himself on. His blue eyes were now brighter and no longer had dark circles under them. His face looked like he'd shed five hard years from it. He occasionally went to the gym I owned to lift weights with me like we did back at Duquesne, but it wasn't as often as I went.

He paused in the doorway, posing in a way he knew would tempt me. "You coming?" He tipped his head toward the bathroom behind him and the corners of his eyes were crinkled because he knew the way he stood, I wouldn't be able to resist.

Honestly, he didn't have to work very hard for me to join him in the shower. "Yeah. In a minute."

"I'll get it nice and hot for you." The way he said it indicated he was talking about more than the water.

With an arched eyebrow and a sly smile, he disappeared.

"Alfred, shower on!" I called out the command, even though my smart home system now recognized Tate's voice. Alfred obediently repeated it in his monotone AI voice and I heard the multiple shower heads turn on.

I also installed the smart lock app on Tate's phone so he could come and go as he pleased from my place and the roof. He also had access to the basement where he kept his car parked next to my Range Rover.

While I wasn't giving him money directly, I did what I could in the background to help him financially recover.

Even though we had promised not to keep secrets from each other, I was keeping a small one. I had set up a small investment account for him with my stockbroker. He could use whatever it earned when it came time for his children to go to college, *if* he wanted. I'd tell Tate about it later since we were only two months in and while things seemed to be going well, that didn't mean it would continue.

No matter what, he was more put together now than when I first saw him checking his mail in the vestibule. Back then, he had been a total mess.

His job was going well and he had bought a cheap, but newer, Toyota. Little by little, he was piecing his life back together after being financially crippled from the divorce. He was still paying off his lawyer, and would be for a while yet, as well as paying alimony and child support, and a lot of other expenses he didn't have to, solely out of guilt.

I hoped once Dahlia found another "catch" to allow her to continue her desired lifestyle, she'd quickly get a ring on her finger and everything but the child support would end.

Dahlia had sunk her claws into Tate because she thought he'd been a "catch." Her scheme backfired when Tate ended up being far from that.

However, that backfire caused a lot of damage for all involved.

I didn't want to dwell on it because it tended to raise my blood pressure and I reminded myself that he ended up where he should have in the first place.

With me.

He just had to take a long and bumpy detour to get here.

He spent more time in my penthouse than he did in his sublet, except for when his kids came to stay with him. When they did, I stayed out of it. We weren't ready to tell them about us. We also weren't ready for Dahlia to know, either.

Especially since we were still working on that "us." The ground beneath our feet needed to be more solid first.

I tried not to think about how keeping our relationship from his ex and his kids reminded me of our college days, when Tate didn't want anyone to know and we kept "us" under wraps as best as we could. Because of that, I still worried about stepping on a rug that could easily be pulled out from under me.

By Tate. Or even worse, by Dahlia.

Those doubts still lingered, no matter how hard I tried to get past them. It was difficult to completely let them go.

But I shared that concern with Tate. So, he knew where I stood every step of the way. I told him it would not work between us if we weren't open and honest with each other one hundred percent. No matter what it was about.

He agreed.

If he hadn't, he wouldn't be in my bed practically every night or we wouldn't be currently recovering from a hot, sweaty and very satisfying session of sex.

With a long sigh, I faced the fact that I needed to get up to shower, too. But the sex had left me boneless and lazy and not wanting to move.

It was even better now than when we were younger and had a lot more energy. In our twenties it was more about getting off. With us in our thirties, we took the time to appreciate each other. We no longer ripped off each other's clothes and began immediately getting each other off. A fun competition of who could get the other off first.

Instead, I spent time worshipping every inch of Tate with my eyes, my fingers and my mouth. And Tate did the same with me.

Like the saying about fine wine, our sex life had definitely improved with age.

Even so, there had been a few times where, as soon as he walked in the door, I ripped his clothes off, bent him over the kitchen island and railed him so hard we both came within minutes.

Then there were the times he'd come in, find me working late in my home office, shove the paperwork on my desk aside and take me on it.

One time I'd been in the middle of a virtual meeting. I scrambled to hit the power button on my computer so we didn't give my employees an unexpected show, where afterward they'd need to bleach both their eyes and brain.

Especially since it involved their boss having unrestrained anal sex. I could imagine the screenshots that would be jokingly used against me and I certainly didn't want to see still shots of my facial expression when Tate was driving himself home.

I later apologized to everyone involved, using the excuse that my power cut out unexpectedly. When in truth, Tate had "powered" me from behind until we both fell to the floor in a sweaty, cum-covered mess.

I smiled at how hot and spontaneous that had been.

It had taken a few weeks before we changed it up and I bottomed for Tate. Now we switched back and forth, depending on our mood or who initiated.

A month ago we had both gotten tested and now went without condoms since we were exclusive. I'd been getting tested on the regular, but Tate hadn't. With both of us having done random Grindr hookups for years, it was only smart to alleviate that worry.

Was going without a condom messier? Absolutely. Was it better? Damn right it was.

Another benefit was, by trusting Tate enough for us to go without one, it took us one more step forward.

With a groan, I roused myself from my comfortable bed and padded naked toward the bathroom.

Tate had a horrible habit of singing in the shower. He never did it in our apartment in college but, since my obnoxiously large bathroom was done up in mostly marble and tile, it had better acoustics. He took advantage of that.

A lot.

While I wish he didn't since his singing was cringe-worthy, he belted out tune after tune anyway. Not once had I told him to stop—though I'd been tempted many times—because if he was singing Britney Spears or Justin Timberlake's greatest hits I figured he was happy.

At least I hoped he was and he wasn't simply putting on a happy face. He was still taking his anti-depressants—and might for the rest of his life—but at least now that his benefits had kicked in at work, he was going to therapy once a week.

What was said between him and his therapist was one thing we did not discuss and I didn't ask. His therapy sessions were his and his alone and if he felt the need to tell me what was covered in them, I'd listen but other than that, it wasn't my business.

I had done some legwork into buying Burgh Media Group in hopes to add it to my ever-expanding portfolio. Besides the fact I was looking for ways to diversify my investments, I figured if I bought it, Tate could skip being a news anchor and I could appoint him as head of the whole organization. I had no doubt he had the skills to run it successfully since he was a veteran in the business.

When I casually mentioned it to him one night over my favorite Korean take-out, he stared at me with his mouth hanging wide open. Then he flat out told me no. He wanted to earn his way into a better position and didn't want me using my money to buy it for him.

I reluctantly nixed that idea, thinking I could address it again down the road. I also toyed around with starting a multi-media group of my own. Pak Media Group, Inc.

It had a nice ring to it.

Again, I was trying to help him become financially stable without actually writing him a check. He had helped me out several times in college and I only wanted to return the favor. Even if nothing else came out of it, he finally understood why I always resisted taking what he offered back then.

He wanted to get ahead on his own merits. Just like I had in college.

I respected that.

When I stepped into the bathroom, Tate's back was to me as he shampooed his dark hair and hit a wrong note while singing *Oops!... I Did It Again* badly. Especially with the accompanying dance moves.

Since he didn't know I was there yet, I smothered my combination laugh-groan and let him get in a few more moves before I joined him and those moves changed to "oops!... *we* did it again."

A large soaking tub sat in front of one of the huge picture windows. I had used it myself maybe twice before recently spending plenty of nights in it together after sex. With the lights dimmed, we could see the view of the city and we'd talk—about everything and also about completely nothing—until the water went tepid.

But the shower in which he was currently putting on the equivalent of an elementary school talent show was the *pièce de résistance* in the room that opened up to both the main bedroom and adjoining massive walk-in closet.

The shower was state of the art with multiple shower heads and massaging jets and surrounded with glass. When I designed it I added so many fancy features that I never used most of them before Tate came back into my life. Now, we found reasons to use them all.

Before Tate, I showered and got out. I only occasionally lingered in it even though it was built like what he called an adult waterpark. All those years I played alone in it. Just me and my fist, assisted by my fantasies. *Hell,* my memories.

But those memories had always been empty comfort. They weren't good company and had made me feel even lonelier.

Worse, the memories you wanted to hold onto the tightest tended to fade away the quickest.

The memories you wanted to forget tended to haunt you forever.

Our goal was to replace those memories with new ones. Even better ones.

And we were about to make one more.

He rinsed the soap from his hair and turned to find me staring at him with amusement. At least it got him to quit butchering one of Britney's most popular songs. "Your shower always makes me feel like I'm a snack in a display case."

"You *are* a snack, T."

Streams of water rolled down his face as he pointed a lopsided smile in my direction and wiggled his dark eyebrows. "One good enough to eat?"

"Always."

His smile, when not forced, had always made him glow and had been infectious. It still was. A precious gift that one can only hope for and be lucky enough to receive. When he gave that gift to me, I always tried to give him one back.

"Are you hungry?" he asked.

"Sure am and I'm about to remedy that." I pulled open the glass door and stepped inside. If we were into it, we could fit another half dozen men in there with us.

But I was never sharing Tate again. With anyone.

Stepping under one of the shower heads, the stream of hot water beat against my skin, quickly washing away the dried sweat and cum clinging to me.

Before I could pump body wash from the dispenser attached to the single tiled wall onto my palm to clean myself up thoroughly, Tate was doing it first. When he stepped toe to toe with me, his mesmerizing blue eyes framed with the thick, wet lashes locked with mine. "Turn around. I'll wash your back."

It seemed like Tate was hungrier than I was.

"Turn around," he demanded again when I didn't move fast enough.

"The shower's big enough that you could give me a wide berth, T. It's not like we're fighting for real estate in here."

His lips twitched and he shrugged. I'd discovered he loved giving me orders to see if I'd follow them.

I sighed with feigned impatience and, of course, did what he wanted.

~

Tate (Now)

I SWEPT my handful of soap across his broad, muscular back. His skin the perfect canvas for his ink, the same as his chest and both arms. One night I had explored each and every one of those tattoos and he'd explained why he got it and if it had any deep meaning behind it.

Since he had a bunch of ink, that explanation took a good bit of time. But as he talked about them, I had touched each and every one with both my fingers and my lips.

I squirted some shampoo from the wall dispenser onto my palm, then dumped it on top of his head before getting more body wash. He washed his hair while I washed his ass, taking my time to tease him before moving up and down both legs, spinning him around and scrubbing sudsy water over his chest, arms, shoulders and face.

I left the best place for last.

With another handful of soap, I swept my fingers between his legs and over his perineum, around his balls and then got to business by using the slippery gel to fist his cock. No surprise he was hard again, even after everything we'd done earlier in bed.

It didn't take much to get him there. A suggestive look, a heated smile, an innuendo. A touch, a kiss, a brush of my lips across the back of his neck when he least expected it…

His eyes focused on mine since we were face to face and practically nose to nose.

I reluctantly released him. "Rinse off."

"I was enjoying that," came his deep rumble, amplified by the acoustics of the immense shower.

"I can tell, but I have a better plan."

He cocked one dripping, dark eyebrow. "Better than jerking me off?"

"You'll have to tell me afterward."

"I don't know, T. You're pretty damn good at jerking me off."

That was because I had years of practicing on myself. With Dahlia, I never knew what got her off, unless she complained that I was doing it wrong. Because I had the same parts as Ronan, it was much easier to figure it out with him. If it turned me on, it probably would turn him on, too. "Wouldn't you rather have me on my knees?"

His sly smile went wide. "Shouldn't even have to ask."

I wouldn't lie, it was his smile that first sucked me in. There was something about it so genuine and, just like he said about mine, his lit him up from the inside out, too.

It didn't matter if it was a sly smile, a happy smile, mixed with a laugh, or even a suggestive one, it got me each and every time. When he wasn't smiling, I had always felt the need to do everything in my power to make him do so.

Right now the very smile I had fallen in love with was lazy and relaxed. But in contrast, those brown eyes that also always drew me in were full of heat.

"How soon are you getting on those knees?"

"Since these knees tend to complain, I think we need to keep a waterproof cushion in the shower."

"Next time." He put his hand on my head and pushed downward.

"Are you getting impatient?"

"I'm always impatient to get your mouth around my cock."

"Now you know how I feel when you text me hours before I leave work and tell me you plan on sucking the brains right out of me when I get home."

Home.

I didn't officially move in yet because of the kids. I figured in time, if things kept moving forward like they were, we'd be living together once again. I was stuck in a year-long sublease so it wasn't like I was in a rush, but saving on rent would help.

"That isn't nice of you. I walk around the offices and studio doing my best to hide my... reaction." I never carried around so many folders full of blank paper in my life.

"Sure, T. I know you go into a bathroom stall and think about me sucking you off while you rub one out."

I rolled my lips inward to avoid laughing. He knew me too well. "If someone catches me doing that, you'll get me fired and I need that job."

"They fire you, I'll buy the corporation out from under them."

"No, you won't. We've discussed this."

He pushed more firmly on my head. "Less talking and more sucking."

I shook it. "You're bossy enough. I can't imagine what you'd be like if you became my real boss."

His face lit up, his eyes gleamed and the corners of his lips tipped up.

"See? That look right there says it all." I lowered myself to my knees and glanced up again.

Even being cocky, Ronan was so damn beautiful.

I had no better way to describe him.

I considered him even more beautiful now than I remembered. And, like Ronan, I remembered those days so long ago like they were only yesterday. Both the good and the bad.

We were currently working on more of the good and no longer focusing on the bad.

We were still considered boys back then and now we were both mature men. Life had banged us up a bit but I was certain we'd be okay in the end.

Sometimes I had to pinch myself to make sure this was my life now.

I had Ronan. I was free of Dahlia… for the most part. I had two children I loved with all my heart. All I had to do was become financially stable once more and I'd be golden.

More importantly, I needed to find a way to spend more time with my kids. I wanted to get to the point where Dahlia and I shared custody instead of the way it was currently.

I hoped Ronan would be onboard with that. Since I wanted him to be a permanent part of my life, he would be a vital part of my kids' lives, too.

Recently, after a long weekend with them, I made it clear to him that Alec and Mazie would always come first, no matter what. He understood and seemed to be fine with it.

However, I dreaded telling Dahlia about us. It might stir up some long-dormant grudge and bitterness. If she got nasty about me and Ronan being back together, my kids might suffer because of it.

I had to handle the whole situation with care.

Unlike Ronan's cock.

As soon as I pulled it deep into my mouth, his fingers weaved into my hair. He loved to fuck my face, not just get blown, so I relaxed my throat and prepared for him to do so.

No matter how rough he got, I still loved giving Ronan head. I did back in college and even that second time on the roof when he'd done it more as a punishment than pleasure.

When it came to sex with him, the only thing I loved more was when he bottomed for me.

While giving him head, I held a lot of power, even when he was thrusting. Depending on what techniques I used, I could make him come quickly, or I could draw out the pleasure as long as possible.

One time I delayed him coming for so long, his legs shook and my jaws began to lock. But when he finally came, I swore his soul left his body. He couldn't move for a long time afterward.

I decided since we were in the shower and I was on my knees, which were already beginning to complain, I would make this a quickie. I knew just how to go about it and also knew my method would guarantee no complaints from him for keeping it short.

Though, I did hear a noise at the back of his throat that sounded like a protest when I leaned back and let his cock slip from between my lips. "I need the lube."

A tube of non-water-soluble lube was kept in the shower for instances like these. Containers of lube were stashed all over Ronan's penthouse because we tended to have sex at any time, in any place.

He knew I didn't need lube for head so, of course, he didn't hesitate to grab it. Especially since it was within arm's reach. But I didn't take it from him, I only lifted my left hand out of the spray of hot water and he applied the perfect amount.

I took his cock back into my mouth at the same time I reached between his spread legs. Since he knew what was about to happen, he pressed the top of his back to the tiled wall behind him for support for when things got intense.

Because they *would* get intense.

I took my time and worked my slick index and middle finger

inside him until I was one knuckle deep, then two, and pushed on until I was finally three knuckles deep.

From experience, I had no problem locating the walnut-sized spot and began to stroke my fingertips back and forth over it. As soon as his hips and his cock both began to twitch and he thrusted even harder into my mouth, I alternated between circling his P-spot and petting it.

I went around and around, occasionally pressing it gently like a start button, because that was exactly what it was. What I did gunned Ronan's engine and he was about to speed down the track. But would he reach the finish line before my knees did?

"Fuck, T... Fuck!"

Oh yeah, I had no doubt he would.

I continued the onslaught and smiled around his cock as I sucked him from rim to root with two fingers squeezing and releasing him at the thick base. How he wasn't sliding down the wall, I didn't know, since we usually didn't do this while standing due to it achieving the best, most intense orgasms.

This method was usually quick but explosive.

It didn't take long before I knew he was getting close when what was hitting my tongue wasn't cum yet but fluid milked from his prostate. The moans, groans and ragged breathing was a pretty good sign, too.

His hips violently jerked forward, then jerked backward, telling me he was shattering from the inside out.

"T... I'm goin—" He didn't even get out the whole warning before he jammed his cock against the back of my throat and spilled his warm, salty cum. "*Oooh fuuuuuck*," came out on a long, deep groan.

Hearing him fall apart made my own cock wake up and pay attention.

As his muscles continued to twitch, his cock throbbed intensely and so did the tight ring of muscle pulsing around my fingers.

With the simultaneous penile and prostate orgasms, he was hit with one big, happy double whammy.

I also looked forward to when he did the same to me. However, I wasn't done with him yet and continued to stroke his prostate until his whole body jerked uncontrollably and I had drawn every drop from him.

It wasn't until he begged me to stop that I finally backed off and glanced up to see his head thrown back, his eyes closed, his mouth parted and his chest heaving.

I did that to him. That gave me as much satisfaction as he got, the only difference was mine was more emotional and his was physical. I took pleasure in taking the man to his knees without his knees even touching the ground.

When I grabbed his hips to use his body to help me rise to my feet, his hand appeared in front of my face. As soon as I grabbed it, he hauled me up and into him.

Wrapping his arms tightly around me, he whispered, "I love you, T," right before he took my mouth in a kiss that showed me just how much he did.

Yes, we were finally making good memories again. And I would damn well treasure every one of them.

CHAPTER 19

Ronan (Now)

I HEARD his bare feet making their way down the spiral staircase. While he had been in the pool, I warmed up one of the dinners delivered earlier in the week.

Tate occasionally cooked for us since he was better at it than I was. But since he worked late and once he got home he liked to swim laps to stay in shape, I still kept the freezer fully stocked by ordering meals from my favorite chef at the local downtown restaurant.

The table was set for two and I had placed a bottle of Cabernet Franc on ice to chill.

As he strode through the kitchen only wearing his damp swim trunks and with his cell phone and a wet towel in his hands, I expected him to keep heading toward the bedroom to quickly rinse off the chlorine in the shower.

He didn't.

He set his stuff on the counter nearby and then went bare toe to bare toe with me.

When he gave me a blinding smile, I cocked an eyebrow, wondering what was up.

"I just wanted to let you know that the whole time I swam laps, I could only think of you. It made me swim faster because I couldn't wait to come back down here and tell you how much I love you."

If that declaration didn't make my heart swell to the point of exploding, nothing would. "You tell me all the time, T."

"It's still not enough."

Damn.

I slowly pulled in a breath. If he asked me for the world, I'd do everything in my power to give it to him. I was that far gone. And here we were only six months in this second time around.

Our second chance at finding our very own forever.

Even though things were going well, I reminded myself six months was only a blip in time. As we both knew, the calm seas that were currently giving us smooth sailing could turn choppy by an unexpected storm at any time.

I wrapped my arms around his waist and pulled him into me. His skin was cooler to the touch than normal from being in the pool, but I could easily turn that around.

He planted both palms on my chest to push away from me. "My bathing suit is still wet."

I tightened my hold, not letting him escape. "I don't care." Pressing my mouth lightly to his, I murmured, "So you know, I don't tell you enough, either." His erection pressed against me. "Obviously, you weren't only thinking about how much you loved me."

He shook against me with barely-contained laughter and I grinned against his mouth. Then I claimed it completely.

We kissed until I was hard, too, and we were grinding our cocks together. If we didn't stop, dinner would burn and we'd end up having to disinfect the counter.

All of that might be worth it, though.

I pulled back with a resigned sigh.

He rocked his pelvis, grinding his hard-on once more against mine. "Do we want to thumb-wrestle to see who bottoms tonight?" he asked a little breathlessly.

"We already know who will win that."

He lifted his right fist and wiggled his thumb. "I've been working on my thumb strength," he teased.

I *mmm-hmm*'d. "You can use that thumb elsewhere."

"If we don't decide now, how are we going to know which one of us should eat light?" he teased, playfully pinching my nipple through my T-shirt.

As I opened my mouth to answer him, his phone vibrated loudly against the granite countertop with an incoming text. Before I could see who it was from, he pulled free of my arms and quickly snatched it up.

With a furrowed brow, he read it and murmured, "Sorry, I have to make a quick phone call."

He walked out of the kitchen and into the living room with his head tipped down as he tapped away at his cell phone, his unruly dark hair falling across his forehead. Even with his tightly-trimmed beard covering his jaw, it was easy to see when it clenched.

He put the phone to his ear and didn't stop walking until he stood in front of the stretch of windows.

I shouldn't listen in. I should mind my own business. But I didn't like his expression. Something was off.

With a quick glance at me, he asked, "Hey, honey, what's wrong?"

He paused as he listened to who I figured was his daughter on the other end of the conversation. She was the only one I'd ever heard him call that endearment.

"Didn't Mommy tell you that I'd see you this coming weekend?" During another pause, Tate turned his back toward me, changing his tone so it was more soothing. "Don't cry, Mazie, it's only a few more sleeps away. I promise."

Silence followed his promise, but his tense shoulders said it all.

"Yes, just a few more days. I'll be there before you know it."

Another long gap occurred as he listened intently to his daughter, who tended to be chatty.

But one thing he had mentioned caught my attention. He had said "there." Normally, he spent the weekends he had with his kids here in Pittsburgh.

"I can't, honey. I…" His head dropped and his voice softened even more. "I don't live there any more, Maze, so I can't sleep there. That's why you and Alec normally come sleep here in my place." After another long gap, he spoke in a rush. "Don't cry, honey. I'm sorry… I'm sorry. I know it's hard for you. It's hard for me, too. I miss you and think about you every minute. I always count the seconds until I see you again."

Pinching the bridge of his nose, he took a quick glance over his shoulder at me with his nostrils flared and his expression pained. Then once again, he turned away.

"Put Mommy on, please. I love you, Mazie girl," he called out at the last second, his voice catching. He cleared the rough from his throat and raised his voice, making it stronger when he said, "Right… Friday… Yes, we can. I'll be there." He nodded. "Okay, see you then. Goodnight."

His head dropped and he tapped the top of his phone against his forehead a few times before he took a deep breath, lifted his head and headed back to me in the kitchen.

He stood there for a moment, looking lost. Then with a frown, he said, "I'm going to go shower."

I glanced over at the timer on the oven. "We're about to eat, Tate."

"I need to shower."

He was shutting down and I needed answers.

"Do you want to tell me what's going on? Why you're driving all the way to Harrisburg to pick them up instead of meeting her at Sideling Hill like normal?"

"I'm staying in Harrisburg this weekend."

My heart stopped. "Why am I only hearing this now?"

"Because it doesn't matter where me and the kids stay, Roe. When they're here with me, I don't see you, anyway."

While that was true, I was still comforted by the fact he was close. And if he needed anything from me, emergency or otherwise, I could be there in a flash. We could easily remind the kids that I was his neighbor.

"But you haven't once stayed in Harrisburg since you moved out here."

I might be going a little overboard but it wasn't the fact that he was going to Harrisburg that bothered me, it was the fact that Dahlia was there.

Was I going to lose Tate to Dahlia again not long after making things right between us? Would she try something? To trick him into getting what she wanted? To guilt him into complying with her demands? Even use the kids against him?

I didn't trust her one damn bit. And that lack of trust made my anxiety spike and unreasonable thoughts spin through my mind.

"Look, I know this is getting you upset. I can see it on your face, Roe. I can see it in how tense you've become. You're white-knuckling the damn counter! But bottom line is, my kids are a piece of me." He slapped his hand over his heart a couple of times. "They're my world."

I pried my fingers from the counter and stepped away from it. "As they should be."

"So, whatever I need to do to keep things civil between me and Dahlia, I'm going to do it."

Whatever I need to do... I'm going to do it. My blood turned cold. "Do you want to explain that?"

"She wants to sit down to talk about the kids and how to better co-parent. She also wants me to attend their teacher-parent conferences."

Panic starting to rise and I had a flashback of that day in our apartment when he announced she was pregnant and that he was going to marry her. It had come completely out of left field and so was this news.

"When are the parent-teacher conferences?"

"Friday. I put in for time off and I'm leaving Thursday night."

This was the first I was hearing of that, too. It wasn't the fact he was going, I couldn't argue that because these were his children and I had no problem with his kids coming before me. If they didn't, I'd actually have a bigger problem with that. But what bothered me—besides Dahlia—was the fact he hadn't given me a heads up about it.

I couldn't call him out for lying to me, because technically, he hadn't.

Had he been worried about my reaction and planned on waiting until the last minute to tell me? Because of course, I would've eventually found out anyway. Especially if he left Thursday and never returned home with the kids.

No matter what the reason, it was bringing some of our old baggage I thought had been laid to rest right back up to the surface again.

"Are you mad?"

"About you spending time with your kids? About doing what a father needs to do? No. But I don't trust her, Tate, and you shouldn't, either."

"I get why you think like that and you have a valid reason for it, but no matter what, she's the mother of my children."

"Children you chose to have with her even after she deceived you to get pregnant with the first one!" burst from me. "Even though at your core, you are gay."

"Roe," he breathed. His disappointment in my outburst was clear.

I was unraveling and worse, I was scared. And I was not one to scare easily.

"We had Alec and Mazie because... I thought it would save our marriage. Spoiler... Having kids doesn't help with marital issues when your marriage shouldn't have happened in the first place. You were right on that. I had this underlying need to keep trying to do right by her. I tried and tried and failed every damn time. But in the end, having kids for the reason we did is not good for them."

"I'll keep that in mind if I ever need to save a marriage I got bullied into. But, here's a thought... Instead of having more children, did you ever think being honest with Dahlia would have been the better option?"

Tate didn't answer right away.

"Truth hurts, doesn't it?" I asked. "And as you know, it's even more painful when that truth is ignored. You lived a lie for over a decade, Tate."

"You don't need to tell me that since I lived it." His voice had risen just like mine had.

We'd been doing so damn well, and here we were stumbling again.

I was starting to wonder if it was all worth it.

"Roe, I promise this weekend won't change a damn thing between us. I want 'us' the same as you do and I'm not going to let anyone destroy us again."

"I want to believe that, Tate. You don't know how much I want to believe that. But I'm not going to lie to you because we promised not to lie to each other… I'm struggling with this whole thing. And because the kids don't know about me, I can't even come along." To reassure myself.

I hated feeling this vulnerable.

We had come so far in the last few months. And now this. I was worried this would turn into a huge setback. Or even possibly break us again.

Worse, I had no idea my self-confidence could be so easily rattled.

The thing was, I knew Tate wasn't doing this to me on purpose. I needed to focus on that fact. And the fact that he'd gone above and beyond to fix our relationship. He'd done anything and everything in his power to do so.

I also needed to remember that he went above and beyond for his children in every way he could. He wanted to be the best father to his children that he could be. Ultimately, he was a good man with a good heart who had made a mistake he spent years trying to make up for. To Dahlia and to me.

Guilt could be a powerful motivator.

"You need to trust me, Roe."

"I do."

"No. Your trust in me is shaky right now. I can see that. But you know I love you."

"You said you love Dahlia, too."

"As the mother of my children. Do I really have to remind you that I'm *in* love with you? *You* are my soulmate. *You* are my one true forever."

I nodded because I wanted to believe that. I did. I guess I had more issues to work through myself. But I'd first wait until I was sure Tate came back to me after spending a long weekend with Dahlia.

Maybe I needed to make an appointment with a therapist, too. Because I loved Tate too much to lose him again. I didn't want to be the one to sabotage us by mistake.

He held my heart in his hands because I had given it to him. I needed to trust him with it. I needed to have faith. In him and in us.

"When you get back, I'll be waiting."

He nodded and I could see his relief smooth out the tension in his face.

At that point, I realized I'd been overlooking the fact he was stressing over the whole weekend as much as I was. I needed to be more supportive and look at the bigger picture.

"And I expect you to call me every night after the kids are asleep," I added.

He grabbed both of my biceps and gave them a reassuring squeeze. "I will. I promise."

I blew out a breath, hoping it would take my worries along with it. "Okay."

"Okay," he echoed.

"Just please… don't get drunk around her," I half-teased.

With a soft snort, he crossed his fingers and drew an X over his heart. "I promise not to touch a drop."

Ronan (Now)

I SAT in my living room with the lights off and a glass of The Macallan in my hand while I stared out over the city skyline.

I didn't move when I heard the lock click on my door. Or when it opened. Or when I heard keys, a wallet and whatever else he'd been carrying get dumped onto the counter.

Or when I watched his reflection kick off his shoes and pad in socks over to where I sat.

I was relieved he was home.

My love for him had never been more apparent than the moment I read his text telling me he was on his way home, followed by two more short messages: *I love you* and *I miss you.*

I sent the same two texts back.

He settled on the couch next to me with a sigh, kicked his feet up on the marble coffee table, then leaned into me.

I wrapped my arm around his shoulders and pulled him even closer.

We sat there quietly for a few minutes simply appreciating each other's company. His closeness quickly filled the emptiness I'd felt all weekend without him.

"How'd it go?" I already knew most of it but I figured I'd take his emotional "temperature."

He took the glass from my fingers and took a long sip of the scotch. He released a long sigh when he was done. "Exactly how I figured it would."

I didn't like the way he said it. Something must have happened that I wasn't aware of. "What didn't you tell me?"

"I told you everything every night I talked to you. But what I'm about to tell you happened after I dropped the kids off at the house before I left."

Immediately my hackles raised. I was ready to go to war to not only keep Tate, but to protect his relationship with his children.

"She sent the kids to their rooms and hit me with something I hadn't expected... She wants me to move home."

She what? She wanted that for herself or for the kids?

"Why did she offer that?" I forced up my tight throat, because the words had to squeeze past my rising trepidation.

"My guess? She's tired of going at it alone. It's a lot more difficult than she thought, even with my financial help."

Well, no shit. She had always wanted an easy life. She expected Tate to be the one to provide it. That was clear when she visited me that day in my dorm room.

He had been paying for everything when they lived together, now he was only paying what the court ordered. She actually had to do for herself for once.

"And what do you want?"

"I want to spend more time with my kids."

Immediately, my heart became heavy and my chest became tight. "Tate—"

He cut me off, probably saving me from saying something we'd both regret later. "But therapy has taught me an important lesson."

I studied his profile as he stared at the lowball glass in his hand.

"I don't want to force a relationship that was never meant to be. I tried that and it didn't work. If I'm not happy, my kids will pick up on that. I want them to witness a loving, healthy and happy relationship, not what Dahlia and I had. Even though we tried to hide it, I'm sure they could sense it. Even if they didn't now, they would when they got a little older."

I lifted the hand I had rested on his shoulder and drew my fingertips along the edge of his hair. "What did you tell her?"

"The truth about us and that I'm never coming home to be with her. I also offered to take the kids more than what the custody agreement says."

"And?"

Tate shook his head. "She said she'd think about it."

"Will she tell the kids about us before you're ready?"

"I don't think so."

"Will she poison them against you because of me?" My distrust of her made me think that could be a possibility.

"I hope not." He didn't sound confident.

"And if she does?"

He lifted his face to mine and his eyes were as sharp as a hawk. "Then she will have an ugly fight on her hands, but I hope to avoid that if at all possible."

"Tate…"

"I know it wouldn't be good for Alec or Mazie but I also need to show them that they need to stand up for themselves. If it comes down to it, that's what I'm going to do. Even if it doesn't, every time I have them, I'll talk to them about everything that's going on, but in a neutral way. I don't want to poison them against Dahlia. No matter what, she's a good mother and she loves them. So, I hope she doesn't do anything that would hurt them emotionally."

"That's a good plan."

"I didn't tell her yet, but once I get my feet under me a little more and can afford a good attorney, I'll be going for fifty-fifty custody."

I blinked. Fifty percent custody meant he'd need to tell them about me, about us, sooner than later.

Realistically, I could front him the funds for a good attorney, or even pay for the fees outright, but I wouldn't suggest it since he was trying to get financially stable on his own. But if he asked, I wouldn't hesitate to help.

He reached up, grabbed my hand playing with his hair and interlocked his fingers with mine. He took another sip of The Macallan, then leaned his head back against the leather couch with a sigh.

"You know, I'll never regret having my children. But I do regret not leaving Dahlia when I began seeking sex outside of our marriage. I regret lying to her about that even though she was aware of how much I loved you when she got pregnant. She sabotaged us, Roe. And then I turned around and sabotaged me and her. Hers was on purpose, mine was not, but I'm still just as guilty. I'll own that to the day I die."

I took the glass of scotch from his hand, downed the rest of it and placed the glass on the floor. I turned us until we faced each other, but stayed quiet because I wanted to listen. It was something I needed to do more of, instead of simply reacting.

Reacting before thinking things through could be damaging.

I could keep my cool during business and that helped make my company successful. I needed to do the same with our relationship, so that could make us more successful, too.

After a few seconds of silence between us, he finally continued. "I also regret not searching for you the moment I walked away from her because I finally embraced who I was and realized that would never change. Honestly, like I told you on the roof that night, I didn't think you'd ever want to see me again. I was afraid if I hunted you down and you only spit in my face—and I'm not saying I wouldn't deserve that—it would have been harder than just leaving you alone. However, not finding you earlier is one of my biggest regrets. And as you know, I have a long list of them."

When the silence descended between us, I waited again to see if he was done talking or had more to say. When he showed no signs of it, I said, "To be completely transparent, I never followed your career, Tate. I never watched one news program that you were in. I just couldn't. I didn't search or stalk you on social media, either. I couldn't do that to myself. Because just you being in my mind and memories was difficult enough. Instead of that, I concentrated on being the most successful businessman I could be. I lost you, but I fought to keep from losing myself. I was afraid if I kept track of you, it would eat me from the inside out until nothing was left."

"It was the same for me."

"And the reason you had no idea I owned this building before you moved in."

He tilted his head as he stared at me. "Out of all the buildings in Pittsburgh I could have chosen, how did I end up in yours?"

"Do you really want that answer?"

His eyebrows rose. "Do you know it?"

"I have a pretty good guess."

"I would have to believe in fate."

"Maybe you should."

He turned his head enough to look out the windows. He nodded. "You're right. I should. Maybe everything that happened in the time between happened for a reason."

"I'm not sure I'd go that far."

He turned back to me, a slight upward curl to his lips. "You don't think it made us appreciate each other more now?"

"I appreciated you back then, Tate. I just didn't appreciate what you did."

He ran the back of his knuckles across my jaw. "I plan on making that up to you for the rest of my life."

"No." I shook my head. "You need to stop doing that and I need to stop expecting it. We need to start fresh from here, this very moment. We said we were going to stop looking backward and only look forward. Let's stick to that."

"That sounds like a great plan."

"I'm good at planning."

He smiled. "What do you have planned for the rest of the night?"

"Besides holding onto you and never letting you go?"

"That's a good start, but yes…"

"Well, first," I began, "I'm going to tell you how much I love you, then I'm going to show you how glad I am you're home and how much I missed you."

"That sounds like a great plan, too."

"Told you I'm good at that."

"You, Ronan Pak, are good at a lot of things."

I slipped my arm from around his shoulders, got to my feet and held out my hand.

As soon as he took it and rose to his feet, I pulled him into me and whispered, "I love you. I'm glad you're home and I missed you more than you'll ever know."

His amazing blue eyes crinkled at the corners. They held a sheen and his nostrils flared slightly. "I love you, I can't wait for us to make a home together and I promise you'll never have to miss me again."

I didn't want to assume our relationship would be perfect.

I thought that before and learned the hard way I was wrong.

Nothing was perfect.

At twenty, I had stars in my eyes.

Now at almost thirty-three? I had stardust.

But we'd continue to build on what we had until I could clearly see those stars once again.

EPILOGUE

WHERE IT STARTED

Tate (A year later)

I PULLED my Toyota Highlander beneath River View Heights and parked it next to the Maserati.

I was home much later than normal since my boss had pulled me into his office as I was getting ready to leave for the evening. He had given me the news I'd been hoping for and I couldn't wait to share it with Ronan.

I grabbed my phone off the passenger-side seat and figured I'd let him know I was on my way up to our penthouse, in case he had dinner already warming in the oven.

I texted, *I'm home. I'll be up shortly,* then hurried to get out of the car. While jogging up the steps to the door, I got an answering text. I glanced at it quickly as I pushed my way into the lobby.

Once the door closed behind me, I paused and read the text again because there was no way I read that correctly the first time.

Meet me on the roof. Be on your knees willing and waiting.

My eyebrows pinned together and I scrubbed a hand over my hair.

What the hell? What was Ronan thinking? It wasn't even ten o'clock yet so the other residents would still have access to the roof. Plus, I was still wearing a suit.

I was also tired to the point I decided to skip my swim tonight. Really, all I wanted to do was head upstairs, get undressed, grab something to eat and then curl up with Ronan for the rest of the night. After telling him the news first, of course.

When the exterior doors opened, I saw the Callahans and Mr. Pibbles heading inside.

Shit.

I stabbed the elevator button a dozen times to hurry the car along, even though I knew that wouldn't work. But desperation made one do desperate things.

As soon as the doors slid open, I just about threw myself inside and frantically pushed the button to close the doors.

I breathed a sigh of relief as my view of the Callahans was cut off before they made it from the vestibule into the lobby. I didn't want to fight off the little shit Mr. Pibbles while he snapped at my ankles. I didn't think my head could take his obnoxious yapping, either. Nor did I want to deal with Mrs. Callahan's sneer that she always pointed our way once they realized Ronan and I weren't only roommates.

I stared at the numbers on the display above the doors as they ticked up one floor at a time. Finally, it arrived at the roof access level and as soon as they opened, I stepped out of the elevator, out of the exit door and onto the roof into the slightly chilly night air.

I glanced around and was relieved the space was empty of any of our neighbors. I'm sure none of them wanted to get to know us any better than they already did.

The regular lights were off and only the pool and string lights were lit, giving the area a soft glow.

I automatically went to the pergola I had kneeled under the time Ronan had used the Grindr app to message me and demand I meet him on the roof.

The hookup app had long been deleted from both our phones. We would never need it again. If something ever happened between

Ronan and me, I swear I'd become a monk and only concentrate on my children.

My lips twitched at my own lie about becoming a monk. Or even becoming celibate. I'd eventually implode if I tried.

I grabbed one of the lounge chair cushions, placed it on the wood platform of the pergola and, with a groan, lowered myself to my knees to wait.

Luckily, it wasn't even two minutes later before the door from the penthouse to the roof opened and Ronan stepped out.

His expression was serious but beyond that, unreadable.

However, he wore a dark, freshly pressed suit that fit him perfectly. In the time we'd been together I saw him wear one once when he was headed to close on a huge apartment complex right outside the city. Even though it was a multi-million dollar deal, he joked about showing up dressed like he normally did—in holey jeans and a snug, worn T-shirt—to prove that no one should ever judge a book by its cover.

As much as he hated wearing suits, I loved him in one. It made him look like he should be on a magazine cover, like Esquire. I actually had to wipe away some drool that caught in the corner of my mouth that day, and I also had to do it again as he strode with a purpose across the roof to where I waited.

When he stopped in front of me, he tipped his face down. I wasn't sure if I should talk or simply listen.

When his head tilted slightly and his dark brown eyes dropped to his waist in what looked like a silent demand, I figured he wanted to do a replay of when I gave him head that second time up on the roof. The time he fucked my face without mercy. I wasn't opposed to it, so I automatically reached for his belt buckle.

But before I could grab it, he grabbed my hands and pulled me to my feet. As soon as I was standing, Ronan dropped to one knee.

If he hadn't been holding onto my hand, I would've stumbled back in surprise.

My heart began to race and my vision became blurry as he pulled a small black velvet box from inside his suit jacket pocket.

I was trying not to freak out, but I was *freaking out*. I was sure they could see the whites of my eyes all the way up on the space station.

How was this happening the same day I was promoted to a top news anchor spot?

"Tate…" he started.

Holy shit! "Yes!" I shouted.

He rolled his eyes. "Can I ask first?"

"No! The answer is yes!"

"Let me—"

"It's yes. Yes! Fuck yes!"

He dropped his head and shook it.

"Okay," I conceded. "Sorry. Ask."

He turned his face back up to me with his lips pressed tightly together. Probably to keep from laughing since this was supposed to be serious.

I slapped the hand he wasn't holding over my mouth and nodded, hoping he'd hurry up before I screamed "yes" a thousand more times.

"Tate Allan Harris…"

Another yes was about to burst uncontrollably from me. I barely managed to keep it contained.

"Will you…"

Now he was screwing with me by asking so slowly. Did he know I was about to collapse into a heap at any second?

I opened my mouth and he glared at me. I shut it.

"Tate Allan Harris, will you love me for the rest of our lives?"

I waited.

He gave me a look.

"Oh… I guess I'm supposed to answer now? Yes!"

He licked his lips and the corners of his amused eyes crinkled. "Will you also become my husband and stand by my side through thick and thin?"

"Damn right I will!" I pulled on the hand that was holding mine, indicating he should stand, too. As soon as he did, I said, "Ronan Pak, will you be my husband and stand by my side through thick and thin?"

"Absolutely."

I smiled. He smiled.

"Do we kiss now?" I asked. I wasn't sure since I'd never proposed before or even been proposed to since my last marriage had been more of an arranged marriage than a willing one.

He shook his head and opened the box in his hand.

As soon as I saw it, I lost my breath. "Is that an engagement ring or my wedding band?"

He pulled the band from the box and slipped it onto my ring finger.

It appeared to be tungsten with three inlays circling the band, the two outer rings were made of glossy polished wood and the center was made from some kind of turquoise shell material, possibly Abalone. It was gorgeous and still very masculine.

I absolutely loved it. He couldn't have picked a better ring and it fit perfectly.

"I'm calling it a promise ring since I promise to love you forever."

I locked my knees so I wouldn't melt into a puddle right there on the roof.

Was this my life? Was this really happening?

Everything was falling into place.

With my career.

With Ronan.

And with my kids.

Now I was going to marry the man I had loved for what seemed like a lifetime, even though a majority of that time we'd been apart.

"We need to start planning a wedding," I announced in my attempt not to blubber like a baby.

Ronan shook his head. "It's already planned."

"What?" I frowned. "When? Where? How did you do all that without me knowing?"

He gave me a look that was so, so Ronan.

"Oh, that's right, you have *people*. Even your people have *people*."

"I did a lot of it myself, thank you very much."

"I want to hear details." Anything to keep me from bouncing around the roof and accidentally tumbling off it in my excitement.

"It's a surprise. Just pack a bathing suit." He rocked his head side to side and added, "Maybe a few bathing suits."

My eyebrows knitted together.

"Think a tropical beach, sun, sand, turquoise water. Me and you."

"Sounds like paradise."

"I've done everything to make sure it will be."

"And when are we traveling to this paradise because..." *Shit.* Work. Ronan didn't know.

"You have two weeks off before you sit behind that desk and in front of those cameras."

"You knew before me?" *Hold on.* "You didn't have anything to do with my promotion, right? You didn't pull strings or something, did you?" Because if he did, I wasn't taking that position. I wanted to earn it all on my own merit.

"No, but when I called your boss to ask when the best time would be for you to take two weeks off—because, again, I wanted this to be a surprise—he told me about it."

"So, he's going to delay my promotion?" I wasn't sure if I was okay with that.

"Just for two weeks."

I was supposed to start anchoring the evening news next week. "That means..."

"That's what it means."

"When do we leave?"

"Monday."

"And when is our ceremony?"

He gave me a look I could clearly read that all my questions were messing up his surprise. I couldn't help that I needed to know all the details. I was a journalist.

"The paperwork has to be in Saba three weeks prior to the ceremony, so that'll be the Saturday after our arrival."

"Saba?" I'd never heard of it.

"It's a small Caribbean island I found that's very welcoming to gay couples. Unfortunately, not many islands are."

No surprise. But... "We're going to be married in a little over a week?"

"You can't back out now."

"No, *you* can't back out now," I reminded him. "You already made me a promise and put the ring on my finger."

"I hope you never take it off."

"I don't ever plan on it." Just like the Circle of Life pendant I wore with Connor's ashes. I would never remove either if I could help it.

"Tate," he said softly with the smile that I loved as much as the man it was attached to.

"Yeah?"

"*Now* we kiss."

I shrugged. "Well, if you insist..."

I crushed my lips to his.

Ronan (Three Years Later)

I PULLED Tate's new BMW X7 into our driveway in Fox Chapel, north of Pittsburgh. We had the house built two years ago since my penthouse, while spacious, didn't have enough bedrooms for Alec and Mazie. We wanted them both to have their own rooms as well as a big backyard.

The gated community was perfectly located. Still close enough to the city and my office, but even closer to Burgh Media Group.

I glanced into the rearview mirror as I put the shifter into Park and waited while Tate, sitting in the back seat, carefully undid the harness from the car seat and lifted the baby from it.

Not only did we have room now for Tate's two kids, since we split custody with Dahlia, but a nursery and plenty of room if we decided to grow our family even more.

Amazingly enough, Dahlia had given us shared custody without a fight. That meant I could no longer despise her. At least as much. After remarrying and dealing with a new baby of her own, Tate believed she was relieved to hand over more of the raising of their children to us.

And now Tate and I had a child of our own together.

It had been a long, exhausting delivery even though our surrogate had done all the physical work. Watching her in the delivery room made me glad I wasn't a woman.

I was thrilled watching the birth of our daughter—officially named Jae Renée Harris-Pak on her birth certificate—but also a bit horrified with the whole process. I was torn with wanting to forget that time in the delivery room but also wanting to remember it forever.

After we left the delivery room, I told Tate I was buying that woman a new Mercedes. A convertible. With every damn option available. He had laughed, but I'd been serious. After what I witnessed, the woman deserved it.

As soon as I got out of the vehicle, I grabbed the diaper bag from the passenger seat and waited for Tate to get Jae settled against his shoulder.

Tate had wanted to pick a Korean name to honor my late father, so I let him choose. He chose the perfect name and my mother was thrilled with the choice.

As we approached the double front doors, one side opened and my mother rushed out with Alec and Mazie right on her heels.

"I want to see her!" my mother and Mazie said in stereo.

"Can we get inside first? And, Alec, don't let the dog escape," I said.

Alec grabbed Harry the Hound's collar just as he was about to bound down the steps and across the yard. Today was not a day for us all to be searching for our beagle as he ran around the neighborhood playing hide and seek. Us seeking, him hiding.

Worse, if he spotted a rabbit, we might never see him again for hours.

With her face lit up and tears in her eyes, my mother immediately held out her hands to take Jae from Tate.

I wasn't sure if he'd let Jae go, but after a second he did and my mother carefully scooped her up and immediately began cooing, crying even harder and smothering our daughter with noisy kisses.

As Tate pulled his hands away, albeit reluctantly, my gaze landed on the tattoo on his inner left wrist. A semicolon. I had a matching one on my inner right wrist since the symbol had meaning for us, both individually and as a couple.

As my mother and the kids filed back into the house, I remained standing on the walkway watching them.

Tate paused while climbing the stone steps and glanced over his shoulder. His dark eyebrows pulled together in concern. "What's wrong?"

With a shake of my head, I told him, "Nothing. Absolutely nothing is wrong. Everything is right."

He smiled the smile I hoped to see for the rest of my life. "It's perfect."

I joined him on the steps, hooked my arm over his shoulders and escorted him inside.

For a moment, while I'd been staring at the house we'd turned into a home and also our family, I worried that I might have died.

Because if there was a Heaven, I had found it.

The semicolon is by far one of the most powerful and inspiring tattoos. In the English language, the semicolon indicates that the writer could have

ended the story simply by using a period but decided the story wasn't finished yet.

Tate and Ronan's life together could have ended twelve years prior on that day in their apartment, but it didn't. Their story had only paused until it could be picked back up again.

THANK you to Maria Louden for letting me use her beloved late uncle's name, Mario Louden, for Tate and Ronan's professor.

Tate's Circle of Life Urn Pendant

Please turn the page to read a preview of Reigniting Chase

Sign up for Jeanne's newsletter to learn about her upcoming releases, sales and more! http://www.jeannestjames.com/newslettersignup

SNEAK PEEK OF REIGNITING CHASE

**Turn the page for a sneak peek of
Reigniting Chase**

About the book:

An unexpected collaboration between two authors that's hot enough to spark a fire...

Chase

After an excruciating loss, I'm desperate for a fresh start.
Away from the painful memories.
Away from everyone I know and anyone who knows my story.
That's how I end up in Eagle's Landing, Pennsylvania.
As a bestselling author, my main reason for moving to a remote mountain cabin is to overcome the writer's block that crushed my creativity for the past two years. My hope is to rediscover my words in the quiet, small town where no one knows me. Or my past.
A place where I can blend in enough that I become invisible.

Rett

Even though Chase, one of my favorite authors, insists he wants to be left alone, I refuse to let him wallow in whatever's drowning him. As a local bookstore owner and author myself, I'm intrigued by the man who's a master of the written word. Unfortunately, his social skills could use a lot of work.
Even so, I'm determined to pull the irritable and frustrating man out of the dark pit he's fallen into and back to the surface, no matter how hard he fights it. I only hope dragging Chase down that fiery path just might reignite his spark and that I don't get burned in the process.

Note: Please check the content warning before reading or purchasing. It can be found at the beginning of the book (accessible by Amazon's "look inside" feature or by downloading the sample) as well as on my website. This standalone gay romance has a guaranteed HEA, no cheating and no cliffhanger.

REIGNITING CHASE (UNEDITED)

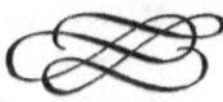

A STANDALONE GAY ROMANCE

Prologue
Escaping the Darkness

Chase

THE FORD BRONCO RAPTOR was put to the test as it rocked and rolled up the dirt lane. As best as I could, I skirted the massive potholes filled with mud from the last storm, overgrown weeds and brush encroaching on the path making it even more narrow, and long, deep ruts reminding me of miniature versions of the Grand Canyon.

I had traded in my Audi A8 for this very reason.

Buying the four-by-four had been the right choice. The real estate agent had warned me about the lane, not to mention the amount of snowfall the area received in winter. I had taken that warning seriously.

Especially after the agent sent me pictures. Tons of pictures.

Of everything. Not just the run-down lane.

Pictures that anyone in their right mind would have them immediately walking away from the property. No, not walk, sprint.

As much as the agent wanted the commission, he also wanted to be upfront with me since I was buying the property sight unseen.

A risky buy for sure.

A risk I was willing to take for privacy and some peace.

I needed a fresh start in a place where no one knew me or about what happened. The remote cabin on a mountain right outside of Eagle's Landing, Pennsylvania, seemed to be the perfect spot.

I hoped so.

I needed to find my mojo again as soon as possible. It had been gone as long as...

I slammed the brakes on that thought before it festered.

I bounced wildly in the driver's seat as the Ford crept up the last few yards of the lane and finally arrived at the edge of the clearing.

A clearing that also needed work like the dirt lane.

I'd paid the agent to have someone trim it back as best as they could, to have the shabby shingled roof replaced with metal, install a large emergency generator—since power failure up on the mountain happened often—and have the five-hundred-gallon propane tank filled. But the rest... I had decided to tackle that after I arrived, either by attempting to do the work myself or finding local people to hire. *Attempt* was the key point since I didn't have any kind of construction experience. I'd never even done any handy work around my previous homes before.

There was a first time for everything. And YouTube was full of tutorial videos for everything under the sun.

I figured being forced to do some hard manual labor could be good therapy. It might also spark my creativity since that had been in the toilet since... that day. The day I was trying not to dwell on.

After shifting the Bronco into Park and shutting down the engine, I stared at what was in front of me. My "new" home.

At that moment, I realized I had really lost my fucking mind.

Now that I was seeing the cabin in person... reality smacked me across the forehead with a sledgehammer. It appeared way worse in person and I hadn't even seen the inside yet.

For a second, I wasn't sure I wanted to.

"What the fuck are you doing, you idiot?" My whisper replaced the silence in the Ford's interior. "What the fuck were you thinking? Why did you ever think you could do this?"

Jesus Christ. I should turn my Bronco around and…

No. I should first burn that rat-trap cabin down to the ground, *then* turn my Bronco around, head back down the mountain, find a comfy motel and then another place to live. Tell the agent to sell the two hundred acres of wooded mountain land to someone who could build something better from scratch. Someone other than me.

I had bought this property mainly because the amount of acreage surrounding the cabin insured I'd have no neighbors. And the fact it butted up against a huge pond or small lake, however the hell it was classified. No matter what it was called, it was a nice sized body of water.

As a bestselling author, I should know how to describe things. But right now, I didn't give a shit about accurate descriptions. Instead, my focus was on how the hell I would survive here.

I scratched at the day-old growth of stubble on my face as I contemplated both my next steps and the cedar-plank-sided cabin before me.

"Fuck," I muttered under my breath and shoved open the driver's door, unfolding myself with a groan.

My forty-fifth birthday had come and gone a few months ago without any fanfare, but left behind gifts that I could've done without. Aching bones, insomnia, stiff joints, blurry vision and more.

Worse, I never expected to grow old alone.

I blew out a sharp breath. I needed to stop procrastinating, go inside, check out the cabin and see if it was possible to sleep there tonight or if I'd have to backtrack into town and find somewhere better until I made the cabin at least somewhat habitable.

With a hand clamped around the back of my neck, I ground it back and forth and gave myself a short and to the point pep talk. "Let's do this."

The wooden steps creaked as I climbed them up to the porch. They weren't spongy and I couldn't see any rot or broken boards, so that was reassuring. The wood porch was tiny, but then from what I'd seen in the photos, the door I was approaching was the back entrance. The true front door faced the ten-acre lake.

Lake *something*. I couldn't remember what it was called.

Not that it mattered. Since I owned it from shore to shore, I could name it whatever the hell I wanted.

Lake Leave-Me-Alone had a nice ring to it.

I dug out the key the agent had overnighted it to me from the front pocket of my jeans. I had never met him since everything had been done virtually. Even the closing.

As I went to slide the key into the lock, I realized the door wasn't completely closed. It was open barely a crack. Did one of the workers leave it open? Or had it already been open and nobody cared enough to close it? They probably did the work they'd been paid for and left as soon as possible.

The hinges squealed as I pushed the thick, rustic wood door open.

Mental note: Grab a can of WD-40 next time you're in town. If that doesn't work, a can of gas and a lighter would solve the problem.

Standing before the threshold, I sucked in a few deep breaths of the warm but clean mountain air. So different from where I just came.

The air wasn't the only thing different. I paused to listen.

So was the quiet.

No traffic. No voices. Pure fucking bliss.

The only sounds besides the birds and small mammals scurrying in underbrush, was the one in my head telling me on an endless loop that I was crazy to buy this place.

Maybe all the silence wasn't the best idea. It might make my own internal voices louder, even deafening.

On the trip here, I'd listened to a couple of long audiobooks since my thoughts tended to drown out music. With audiobooks, I was forced to concentrate. A good, well-written mystery was able to pull me from those dark and wandering thoughts and into someone else's story. One other than my own, both the crime thriller I needed to write and the Nicholas Sparks story I was currently living.

But it also reminded me that I needed to find my creativity again. I sure as hell hoped this place would help with that.

That was the whole point of moving to this remote area.

I stepped over the threshold and had to stop myself from turning around and escaping as fast as possible. The pictures didn't make it look this bad. Now I wondered how long ago they were actually taken and why the agent hadn't provided a virtual tour. But in truth, the agent hadn't been lying. It certainly was an old hunting cabin that was, at this point, not much better than camping.

Unfortunately, I knew nothing about roughing it or living off the grid. Even though, it was debatable whether this cabin was actually considered living off the grid. Mostly because it had well with a working pump and water that had already been tested and deemed safe. It also had electricity and soon would have satellite internet so I could get back to being productive.

If that was actually achieved, my agent might do some backflips. So would my reader base, who'd been clamoring for the last two years for the next book in my bestselling series.

When it came down to it, so would I, since writing was my sole source of income and my royalty payments had been slowly dwindling every month I went without a new release.

While I currently had a nice cushion in my bank account, it would be quickly eaten up by getting the cabin and its sparse amenities into shape.

No matter what, I'd have to actually *write* a book first. And with all the endless work that came after the first draft—editing, cover art, marketing, etc.—it wasn't like it would be published soon after.

I was giving myself six months to write the next book in my popular crime thriller series. By the time it hit my readers' hands, it would probably be a year and a half from now. If not longer.

I didn't want to think about it. I might be dead broke by the time I received my first royalty payment, depending on how generous the publisher's advance was.

The publisher had been hesitant to give me one this time after I'd spiraled into a dark place. They told my agent once at least three "well-written" chapters landed in their hands, they'd consider sending an advance.

Just fucking great.

Reluctantly, I couldn't blame them since severe writer's block had crushed some authors' careers. I held out hope that it wouldn't end mine.

Hence, the reason I stood where I currently did.

Shoving those depressing thoughts aside, I concentrated on the depressing view directly in front of me, instead.

It appeared as if no one had been inside recently except for local wildlife.

I walked deeper into the fifteen hundred square foot cabin. It wasn't a bad size for me since I'd be living alone and I didn't need much in terms of space. A place to sleep, a place to eat and somewhere to write.

The cabin had two rooms walled off—the bedroom and bathroom—but other than that the floor plan was completely open. Dust kicked up as I wandered around the main area of the cabin checking out everything a bit closer and making a mental checklist of what needed to be done.

Maybe I needed to actually write shit down since the list might be longer than my brain could handle.

The little bit of furniture left behind from the previous owners was covered in an inch of dust or was broken. All of it needed to be tossed or broken up and used for firewood. The kitchen cabinets were empty but the doors hung wide open as if the contents inside had been either stolen or packed up and removed.

Ghost-like cobwebs clung to every corner.

All of the windows were cloudy from years of neglect. One was completely shattered and would need to be replaced. Actually all would need replaced with new double-paned windows to help keep in the heat come winter. Even with the light early spring breeze, drafts were detectable when I ran my hand along the edge of the nearest window frame.

I shook his head and spotted scat on the floor. Lifting my gaze, I saw why. A half dozen bats clung to the open rafters above having a little afternoon snooze.

Fuck.

Besides the bat shit, I recognized what animal the little black grains of rice belong to. A small animal related to Mickey.

"You're all getting your eviction notice in the next day or so," I warned the bats and any mice listening. "Freeloaders."

I continued around the main living space. Luckily, the large fireplace made with mountain stone seemed to be in good shape as was thick, wide wood mantelpiece over. At least something was.

Actually the structure of the cabin was basically sound. It had "good bones." Most of the repairs would be cosmetic or to make it more energy efficient. The wide-planked wood floor boards just needs a good scrubbing as did the kitchen sink and appliances.

Luckily, that was something I could easily handle on his own. I didn't mind using a little elbow grease.

The filthy woven rug in front of the hearth needed to be tossed. Firewood scattered on the floor needed to be stacked neatly. The pile of cold ashes in the fireplace needed to be removed and a chimney sweep needed to be hired to avoid any fires in the flue.

I peeked my head into the bathroom. Since it was the only one, it was a decent size. No tub, just a stand-up shower stall needing a shower curtain, a window, a toilet that needed scrubbed, and a sink marred with hard water stains.

Next to the bathroom was my bedroom. Also not a bad size since it was the only one. A metal bed frame sat in the center of the room, and an old wood dresser was against one wall. I was afraid to open the drawers since I was sure families of mice had turned it into a condominium complex.

But it was the large windows in the room that caught my attention. They might be dirty now, but the view of the lake from them was spectacular. I imagined myself opening them wide and hearing owls, fox and even loons at night along with getting a breeze.

I added several ceiling fans to my list. One for the bedroom as well as a couple for the main living space.

My king-sized bed would fit perfectly in that room as well as the one dresser I brought along and was waiting in the U-Haul parked at the bottom of the mountain.

Both my SUV and the enclosed trailer were packed full with only the necessities, like clothes and my bed. Everything else I had given away to organizations that helped veterans and the homeless after selling my house on Long Island.

I stepped out of the bedroom and headed to the back door... No, the front door... to find it had been left unlocked, too. Pulling it open, I walked out onto the covered porch that spanned the whole length of the cabin and stared out at what I now owned.

The spectacular and breathtaking view of the lake from that wide porch had called his name when he scrolled through the pictures. Beyond the lake were more trees and the mountain continued rising as a backdrop. That picture perfect view had been what sold me on the property. I had to don blinders and ignore the rest of the issues.

I imagined myself in a rocking chair enjoying my morning coffee. Or setting up a little place to write.

Suddenly the tension I'd been holding in my shoulders disappeared and they dropped a couple of inches. My spine softened and my thoughts immediately became clearer.

This. This was what he needed.

At least once the major work was done. Like the rest of the cabin, the porch needed a fresh coat of stain and protective coating, something I could handle on my own.

I glanced over to my right to find a three-sided open shelter half-full of split firewood along with a stump clearly used for chopping that wood. After descending the three steps, I made my way around to the front of the cabin—no, the back—to where I was parked.

On my my route back to the Bronco I paused at the large propane tank along the exterior wall on the same side of the cabin as the kitchen to check the gauge. Thankfully, it was completely full as promised.

I kept going until I stood next to the Bronco and gave the outside of the cabin another once over.

My home.

It would do.

It had to.

I undoubtedly needed a change and this would definitely be a big one.

If moving here didn't help, then I'd need to face the fact I was helpless.

But for now, I needed to head back to town, find a place to stay for the night and buy a bunch of cleaning supplies so I could tackle the filth.

Before I could do that, I had to empty out my Bronco since it was packed full and only take an overnight bag and my laptop along. On my way back to town, I should double-check the U-haul to make sure it was locked since it was left in a small cut-out area meant for parking if the mountain lane—it certainly couldn't be considered a driveway—was impassable. However, where it sat was visible from the road.

When I came back tomorrow, I'd begin cleaning as best as I could, then attempt to tow the U-Haul up the lane without it breaking an axle.

Also while in town, I'd ask around at the diner and motel to find someone to replace the windows. In the meantime, I'd buy some plastic sheeting to cover the broken one to keep the bats and critters out.

I also needed to rent a post office box.

Damn. The list was endless.

I sure as hell hoped that by the time the cabin was in a somewhat livable condition the words would be ready to flow.

If not, I needed to find a new career.

Get Reigniting Chase here:
mybook.to/ReignitingChase

IF YOU ENJOYED THIS BOOK

Thank you for reading Everything About You. If you enjoyed it, please consider leaving a review at your favorite retailer and/or Goodreads to let other readers know. Reviews are always appreciated and just a few words can help an independent author like me tremendously!

Want to read a sample of her work? Download a sampler book here: BookHip.com/MTQQKK

ALSO BY JEANNE ST. JAMES

Find my complete reading order here:

https://www.jeannestjames.com/reading-order

* Available in Audiobook

Made Maleen: A Modern Twist on a Fairy Tale *

Damaged *

Rip Cord: The Complete Trilogy *

Everything About You (A Second Chance Gay Romance)

Reigniting Chase (An MM Standalone)

Brothers in Blue Series:

(Can be read as standalones)

Brothers in Blue: Max *

Brothers in Blue: Marc *

Brothers in Blue: Matt *

Teddy: A Brothers in Blue Novelette *

Brothers in Blue: A Bryson Family Christmas *

The Dare Ménage Series:

(Can be read as standalones)

Double Dare *

Daring Proposal *

Dare to Be Three *

A Daring Desire *

Dare to Surrender *

<u>A Daring Journey</u> *

<u>The Obsessed Novellas:</u>

(All the novellas in this series are standalones)

<u>Forever Him</u> *

<u>Only Him</u> *

<u>Needing Him</u> *

<u>Loving Her</u> *

<u>Tempting Him</u> *

<u>Down & Dirty: Dirty Angels MC Series®:</u>

<u>Down & Dirty: Zak</u> *

<u>Down & Dirty: Jag</u> *

<u>Down & Dirty: Hawk</u> *

<u>Down & Dirty: Diesel</u> *

<u>Down & Dirty: Axel</u> *

<u>Down & Dirty: Slade</u> *

<u>Down & Dirty: Dawg</u> *

<u>Down & Dirty: Dex</u> *

<u>Down & Dirty: Linc</u> *

<u>Down & Dirty: Crow</u> *

<u>Crossing the Line (A DAMC/Blue Avengers Crossover)</u> *

<u>Magnum: A Dark Knights MC/Dirty Angels MC Crossover</u> *

<u>Crash: A Dirty Angels MC/Blood Fury MC Crossover</u>

<u>Guts & Glory Series:</u>

(In the Shadows Security)

<u>Guts & Glory: Mercy</u> *

<u>Guts & Glory: Ryder</u> *

<u>Guts & Glory: Hunter</u> *

Guts & Glory: Walker *

Guts & Glory: Steel *

Guts & Glory: Brick *

Blood & Bones: Blood Fury MC®:

Blood & Bones: Trip *

Blood & Bones: Sig *

Blood & Bones: Judge *

Blood & Bones: Deacon *

Blood & Bones: Cage *

Blood & Bones: Shade *

Blood & Bones: Rook *

Blood & Bones: Rev

Blood & Bones: Ozzy

Blood & Bones: Dodge

Blood & Bones: Whip

Blood & Bones: Easy

COMING SOON!

Double D Ranch (An MMF Ménage Series)

Beyond the Badge: The Blue Avengers MC™ Series

ABOUT THE AUTHOR

JEANNE ST. JAMES is a USA Today and international bestselling romance author who loves writing about strong women and alpha males. She was only thirteen when she first started writing. Her first published piece was an erotic short story in Playgirl magazine. She then went on to publish her first romance novel in 2009. She is now an author of over fifty-five contemporary romances. Along with writing M/F, M/M, and M/M/F ménages, she also writes under the name J.J. Masters.

To keep up with her busy release schedule check her website at www.jeannestjames.com or sign up for her newsletter: http://www.jeannestjames.com/newslettersignup

www.jeannestjames.com
jeanne@jeannestjames.com

Newsletter: http://www.jeannestjames.com/newslettersignup
Jeanne's FB Readers Group: https://www.facebook.com/groups/JeannesReviewCrew/
TikTok: https://www.tiktok.com/@jeannestjames
Audible: https://www.audible.com/author/Jeanne-St-James/B002YBDE7O